TANKS

Evil Lurks on Whidbey Island

Ted Mulcahey

Other Works by Ted Mulcahey Featuring the O'Malleys

Bearied Treasure
Teed Up for Terror
Little Dirt Road
Juiced
Punch Down

One

He waited until the Duke Water treatment truck backed down the gravel road that served the concrete reservoir. It was five p.m. on April 20th on Whidbey Island, and he still had to wait three hours until it would be dark enough.

Concealment was not an issue here in the thick pine and fir forest, and his excitement trumped any boredom that might have crept in. With clear skies, the temperature fell quickly, even at this time of year; he was glad he'd worn his jacket.

After intermittently watching the tank for almost a month, he'd gotten used to the routine of the monitoring company. They came once a week, on Tuesdays, and always between four and five p.m. Sometimes she would be there for half an hour and sometimes only ten minutes. Today it took longer, so he had to wait behind the deadfall from one of the fierce winter storms.

At a shade under five-ten, his slight build and unremarkable features were excellent attributes for a man who preferred to remain overlooked. A closer inspection would reveal very dark eyes that were perhaps just a smidge too close together and a thin-lipped mouth with a perpetual cruel smirk leaking from the right corner. Wispy brownish hair of medium length was concealed by a generic ballcap absent of any logo.

As dusk turned to twilight, he made his way to the access ladder at the rear of the 35,000-gallon reservoir. He thought it comical that the drinking water for a hundred or more homes had little or no security, but hey, *tough shit for them,* he figured.

With his Mini Maglite between his teeth, he climbed the rusty steel ladder twenty feet to the top, where the vent pipe and the access port were located. He would be here all night if he had to remove the rusted bolts from the cover; fortunately the vent pipe was all he needed.

Keeping his gloves on, he removed his backpack, still securing the LED light with his teeth, and removed the tools he needed to complete his task: A saw, a PVC fitting and cement, his respirator, and three quarts of a unique blend he'd been working on.

He used the saw to cut off the three-inch "U" at the vent termination and stuffed it in his pack. Next, after taking the flashlight from his mouth and placing it on the concrete surface, he securely fastened his mask and dumped the contents of the quart bottles into the tank via the vent. After placing the empty bottles in his pack with the sawn-off fitting, he swabbed the vent pipe and fitting he'd brought with PVC cement and immediately twisted them together.

Standing back to admire his handiwork, he removed the mask. The risk of airborne transmission was remote, but the virulence of his creation made the additional precaution necessary. The vent stack was now several inches shorter, but no one would ever notice. Making sure nothing was left behind, he climbed back down and walked to East Harbor Road. Traffic was sparse; even so, he took care to avoid any cars. Several passed by during the time it took to get back to the truck, which he'd parked at a seldom-used trailhead, but he avoided them by stepping into the brush long before their headlights reached him.

Getting back inside his ten-year-old Toyota Tacoma pickup with the heater cranked up felt good. Now all he had to do was wait a few days. He was confident of his calculations, and soon there would be illness in the small community on the east side of Holmes Harbor. He relaxed and listened to the reggae sounds of Bob Marley on the twenty-minute drive back to his home.

Two

"You going off-island today?"

"Nope. Got a meeting with the HOA board."

"Sure sounds like fun; sorry I can't be there." Jenne knew sarcasm when she heard it but chose to ignore me.

"And you? The links calling?"

As spring morphed into summer, the soggy dark days of winter were becoming a distant memory, and the ball-drop boys at Mutiny Bay Golf Club would be teeing it up—and I'd be one of them.

I'm Kevin O'Malley, and my wife is Jenne, same last name. We live on Whidbey Island and have done so since we sold our interior design firm a half dozen years ago.

Our home is on a high bluff overlooking Saratoga Passage in a small community of fewer than fifty homes. When the weather was pleasant, Jenne was happy to join me on the course. During most of the winter, however, it was either cloudy, cold, or rainy, and she opted for workouts at the gym, hikes among the many trails on the island, or the occasional foray across the water to meet up with her good friend.

Of course, now that she had joined the HOA board, she had less time for more enjoyable pursuits and frequently teased me for encouraging her to volunteer. I often reminded her that her executive experience and talent were a perfect fit for dealing with mundane complaints and silly disputes among homeowners. The reality was that it was a thankless job, but the folks who served had genuine responsibilities.

The private roads and the bluffs were constant maintenance headaches, and overseeing the community water system was paramount. Unaware of the responsibilities before, I was now exceedingly appreciative of my wife and the others who chose to serve.

"Anything earth-shattering on the agenda today?"

"Nah, just the usual. There are some dues issues and a few complaints about neighbors, but that's about it."

"I guess I'll go tee it up. Want me to hit the grocery store on the way home?"

"I'll go; it'll give me a chance to leave the house. Better yet, how about I take Emma for a walk and you can pick me up when I get to the bottom of the hill?"

Emma was our aging GSD who still enjoyed a leisurely walk—as long as it was downhill. If I timed it right—and I would—Jenne would get some exercise, as would Emma, and then we'd continue to the store.

"Sure thing. Hopefully I'll be there on time."

"You *will* be."

Her reply might have sounded like a threat to another, less confident husband. To me, it simply showed her faith in her loving and considerate partner, a fellow who knew better than to venture onto thin ice.

"Of course I will, dear." I kissed her and left for the course. I needed to make sure I was first off, because no way was I going to be late.

Three

Cassie's stomach started bothering her at four a.m. She knew because the damn bedside clock stared at her while she writhed in pain.

After two trips to the bathroom to empty both her stomach and her bowels, she felt no relief. The cramps started well below her waist and didn't stop until her sternum. She had been sick before, but not like this.

Last night's dinner with her boyfriend was the usual Friday night fare—pizza. The local pizza kitchen in Langley, their favorite, had readied it for seven when John picked it up. They shared a bottle of wine from a local winery, watched a rom-com, and had sex. As usual, John returned to his place while she hit the sack by eleven. They had been together for six months but still enjoyed their space.

She wished like hell he was there now. Whatever this was, it wasn't going away and seemed only to be getting worse. She had experienced food poisoning once during her thirty years, and it had been brutal, but this was far worse.

Now, at six a.m., she called him. "John ... I'm sick. Can you come over?"

Within fifteen minutes her boyfriend had arrived, assessed the situation, and promptly bundled her into the car to take her to the hospital in Coupeville. Her moaning and thrashing throughout the half-hour trip confirmed his evaluation.

The admitting nurse took one look at Cassie and commented to her associate, who was busy with another patient, "Shit, another one."

"What do you mean?" As John allowed the nurse to attempt to seat Cassie in a wheelchair, he noticed two nearby gurneys occupied with patients who were in obvious discomfort.

"This is the fourth patient we've checked in within the last hour. The doctor on call is looking at the first one now. This chair isn't going to work; she's too cramped up. Let's see if we can make her a little more comfortable."

The two medical professionals got Cassie onto a gurney, then one grabbed several warm blankets to put over her midsection.

"The heat should lessen the severity of the cramps in a few minutes. The doctor shouldn't be too long."

John Bender stood next to Cassie and held her hand while they waited. When she wasn't shivering, she was lying still with her eyes closed or squeezing the shit out of his hand. The two patients he had seen when they entered had been taken through the swing doors and were presumably being tended to.

A small, youngish man came over to greet him. "I'm Dr. Ericson, and I'll be looking after your friend here."

"Thank you."

"Did she have anything unusual to eat last night?"

"No. Just pizza and some wine."

As Dr. Ericson prepared to ask another question, the admitting nurse interrupted and took him aside.

"Doctor, I was reviewing the admitting forms and noticed three of the four patients live on the same street."

"This one?"

"No—hers is different."

"Look it up on the computer. I need to know if she lives near the others."

He returned to an obviously worried John.

"We'll get her set up in the treatment area with an IV and get some fluids into her so she won't get dehydrated."

"Will you give her antibiotics?"

"No, not until we're certain of the infection. If it's E. coli, we'll stay with fluids and rest. If we use antibiotics, we could worsen the situation by allowing the bacteria to multiply too rapidly. We'll need to run some tests, but this initial course of treatment should begin to help within a few hours."

"Will she be okay?"

"The first case we admitted is already showing signs of improvement, so if this is the same thing, we should be fine."

As the doctor finished with John, the nurse beckoned once again. "Doctor, Cassie's street is just around the corner from the other three. There's gotta be something going on there."

"I've treated too many bacterial infections not to recognize them when I see them. As soon as we get the samples back from the lab, report this to Island County Health. I'd like to get ahead of it if we can."

Four

I walked off the eighteenth green by four p.m., had a beer while I paid the vultures their spoils, then got on the road to pick up Jenne at the bottom of the hill, where Brainers Road intersected East Harbor.

When I crested the hill on East Harbor, I could see her dayglo yellow vest from half a mile away. As I got closer, I saw Emma sitting by her side, alert to anything she perceived as threatening. It always warmed my heart to see them.

"Cutting it close there, buster."

"Nuh uh, had a minute to spare."

"You're lucky there was no traffic."

"It's Whidbey Island, dear; there's never any traffic."

"No argument there. How was the golf?"

"Shitty—three-putted four times and lost thirty bucks."

"Too bad, so sad, baby. Did you have fun?"

This is why I love my wife; she makes fun of me, then wants to know if I enjoyed myself. What a gal.

"Yup, great fun."

"Good; let's talk about something else."

See. She wanted to talk about something else all along, but we had to get me out of the way first. "What's that, honey?"

"I passed Ginnie when I left the house. She said a bunch of folks near Holmes Harbor got sick."

"Yeah. I guess there's some flu going around, and the COVID is still popping up here and there."

"No, it's not that; she said it's bacterial, like E. coli or something."

"That's not good. How does she know?"

"You know Roger Wilkie, right?"

"Yup."

"She's his cousin. She said the county health department asked him to follow up on the outbreak."

"Okay, well, I guess she'd know, then. Isn't that from bad food at a restaurant or something?"

"It could be, but according to her, all the folks who got sick are from the same community, and none ate at the same place."

"Sounds weird. Maybe something from the grocery store?"

"She says not. Two just returned from the mainland, and the other two hadn't been to the store in a week."

"Well, maybe Wilkie can figure it out. He was a big help when we were involved with Sharon Waffle's place."

"I agree. Still, it's odd."

Whidbey Island is almost forty miles long, its geography lending itself to distinctly different lifestyles.

The island's north end is identified as the city of Oak Harbor and, further north, Deception Pass. Whidbey Naval Air Station dominates its economy, and most businesses and services support those stationed and living there.

The stretch from the town of Coupeville to the southern tip of the island is considered South Whidbey. The population of approximately 15,000, only 20 percent of the island's total, depends on an economy supported by tourism, agriculture, and the arts.

With most of the residents in the south living in rural settings, the Sheriff's Department had its hands full policing the territory.

We met Wilkie several years ago when an elderly scientist's death resulted in Jenne inheriting the woman's small cottage in the woods. The surprising windfall led to a statewide escapade featuring arson, larceny, miscellaneous treachery, and a paradigm-shattering discovery that was changing the world. But that's another story.

Right now, we found ourselves in the bulk foods aisle at the Payless Market in Freeland, and who should we bump into but Roger Wilkie.

"Hey, you two, picking up some prunes? Because, you know, your age ..."

If I hadn't mentioned it before, Roger considers himself quite the funny man.

"Good one, Roger. You been saving that up?" I asked.

"Nah, spur of the moment thing. Have you guys been keeping out of trouble?"

While Wilkie kept tabs on most of his flock, our recent adventures were mainly off the island. Although the latest events in Walla Walla were far from his patch, his network of information was legendary.

"Of course."

"Not what I hear. That thing near the boat turned out to be something after all."

Rather than flash back to the psycho who had almost killed my wife, I thought a change of subject was in order. "I hear a bunch of folks up the road got sick. Any idea what caused it?"

He raised his eyes, perhaps thinking he wasn't the only one with sources. "I guess nothing stays quiet for long on the island. Yeah, four were hospitalized, and another half-dozen had similar but less serious symptoms."

"Were they all from that East Harbor area?" Jenne asked.

"They were—that's what's odd. The bacteria that caused it was similar to E. coli, but according to the lab, it was more virulent. The complications could have been life-threatening if they hadn't forced fluids on those admitted."

"Any ideas on the cause?" I asked.

"We know it wasn't food because everyone had something different. About ninety homes are in that community, but some of the snowbirds are still away, so only fifty or sixty homes are occupied."

"So 20 percent of the folks there got sick?" My math skills at least got me in the ballpark.

"Yes. The only other common denominator is the water supply. We talked to Duke Water and they sent the weekly report from Tuesday; everything was within normal ranges. No increased levels of bacteria or arsenic."

"So if not the water, then what?"

"I don't know. There's a scientist from UDub coming up next week, and maybe he'll have some idea." Looking at his watch, he added, "Shit, I'm late. I gotta pick up one of those rotisserie chickens and get back in time to see the start of the Mariners game. See ya, bye."

We both watched as he hurried down the aisle to the chickens. "Kinda weird, huh?" Jenne muttered under her breath.

"You mean that he likes chicken? Nah, lotsa folks do."

My response received a well-deserved poke in the ribs, but I agreed with Jenne. I suspected we hadn't heard the last of whatever this was.

Five

Harry disliked driving to the island's southern tip, but it was part of the plan.

The Cultus Bay area was home to several small communities, each with its own private water system and reservoir. The East Holmes Harbor trial had gone perfectly, but he needed more data to be sure of his intended results.

His choice for the initial trial was random. The location was convenient, just off a well-traveled road, and it was easy to determine the schedule of the testing company. This one, the Cultus Bay Beach Village, was approximately the same size as his first test, but most residences were year-round homes.

He'd made several trips to the area and eventually determined the routine of the Duke Water tech for this part of the island. It would have been far simpler if he'd had access to their scheduling.

Since this section of Whidbey was mainly rural, it was a matter of driving the roads aimlessly for a few days until he stumbled across a company vehicle. Most trucks on the two-lane roads were pickups or UPS, FedEx, or Amazon vehicles. Fortunately the Freightliner Sprinter vans with the bright blue "Duke Water" signs plastered on the side were easily seen.

It appeared this particular tech made the rounds of the south end on Wednesdays and Thursdays, which was ideal for his plans. Only a few hundred yards from the 30,000-gallon storage reservoir, the community soccer field offered a perfect location to observe the Duke Sprinter.

On Thursday at two p.m., the water tech wrapped up his fifteen-minute stop. It looked like he had filled several containers with water from the tank and would run the tests back at their facility.

After confirming the tech's visit, Harry killed time by reviewing the data he had accumulated while experimenting with untold numbers of fecal combinations.

The access ladder to the top was opposite the road leading to it, as most of them were, he was discovering. *Strange*, he thought; *it's as if the designers and contractors who located the reservoirs wanted me to remain unseen.*

As dark as it was, being seen by anyone was unlikely. Much as he had done for the first attack—that was what he considered them—he quickly climbed to the top armed with his Mini Mag and followed the same procedure he had previously used.

This time he poured four quarts of the liquid into the tank before regluing the vent termination fitting. He knew the investigators would suspect the infection came from the water system sooner or later, so he waited until just after the weekly testing samples were taken. They would show a safe water supply, and by the time the next weekly samples were taken, the dilution factor would be significant enough to obfuscate his tampering.

He removed his mask—even in the cool evening, the damn thing was hot—and climbed back to the ground. He was anxious to see what the coming days would bring.

Six

"Where's Don?"

"You didn't hear?"

"What?"

"Both he and his wife ended up in the hospital over the weekend. They got some weird stomach bug and had to be put on IVs. Took them two days to feel better."

It was Tuesday afternoon and one of the few days over the past week that it wasn't raining. It was still overcast, but the temperature in the upper fifties meant I was on the golf course. Don Dempsey was one of the regulars of the Ball Drop group, so his absence was notable.

I was on the fifth hole at Mutiny Bay GC, getting ready to hit a nine iron to a back pin, when I realized I hadn't seen Dempsey. Our foursome was made up of guys I'd played with numerous times, and I enjoyed their company.

I suddenly forgot about my shot, looked at Billy Pike, and asked, "Did anyone else get sick?"

"One of the guys talked to him before we teed off. He said he was feeling better, but whatever it was kicked the shit out of him. I guess it was mighty contagious too, because he said a bunch of the neighbors came down with it, and a few of them ended up in the hospital too."

"He lives down by Cultus Bay, right?"

"He does, yes."

The similarity to the outbreak at East Holmes was too much of a coincidence, and I couldn't wait to talk to Roger about it. The rest of my round was forgettable.

Although we were retired and in our sixties—me middle and Jenne a half-dozen years younger—we were still curious about life and why folks do what they do. Since we hung up our professional work clothes, in the last few years we've somehow gotten involved in several situations featuring participants from the other side of the law.

Don't get me wrong, in no way are we qualified to investigate or in any way assist those whose job it is to keep the public safe. For some reason, though, trouble seems to find us. My best friend is the head of detectives for Bellevue, and I'm sure if he were asked, he'd say I was a shit magnet. I think he feels the same about Jenne, but he knows better than to say anything about it to either of us.

Roger Wilkie, on the other hand, is keenly aware of our propensity for getting into trouble, but he also knows that more often than not, we end up unraveling the mystery. Because of this—and probably also because of his woefully understaffed department—he is willing to listen to us and sometimes even confide in us when he's stumped. I managed to catch him at his office while on the way home.

"You heard?"

"Yup. Cultus Bay, right?"

"Yeah, another outbreak. We had eight admitted and another dozen or so with less serious symptoms."

"Last time we spoke, you said someone from UDub would take a look at things. Did he find anything?"

"She, not he; her name is Andie Saunders, PhD in epidemiology. She seemed pretty sure the Holmes outbreak was bacterial, and she said she would be shocked if it didn't come from the water supply, since it's the only common denominator."

That was what I thought too. I asked, "Did she take samples?"

"She did. Said I'd hear back from her after she had a chance to review the results, but nothing yet. I've got a call into her about the Cultus Bay thing."

"What are the odds of two bacterial outbreaks, both in communities with their own water systems?"

Wilkie shook his head and rubbed the back of his neck. "Shit, I don't know—they gotta be off the charts. Thing is, those wells are ten miles apart. Sure, it's the same aquifer, but the odds of it being contaminated are infinite. Every so often, one of the reservoir tanks will have high levels of bacteria, but nothing like this. Remember, they test those things weekly."

"I know, I know, but it really is strange. Would you mind letting me know what you hear from Saunders?"

"Hell, no; I'm not too proud to take your help, regardless of what your buddy Bill Owens says." A wide grin broke across his tanned face as he said this.

Uh oh. "You've been talking to Bill?"

"Of course. Saw him just the other day. I was in Bellevue for a conference last week, and we had a beer after the meeting."

Bill and Wilkie exchanging information? This couldn't be good.

"After that deal with the batteries and then the boat thing, we got to know each other. He and Shelly are great folks."

"Um, what did he have to say?"

"He says whenever the shit hits the fan, you and your wife can't be far away. He says somehow you're always in the middle of things."

"I guess ..."

"He also says—but I promised I wouldn't tell you—that without you two, most of these crimes wouldn't have been solved. Don't let on that I told you."

It sounded like Bill. I think he's mostly concerned for our well-being but tries to hide it.

Wilkie spoke again. "This'll be our little secret, Kevin. I'll call you when the lady from UDub gets back to me."

*****

"That Roger?"

"Yup."

"Are you going to tell me what he said, or do I have to threaten you?"

It was the day after I'd visited with Wilkie, and I had just gotten off the phone with him. I'd brought Jenne up to speed with things the previous night, which meant I needed to provide up-to-the-minute updates on the situation now. Her threats were mostly idle, and she did so jokingly—mostly. When she got serious about things, though, it meant yours truly might have to live the life of a celibate monk for an indeterminate amount of time. Needless to say, that condition needed to be avoided at all costs.

"I was just about to update you, dear. He heard from that professor at UDub. The results from the patients show that E. coli is definitely the culprit, but the water tests from the tanks at both sites show well below acceptable levels. She's never seen such an outbreak without being able to locate the source."

"It's lucky there haven't been serious complications with any patients. I did a little reading and saw that elderly patients and those with compromised immune systems could have complications that might even cause death."

"Yes, I looked at some outbreaks across the country where a few folks have died. It seems that bacteria from fecal matter, usually livestock, enter the food chain. Most of the south end of Whidbey is rural with lots of small farms and ranches, so I guess somehow it got into something they ate or drank."

"But why so specific an area? And how? It's not like they all ate the same foods. It *has* to be in the water."

I couldn't find any holes in her reasoning, but the testing suggested otherwise. "Do you think they screwed up the tests on the water in the tank reservoirs?"

"I doubt it; those scientists are world famous. If they messed anything up, I'd be shocked."

"So?"

"Let's ask Roger if we can visit the two communities and ask some questions. Maybe we'll find out something he missed."

"You think he'll be pissed that we're suggesting he missed something?"

"You're an idiot. We're not *suggesting* he missed something. We're going to interview the folks in-depth—something he surely doesn't have time for because he's so over-worked—to see if we can help lighten his load."

"It doesn't seem so bad when you put it like that."

She showed the beginnings of a smile, similar to the ones I displayed while watching Emma discover a long-lost tennis ball, slowly shaking her head from side to side. "Kev ... just call Roger and tell him what we're thinking."

I convinced Jenne it made more sense to have her present our case to Wilkie, suggesting I might inadvertently say the wrong thing. I'm pretty sure she saw through my attempt at avoiding the awkward request, but when she balked, I reminded her that an idiot might screw something up. She caved, and Roger was only too happy to have our help.

We started with the residents at East Holmes Harbor. It was a sunny afternoon in May, the temperature in the low 60s. After the long, dark winter, any day with sunshine would be celebrated, and the homeowners took full advantage of Old Sol. Gardening, lawn mowing, and car washing appeared to be projects of choice, which made our investigation considerably easier.

Using the names Roger gave us, we began with the folks admitted to the hospital. By the time we had finished interviewing Cassie Gray on her porch, most of the others who were infected had gathered around us, eager to see if we could shed any light on their regrettable misfortune.

As cocktail hour approached, we said our thanks and goodbyes and headed to the bar at Mutiny Bay for an early dinner. The place was bustling with golfers finishing up and diners coming and going. We welcomed the decibel level for the privacy it gave us.

"We spent the afternoon with those folks and are no further ahead than when we started." Jenne's frustration appeared to mirror my own.

"I agree. The one thing those who got sick have in common is where they live. Most of them use bottled water for drinking, but even if they don't, it's almost impossible to avoid ingesting water from the community system."

Jenne nodded her agreement and said, "Right; whether it's teeth brushing or rinsing dishes or taking pills, it's got to be the water."

"Yeah, except it isn't. The tests by the water company show very little bacteria and those by that PhD confirm it."

At an impasse, we decided to table the discussion for the evening and enjoy ourselves. Tomorrow morning we would do it all over again at the Cultus Bay community.

***

We arrived at the home of the Dempsey family shortly before noon. I had called Don the previous evening and told him we were doing some legwork for Roger Wilkie.

In his early seventies, Don lived with his wife in a modest cottage on a slight rise overlooking Puget Sound. Although I had seen him a couple of weeks earlier, I was surprised at how much weight he'd lost. He'd never been concerned about the protruding stomach that draped gently over his waistline, but now it was hardly noticeable.

"Looking good, Don; trying the Atkins diet?" As a golf buddy, he'd be hurt if I didn't zing him immediately, but Jenne looked at me as if I was insensitive.

"If you call barfing and shitting your guts out for three days a diet, then yes, I was on the Atkins diet. That was miserable. I'm just now getting my appetite back."

We sat in his kitchen with his wife, Connie, sipping the coffee she had made. An avid hiker, she was several years younger than her husband and an abject failure at convincing him to stray from his miserable eating habits. It was a distinct possibility that the condition of their immune systems accounted for the difference in the severity of their infections.

"I know you were in the hospital, Don, but how sick did *you* get, Connie?" Jenne started things off.

"I had diarrhea for a day or two and was a little nauseous, but that was it. Don was so bad I took him to Coupeville, but you know that." Her husband reached across the table as she spoke and gently squeezed her hand. It was obvious the years hadn't diminished their affection.

"We understand the other folks who got sick were from here, and everyone had something different to eat. The tests from the university came back negative, so even though it seems the water is the only common denominator, we can't find high enough levels of bacteria to confirm it." I wasn't telling them anything they didn't know, but sharing my thoughts seemed to be welcomed by them.

"Everybody is better now, but since we don't know the cause, folks are leery of getting sick again. Will you keep us in the loop on your findings?" Don asked, clearly not relishing another bout of gastrointestinal fury.

"We will. We're going to question a few of your neighbors, then get back with Roger and see what we come up with if anything. I'll make sure to fill you in."

Because the Dempseys were kind enough to notify the neighbors we planned on visiting, the rest of our interviews went smoothly. Unfortunately, when we were done, we were no further ahead than when we started. It was clear that the sickest residents were those with weakened immune systems or underlying medical conditions, but that was all we learned.

"The only thing that makes any sense is something in the water." Jenne sounded as frustrated as I did.

"I know ... problem is, the tests are negative."

"Maybe they made a mistake."

"Two different labs checked the water at different times, so doubtful."

"So it's a mystery?" Now I knew she was annoyed.

"I guess it is. I just hope we don't have another outbreak before we figure it out."

We called it a day and headed home to take Emma for a walk. We thought it better to sleep on things before we got back to Roger Wilkie

Seven

Whidbey Island is heavily forested, especially on the south end of the oddly shaped land mass. Harry Hogan's place, a ten-acre parcel north of Freeland and south of Greenbank, had been in his family for two generations.

A gravel single-lane road peeled off the main thoroughfare and wound through massive firs and cedars, most exceeding two hundred years on the planet. The quarter-mile drive led to a seven-foot cedar fence that shielded the compound from anyone stumbling across it. The Hogan property backed up to a state forest preserve that effectively provided absolute privacy even without the imposing enclosure.

Even though "No Hunting" signs were posted throughout the forest, deer hunters often didn't care or were too stupid to pay attention to them. Harry countered this unavoidable nuisance by installing video cameras and two-way intercoms throughout. When the inevitable occurred, an alarm would sound, startling the intruder and alerting Harry. Ninety percent of the time, the shocked hunter would take off running, while the other ten percent were informed that the law would be on the way if they didn't depart immediately.

The view from Google Earth showed a modest cottage-style home in the center of the parcel, a small barn and corral to the rear of the house, and another larger building to the right of the barn. If it were possible to see this third structure on the ground, its only noticeable feature would be the location of the windows.

A perfect 25 × 50 rectangle, the steel-sided, fifteen-foot-tall shop featured six two-by-three windows placed ten feet high on each end. The long sides were utterly blank, just two solid walls of yellowish paint, the only blemish a three-foot steel door on one side and an eight-foot overhead door on the other.

With two successful operations under his belt, Harry felt confident enough to prepare for his ultimate objective. When his father had died twenty years ago, he had inherited the property and a healthy stock portfolio.

In the early forties, his grandparents had purchased the land to use in their retirement years. They took their time, planned, and meticulously built the cottage during vacations and holidays. His grandfather, a skillful craftsman who worked for a general contractor, would have completed the home faster, but they were blessed with a son after years of failed attempts.

Young Ivan Hogan turned out to be more of a curse than a blessing. At an early age, he displayed above-average intelligence that somehow became directed at finding unique ways to injure small animals.

First it was frogs and various acids and chemicals commonly found around the house. When his parents removed those, he progressed to electrocuting larger specimens; squirrels and chipmunks were his favorite victims. While his classmates held their breath during countdowns to launching toy rockets, he did the same in anticipation of throwing a switch while 110 volts of electricity jolted the life from a poor forest rodent.

Predictably, his antisocial tendencies led to him being discouraged from attending school, resulting in his poor mother's attempt at homeschooling. It did not go well, and shortly before his sixteenth birthday, he announced he was leaving his Ballard home, never to return.

His parents felt terrible and blamed themselves for their son's character flaws. However, that's not to say they weren't secretly thrilled to be rid of their rotten progeny. To ensure he managed to stay away, they established a trust fund that could be accessed monthly up to a specified amount and prayed to God they would never hear from him again.

Like most rebellious teens on their own, Ivan turned first to alcohol and then to drugs. He found a weekly rental in a shabby motel in Tacoma, where he lived from monthly draw to monthly draw. His animal torture trials, which had progressed to feral cats and tiny abandoned chihuahuas, were put on hold when his landlord threatened to evict him if that awful smell persisted.

Meanwhile, their son, thankfully gone, the Hogans completed their retirement cottage on Whidbey Island. Nine years to the day of its completion, tragedy ensued. Planning a weekend of rest at their vacation home over the Christmas holidays, the Hogans luckily made the five o'clock ferry, leaving from Mukilteo. Being the last vehicle to board was always considered good karma, but this time was an exception.

The ferry attendant dutifully blocked their rear wheels and attached the netting across the massive rear opening of the boat. As often happens during December, a vicious storm was battering the sound from the south. Gale warnings were posted, but the ferry captains were used to this weather. Midway through the twenty-minute crossing, the Suquamish ferry plowed into the carcass of a 300-year-old Doug fir. The vessel shuddered with the collision, causing the blocks behind the wheels of the Hogan car to shift to the right.

In his delight at their good fortune of being the last car on the boat, Grandpa Hogan had neglected to engage his parking brake and, worse yet, had forgotten to put the vehicle in park. When the ferry recovered from the blow and surged forward, the Hogan automobile rolled slowly back into the flimsy nylon webbing stretched across the opening.

They discovered their dire predicament only when they felt the rear wheels roll over the edge of the steel deck, but by then, it was too late. Grandpa Hogan frantically pulled up on the brake, not realizing the rear wheels had no purchase. When the people in the car in front of them looked up from their newspapers, the Hogans had made history by becoming the first vehicle ever to have fallen from a Washington State ferry. The sound was just under 600 feet in that location and home to some of the most ferocious tidal currents in the country. Neither the Hogans nor their car were ever recovered.

Now in his early twenties, Ivan was notified by the state police of his parents' accident only hours before the story became a national headline. Although he'd had no contact with them for over five years, he was their only child and, by default, inherited their entire estate.

With a tidy sum of money and a Whidbey Island home now at his disposal, Ivan traded in his smelly Tacoma rental for island life. His warped sense of morality was not conducive to a lively social network, so his inherited real estate's solitude suited him perfectly.

His hermit-like existence was acceptable for a few years, but even the antisocial Ivan acknowledged his need for companionship befitting the bodily appetites of a young man. With little opportunity for meeting members of the opposite sex on the island, Ivan started making daily visits to one of the larger grocery stores.

Always a chubby fellow, he went on a low-calorie diet to improve his chances of scoring with one of the checkout gals at the store. He gradually became known to most of them and eventually zeroed in on one of the cuter but less intelligent employees; he began going to her station, even if it meant a longer wait.

A fifteen-pound weight loss did little to distract from his closely spaced gray eyes and flattened nose, but it was enough to attract a sympathetic second look from Margie, the checker, barely old enough to drink. After another week of daily visits, he asked her out, and before long, they were an item.

She soon moved in with Ivan, became pregnant immediately, and nine months later, Harry was born. Ivan considered this event a terrible inconvenience because it meant curtailing his need for sexual release. He busied himself building a steel pole building where he could be alone to continue his deviant experiments. Most construction projects in Island County require permits and inspections. Still, the place's rural and heavily forested nature meant owners seldom observed those requisites, and they were difficult to enforce.

After Harry's birth, Ivan had little to do with the kid and grew to resent Margie and her motherly instincts, preferring to spend more time in what he now considered his *laboratory*. Eventually even the slow-witted Margie grasped that her future with the man would be limited. While Ivan was experimenting with something one morning, she packed two-year-old Harry into her ten-year-old Honda and left for her mother's home in Portland. It was the last she saw of Ivan Hogan.

***

Harry, unfortunately, turned out to be a chip off the old block. Always small for his age, he developed a technique for dealing with bullies early in life. While in the third grade, Bobby Oziemblewski, the biggest kid in the class, thought shoving little Harry during recess one day would be fun.

The overweight "Ozzie," as everyone called him, had inherited a much smaller brain than his size would accommodate. As Harry stumbled onto the dirt play area, his tormentor stood by with his finger up his nose, guffawing along with several of his cronies.

Harry dusted himself off, flipped Ozzie the bird, and retreated to a safer section of the playground. He stood there, glaring at the big dufo, contemplating his revenge. The following day the class shuffled in at eight o'clock, placed their packs in their assigned cubbies, and proceeded to their desks. That is, all but Ozzie.

While the rest of the class was seated, a high-pitched scream arose from the big kid in the back, still holding his pack and staring at his small storage shelf. The entire class, save for Harry Hogan, turned to see what might have caused such an uproar.

By then, young Oziemblewski, tears streaming down his face, had bolted for the exit. The teacher, Miss Donnelly, unsure of the nature of the problem, immediately addressed her students: "Class … class, please turn around and study your readers for a few minutes."

She walked to the back of the room and peeked into Ozzie's cubby to see what could have caused the boy to freak out. Stuffed at the back of the storage cube was a small, bloody, furry head, a note stapled to its ear. She kept her distance, hand over her mouth, and silently read it: *It's your cat this time, asshole. Don't fuck with me again.*

Only a few kids knew about the altercation between Harry and Ozzie, but that was enough. Word spread like wildfire, and Harry became an outcast. It wasn't so much that Ozzie was well-liked—more that at such an early age, it was tough to comprehend someone deranged enough to cut a cat's head off. Ozzie was severely traumatized and refused to return to school. Harry endured the balance of the school year but told his mom he wasn't going back.

Margie successfully found a checkout clerk job at the local grocery store and worked the second shift so she could homeschool Harry. That her less-than-Mensa-material daughter was attempting to school a brilliant, although certainly disturbed, kid was not lost on her mother, who busied herself watching right-wing cable news from morning till night.

By the time Harry was in his teens, the only contact he had with his mother or grandmother was if he bumped into them while using the house as a place to crash. Still a loner, he spent a considerable amount of time at the library—so much so that he was asked if he'd like to work there part-time. Needing some source of money besides what he stole from his mom or grandmother, he accepted.

Most of his work hours were spent shuffling books and papers around with minimal contact with the public. The head librarian was happy that Harry enjoyed the place, but she suspected something off about him that was best hidden from regular folks.

One week after his sixteenth birthday, he received word that his father, Ivan, had died in a laboratory accident. Somehow, the shop on his Whidbey Island property had erupted in flames, and he was unable to escape. Harry had had nothing to do with the man since he was a toddler and couldn't have cared less.

He was unaware that he was the sole heir to his father's estate since Margie and Ivan had never tied the knot. After being informed of his windfall and having researched the age of emancipation in Washington State, he packed his things and moved to Whidbey Island. He felt no obligation to repay his mother or grandmother for their kindness, a behavioral quality unfamiliar to him.

Ivan had never been much of a housekeeper. It took three months for Harry to clear the detritus from his new home on Whidbey and another three to clear out the fire damage from his father's lab. The flames had destroyed numerous cages and storage cabinets, save for one, and an unknown number of custom-made tools and contraptions. An undamaged Mossberg 500 twelve gauge sat in the corner, covered with soot and ash.

While he never knew what sorts of things his father had worked on, judging by the remnants of his experimentation, they were far from the mainstream work of other researchers.

Along with the Whidbey property, Harry inherited a substantial stock portfolio. The funds, initially invested by his grandfather and then passed to his father, had grown considerably over the years. The moment he was informed of this additional good fortune, he began refurbishing his father's laboratory.

Eight

"Guess who I bumped into on my walk?"

Jenne had just returned from her three-mile loop around East Harbor and Saratoga Roads, her face flushed with exertion and a reflection of the brisk 58-degree temperature. It was a little before noon, and I planned to spend the day doing yard work.

"I give up. Who?"

"Alice and Seth. They were doing some pruning on their apple trees."

"Are they going to be home for a while?"

"Yes. After meeting with scientists, manufacturers, and politicians worldwide for the past year, they're looking forward to enjoying life on the island for a long time. Seth said they can visit him at their home if anyone needs to see him."

"Can't say as I blame him. With the royalties they're getting, they'll never have to worry about money again."

Seth Robbins and his wife Alice lived less than a mile from us. Their lovely home sat on a five-acre parcel the previous owner had left to my wife. The woman, Sharon Waffle, was a world-renowned scientist who had chosen to live off the grid. Jenne had befriended her on the day she died, and with no relatives surviving her, she had left her estate to Jenne.

Seth, a scientist with the PNNL—the Pacific Northwest National Laboratories—had corresponded with Sharon. Upon her death, we uncovered a trove of research notes that eventually led to a unique battery concept, but unfortunately, all her research was written in Dutch. Jenne and I tracked down Alice DeGroot from the University of Washington, who volunteered to translate, and after working closely with Seth, sparks flew and now they are married.

Naturally, the lithium producers were unhappy about Seth's discovery, and an unscrupulous corporate officer sent a pair of thugs to stop the research at all costs. It was surprising how things ended, but Jenne sold them the property at a bargain price, and we were thrilled to have them as neighbors.

"We're having dinner with them this weekend."

"Wonderful. It'll be fun catching up with them."

"Oh, Bill and Shelly are coming up too."

I wondered how this woman could hustle three miles, stop to talk to the Robbinses, *and* set up a dinner party for the weekend. I was also smart enough not to say anything, although I did stick my toe in the water by asking, "Um, when you say we're having dinner with them, does that mean at their house?"

"Don't be silly, of course not; they're coming here."

"Do you have some idea of what we are going to serve to these lovely people?"

"Yup. You're making a big pot of that famous chicken chili. It'll be easy."

It *was* easy, but it was a full day of prep the day before, and that could only mean golf this Friday would be a casualty. They *were* great friends, though, and it would be fun seeing everyone, so it would be a small price to pay.

"Geez, hon, pulling this together at such short notice was nice of you."

"Nothing to it. I did it on my walk after I left Seth and Alice. Francis and Jake had to call me back, but they did, and it's cool with them, too."

"The Earlys?"

"Of course. We gotta have them, too, right?"

Silly me, we just *had* to. "Well, sure. I would have brought it up if you hadn't."

The Earlys were brothers who lived on the island and were the principal players in a foiled effort by a cartel drug kingpin to murder them, the Owenses, and me and my lovely wife. We saw them occasionally, but this would be our first time together in a year.

"Thanks for including them, Jenne; it'll be great fun."

Saturday was May 10th, and it arrived with clouds and drizzle. It would be another month before the skies would abandon the dreariness for certain, and a glorious twenty weeks of sunshine would follow. This time of year usually offered an occasional sun break, but the overcast ceiling was more the norm.

Jenne promised that the afternoon and evening would offer a break in the cloud cover and that serving pre-dinner cocktails on the deck would be comfortable. I had my doubts but knew better than to challenge the weather guru.

Because the entire previous day had been spent chopping, marinating, sautéing, grilling, and simmering, all that was left for me to do was to put the twelve-quart pot on a low simmer and watch while Jenne prepared the cornbread muffins. At least, that was what I thought.

"Kev, do you think you can sweep off the deck and maybe pick some things from the garden for me to make a centerpiece?"

Now, I certainly *thought* I could, but I had a sneaking suspicion that she cared less about what I thought and what she really wanted was for me to perform those duties. It's by keeping these musings to myself that I can experience a relatively conflict-free relationship, so I nodded and said, "Got it, hon. Let me know if you need anything else."

With at least an hour before our guests arrived and the final bale of German Shepherd dog hair vacuumed away, all was ready. That is all but the last womanly ablutions necessary for a flawless presentation, which were still being administered when Jake and Francis Early arrived in their fancy handicapped-accessible van.

Jake had been injured in Vietnam and had used a wheelchair ever since. Up until two years ago, he was also agoraphobic and, even now, was still constantly astonished at the things he'd missed while cooped up in his house. Francis, an ex-con with a heart of gold, was a thick fireplug of a man with a completely shaved head and still sported prison tears on his face. He had been the catalyst for saving the day when the cartel kingpin appeared.

Jenne somehow miraculously appeared to greet them as Jake, with Francis's assistance, rolled down the van's ramp. Emma dutifully sat nearby, making sure all the visitors were acceptable. With hugs all around, we made our way to the deck to await the other guests.

"Hey, Kev, I heard you two got in some hot water at that winery in Walla Walla." Jake's awareness of all things news on the island was legendary.

"You heard about that, did you?"

"You're kidding, right? Hell, I've been a club member at Uva Cellars since they won that platinum from *Decanter*. I've known Butch for years."

I shouldn't have been surprised. Jake was a shrewd investor, and Butch Carlson, a hedge fund manager and the owner of Uva, was a close friend who was recently killed. The entire episode was difficult to revisit, and Jenne's escape from certain death was still too terrifying to think about.

"We're trying to leave that episode in the rearview; it's still a little recent to talk about." Jenne looked over at me and nodded her thanks for my redirection.

"Hey, Jake, tell the O'Malleys about the big news." Francis, a man often underestimated, was wise enough to know when to move on to other topics.

"Sorry, guys. I can't imagine what you went through, Jenne." Jake quickly picked up the mood then continued, "Francis goaded me into running for the empty county commissioner's seat. I'm on the ballot for the special election in June."

"Wow, congrats, Jake. You're perfect for the job." Jenne's enthusiasm matched my own.

"I don't know about perfect, but I've lived here on the island for a long time, and now that I'm more comfortable in public, maybe I can do something to give back a little."

Just as I started to respond, an SUV with four occupants pulled into the gravel drive. Emma bounded off the deck, making a herculean effort to be the loudest barker in the state. I hurriedly followed; letting a GSD greet your guests alone was never a good idea.

Bill and Shelly Owens and Seth and Alice all exited the vehicle simultaneously. Knowing the drill, they stopped immediately and let Emma sniff before stepping forward. Shelly and Alice fawned over the dog and rubbed her ears while I greeted Bill and Seth.

"I see Emma's still taking care of things, eh?"

"With everything we've been through, Bill, it's reassuring to have her around."

"You don't have to tell me, remember? I've been there for most of your escapades."

We took the steps to the deck and joined Jenne and the Earlys.

***

Time passed quickly as the eight of us caught up on the events we'd missed, those we weren't aware of, and those that might happen in the future. Because we were such good friends and genuinely liked each other, the conversation, jokes, and sarcastic digs were shared equally among the men and women, with no particular gender bias.

The conversation eventually turned to the recent outbreaks of the intestinal bug that had invaded the island, and I updated the group on where the investigation was. I could tell Wilkie had kept Bill in the loop because he didn't bother scolding me or interrupting. That was until I was finished.

"Couldn't let it slide, could you?" He said this with enough of a smile that I knew there was a hint of admiration in his demeanor.

"We know Roger is stretched pretty thin here, and we thought we could lend a hand."

"Of course you did. Plus you love the puzzles, and when I say you, I include you in there, too, Jenne. I don't know how you manage to get in the middle of everything, but you do. I hate to admit it, but somehow, you both find a way to get to the bottom of things. And to the rest of you, if you ever repeat what I just said to anyone, I'm coming for you."

All of us were stunned. Bill was as solid as they came and an excellent detective. If he came across as curmudgeon-like, I was sure it was out of concern for our safety, but this was the first time he had complimented us in front of anyone, and we were at a loss for words.

Until Jenne spoke up. "Geez, Bill, are you okay? Is there something terrible killing you that we should know about?"

I had to hand it to my wife; the woman knew how to break the ice. With an eye roll and a sheepish shake of his head, he raised his hands in surrender.

"Okay, I give, uncle ... Look, you two are our best friends. If anything ever happened, well ... and this last narrow escape with you, Jenne, was too close. Things could have turned out differently if it hadn't been for Michelle."

As he looked down at his drink, I rose and gave him a quick hug. "Thanks for watching out for us, buddy."

It was an unusually honest display of affection, which neither of us expected. The quiet stretched out until Francis could no longer stand it. "So, what does an ex-con have to do to get some food around here?"

Warm and happy laughs followed as we moved into the house to prepare for the chili-fest.

After we'd eaten our fill of chicken chili and cornbread, the conversation returned to the local illness.

"You said earlier that someone from UDub was working on this for the county. Do you know who?" Alice had taken a sabbatical from the university while she and Seth were traveling, and she was up in the air about returning to work or doing something on the island. Even though her area of expertise was in languages, her tenure at the college was such that she knew many of those on staff.

"She's got something to do with epidemiology," I said, "but I can't remember her name. It's like a name that could be a man or a woman; I think Bobbie, Billie, or something like that."

"Could it be Andie?"

"That's it!"

"Andie Saunders?"

"You know her?" Jenne asked.

"She's a good friend and my running buddy. We ran together all the time." Alice was a marathoner and had run two or three annually until the previous year.

"If she's helping on this, you're in great hands; her research is recognized worldwide. I don't know any details, but I think she's even discovered several new bacteria. She's a very smart cookie."

I nodded my agreement and said, "I think she's coming up next week to meet with Roger and the folks from Duke Water. She told him it made sense for everyone to get together in the same room and try a little brainstorming. He wants us there to report on our interviews with the two involved communities."

"I'll call her tomorrow and tell her that the four of us are close friends; I'm sure she'll want to get together."

I wasn't sure how much fun it would be to have coffee with a famous epidemiologist, but I kept those thoughts to myself.

Nine

For years, Harry Hogan did his best to keep a low profile. While the south end of Whidbey is primarily rural, it still has a small-town personality. There are only two post offices, very few fine dining establishments, and a limited number of grocery stores.

It was impossible to avoid seeing the same folks repeatedly due simply to the logistics of daily life. It was marginally easier during the summer months, when South Whidbey's population increased by a whopping 32 percent and the return of the snowbirds helped to dilute the recognition factor considerably. Still, after two decades, Harry Hogan's reputation had evolved through snippets of whispers, sightings at grocery and hardware stores, and infrequent fill-ups at the local gas station.

No one thought poorly of the man, only that he preferred to keep to himself and his politics were drastically tilted to the right. The tale of his father's demise was brought up occasionally, but other than aimless falderal, it served no purpose. His penchant for privacy led to suspicions of nefarious activities, but no corroborating facts were ever brought to light to back them up.

Deliveries were instructed to be left by the front gate to discourage any of the local drivers from seeing what went on beyond the fence surrounding the property. The nearby residents occasionally reported strange smells and infrequent smoke from a fire or incinerator, but these occurrences were expected and ordinary for such a rural location.

During the season, a wayward hunter would sometimes wander a smidge too close for comfort, but the automated warning system or a blast from the Mossberg pump action was enough to chase them off. After all these years, Harry was considered just another eccentric choosing a solitary life on the island.

The cosmic forces that conspired to develop the brain of Harry Hogan started with his father. Ivan had inherited *his* father's intelligence and patience, but for no discernible reason other than to see what might happen, the gods supplied enough of a dose of fucked-uppedness to rewrite the sanity code in his psyche. Ivan nurtured and fed this character flaw until it was passed on to his son, where it found fertile ground to prosper.

Whether it was Oziemblewski's bullying, his grandmother's penchant for disbelieving known facts, or something else, it was difficult to identify a single point in time that initiated Harry's animosity toward the vast majority of the human race. Even those who tried to help—the librarian in Portland, for example—were considered irrelevant in the grand scheme. The raw material for a life of vengeance and retribution for some real or imagined slight was inherited, but its realization was solely the chosen path of its owner.

Severing the head of Ozzie's cat may have been the first of Harry's forays into the realm of the depraved, but it was far from his last. The thrill he received from watching a helpless animal die was difficult to describe. It wasn't sexual; it was more a feeling of power, being the sole arbiter of life or death. While living with his mother and grandmother, his experiments with this control were only sporadic. Living with the two women was tedious enough without giving them something to bug him about.

After relocating to Whidbey Island and overhauling his father's lab, he could pursue anything that satisfied him. The one storage cabinet that had survived the fire contained several useful substances, but still, only so much could be done with squirrels, coyotes, and black-tail deer.

While his formal medical training was nonexistent, his commitment to online study was exemplary. Although the chemicals and paraphernalia found in his father's old storage cabinet were outdated and mostly useless, one material was hermetically sealed and packaged in a container labeled "Wildnil."

When his investigation showed it was a trade name for carfentanyl, a substance used by veterinarians for anesthetizing elephants, he started experimenting with it on the animals unfortunate enough to wander onto his property.

Even though his research suggested the strength of the powerful opioid was off the charts, its potency was still difficult to grasp. It had taken over four black-tail deer to get the proper dosage for anesthesia rather than death by overdose. He carefully noted the minuscule amount required by weight and began using it for subsequent experimentation.

After several months of testing with these members of the animal kingdom, the carcasses began piling up, and disposal became an issue. Burying the damn things took too much time and work, and burning them was too smelly even for him.

Fortunate to have high-speed internet service, he resumed a topic of his earlier interest while working in the library. It was one thing to lord power over the creatures of the forest but quite another to affect fellow members of the human race. Because he lived on an island with a rural infrastructure, he could selectively experiment on small groups of people without their knowledge. It was as if he were the puppet master, pulling the strings, controlling their health and well-being.

His constant exposure to the "fair and balanced" propaganda cable news channel had done sufficient damage to his political outlook that he considered anyone with an open mind or even a smidge of tolerance an enemy.

How ironic that his far-right view of life would continue to advance even while living on an island where the left outnumbered the right by two to one.

Ten

Dr. Andie Saunders didn't get to Whidbey until Friday. There were new outbreaks of a flu-like disease in Brazil, and the fear that it could spread quickly was enough that the CDC had requested her presence earlier in the week. Jenne and I were seated with Roger Wilkie and Dwayne Callison from Duke Water when the forty-something epidemiologist entered the room.

Although tired-looking, her warm smile and crystal-clear blue eyes hinted at the intelligence within. Her thick brown hair sported streaks of gray and was cut in a short bob. Her slight build and athletic presence screamed *runner*, and already I was envious.

"Sorry I'm a little late; I just missed the ten-thirty. I went to the Edmonds/Kingston terminal by mistake."

It wasn't unusual for first-timers to the island to make the same error. The terminals were only thirteen miles apart, and the signs on I-5 boldly announcing "Ferries" were often assumed to indicate the only ferry terminal in the area. Had she embarked on the Edmonds ferry, she would have been on her way to the Olympic Peninsula and probably a three-hour detour. I still recall taking that journey on my first trip to Whidbey Island.

"At least you discovered your mistake in time. Some people end up going the wrong way."

"Ignore him, Andie; he's only trying to excuse his poor sense of direction." Once again, my wife was adept at ice-breaking, "I'm Jenne, this one's wife. He's Kevin."

Her laugh was deep and genuine; it was easy to see why she and Alice were good friends. As the rest of the group introduced themselves, I fetched the coffee and scones that someone—me—had thoughtfully brought to the meeting.

Roger assumed the administrator's duty and began by summarizing the known facts to date. "This will be old ground for some of you, but let's do it anyway. We've had two outbreaks of bacterial contamination, infecting only the members of specific HOAs. The fecal tests on the victims have confirmed that the culprit is a strain of E. coli. We tested the water before the outbreaks and again when we became aware of the infections, because it's the only thing the victims had in common. In both instances the tests were negative for E. coli pollution. Dwayne, have I got this right?"

The burly tech from Duke Water nodded and confirmed, "We test these reservoirs weekly, and we found them safe both before and after the outbreaks."

"Do you normally test for E. coli?" asked Saunders.

"No, only when asked, but after the outbreaks, we thought it made sense to test for it, and the HOAs agreed."

"There wasn't even a trace?"

"There was a trace in both systems, but it was less than 1 mg per cubic meter, so negligible."

After the back and forth with Dwayne, Andie addressed all of us. "I'm sure you know this, Dwayne, but let me give the rest of you a quick primer on this bacterium. E. coli lives in the gut, and most strains are harmless and help us digest food to absorb it.

"There are several strains of these bacteria that can cause diarrhea and vomiting, and they are known as Shiga toxin–producing E. coli or STEC. This Shiga toxin damages the lining of the small intestine and can lead to serious complications, especially in immunocompromised individuals. The chief culprit in North America is known as E. coli 0157. The tests we ran from the samples we received showed a structure very similar to 0157 but not exactly the same. When we cultured the strain, we found it much more aggressive than known Shiga producers."

As the four of us absorbed this lesson in epidemiology, the meeting room was quiet save for the ticking of the coffee urn. I finally asked, "Is this something new?"

"Well, it's new to me. I'm brought in to consult on strains worldwide, and I've never seen it before. The real issue here is how it got inside these people. I trust the testing done by Duke, but I haven't yet conceded that it *isn't* the water supply."

"What about the E. coli tests we ran?" Dwayne sounded slightly defensive, but I couldn't say I blamed him.

"I have no reason to doubt your results, but you did say you found a trace."

"But nowhere near enough to cause a problem."

Instead of getting into a debate, Andie began looking for answers. "What is the recovery rate on most of these island reservoirs?"

"Huh?" I hated to seem stupid, but it appeared I was getting over my skis quickly.

Andie continued, "Most of these shared water communities have reservoirs anywhere from twenty to forty thousand gallons. Drilled wells constantly pump into them to make sure there's ample water available when they need it. Usually, peak demand is morning and evening, which means the wells are pumping during the day and at night. The recovery rate is the time it takes to refill the tank to its capacity."

"Right, that's what I thought." Jenne looked at me with that headshake she does when she thinks I'm a child. Of course, this brought a smile from Andie, once again proving that women seem to have an unspoken language only known to them.

"They're all a little different," Dwayne answered, "but they're designed to recover during the nighttime to be ready for the morning."

"Got it. Let me see if I've got this right. You tested the water in both instances three days before the outbreak, which incidentally is the incubation period for this bacterium. Then you tested them again a week later, meaning the water in the tanks could have been changed almost a dozen times."

Dwayne nodded, suddenly aware of where the professor was going. "You're saying even if the contamination were from the water, it would have been so diluted by the time we tested again that only a trace might show."

"That's my guess. It's the only answer. It *has* to be the water, and I think someone or something is timing the introduction of the bacteria so that it won't show up when it's tested."

"Shit. You're suggesting someone is sabotaging the drinking water?" Roger was fully engaged now that there was possibly a bad guy out there.

"I can't think of another solution. It's *got* to be the water."

"Thank you, Dr. Saunders. This helps a great deal. Is there anything else you think might help us?" Roger was ready to start hunting for whoever was poisoning his island brethren.

"I'd like to spend a little more time studying this strain. If it gets out there, we need to know what to do about it."

"We welcome your help. Let me know whatever you need."

We all stood to leave, and Andie turned to Jenne and me. "I'm heading over to visit with Alice. She convinced me to spend the night and made me promise to invite you two over for dinner. You'll come, right?"

"Of course, we'll be there, and we're looking forward to it." Jenne apparently didn't see the need to check with her husband, probably rightly assuming that I'd never pass up free food and wine anyway.

***

While I hit the links for the afternoon, Jenne was invited to go hiking with Alice and Andie. This worked perfectly since I could play without guilt, and Jenne could enjoy some female bonding time. I asked Seth, but his involvement in the battery thing seemed to have no endpoint.

On the way home, I posted a few yard signs saying "Elect Jake." We tried to avoid local politics, but Jake was a buddy, and I'd promised to spread the word. Although he was relatively unknown until the shootout two years ago, his only competition was a trust fund youngster who had just moved to the island from Los Angeles. I was confident he'd be elected.

I met up with my wife at our home shortly before heading to Seth and Alice's. "How was the hiking?"

"Great. We went to Ebey's Landing and did the cliffs and the beach. It was spectacular."

The National Historical Reserve was one of the many treasures of Whidbey Island. Vast stretches of prairie farmland nestled up to the Salish Sea with breathtaking views of the Olympic Mountains. It was a favorite hiking destination, and those who visited once wouldn't soon forget its grandeur.

"How was the golf?"

"Fun—some good shots and some bad ones, but the sun was shining, and the company was enjoyable. I put some signs out on the way here. Sorry I missed the hike."

"No worries, it was mostly girl talk. That Andie is no dummy, by the way, and she's on all these world-famous committees and boards. Nice job on the signs."

"That's good to know; we're lucky to have her looking at our little island issue, and thanks."

"She seems very interested. She says this bacterium she cultured from the fecal samples could do serious damage if the concentration were high enough. I think she's worried about where it came from."

If one of the preeminent epidemiologists in the world was concerned about this outbreak, then it bothered the shit out of me. "Did she say anything about her plans?"

"Not much; maybe you should ask her tonight."

Seth and Alice lived in a prefab home. While the term *manufactured* is often associated with slapdash construction and the ultimate goal being affordability, nothing about their house could have been further from the truth.

They'd used Stillwater Dwellings, an exclusive architectural firm specializing in custom high-end prefab homes. In only six months, they went from a cleared lot with septic and water on the property to an ultra-modern single-story structure reminiscent of some of Richard Neutra's residential masterpieces. Their wooded parcel was the ultimate in privacy and serenity and one we thoroughly enjoyed visiting.

Alice and Andie were regaling Seth with their day's activities when we arrived. He appeared genuinely interested in their descriptions of the hike and promised to be there for the next excursion.

"Kevin, sounds like you missed a fun time with these three."

"I agree. That place is special. Next time we'll all go. How did you like it, Andie?"

"I can see why you love it up here. Compared to the hustle and bustle of life in Seattle, this place is heaven. Maybe I'll keep my eyes open for a small place to chill out."

Instead of skirting around the issue all evening, I figured I'd just come out and ask: "Andie, how concerned are you about this bug we have here on Whidbey?"

She took her time answering, choosing her words carefully. "I always worry about a strain of bacteria or a virus that I've never seen. It means that while we can predict what might happen with it, we don't know for certain, and bad things can happen when we don't know for sure how it will behave."

Her answer caught everyone's attention. I followed up with, "Could it just disappear?"

"I suppose so, but it's unlikely. I'm convinced this isn't a naturally occurring bacterium. Someone would have seen it before if it was. I've contacted most of the leading epidemiologists in my circle, and so far, it's also new to them. Somehow, this thing contaminated those two water tanks, and I believe it was done intentionally. It's the only thing that makes sense. You've got one sick puppy here on the island, and he or she is making folks seriously ill."

Eleven

As a youngster, Harry never paid much attention to anyone naïve enough to offer him advice, but there was one tidbit the head librarian bestowed upon him while he worked there.

He remembered her exact words. "If you want to become an expert on something, Harry, read about it for just one hour a day and do it every day. In a year, you'll know more than a college graduate. In five years—that will mean over seventeen hundred hours—you'll know more than all but a few people in the world."

Harry had been absorbing data about bacteria, infectious diseases, poisons, and other exotic potions for over two decades. He started while employed at the library, paused for a time while screwing around with forest animals, and then resumed his studies when it became clear that affecting the lives of human beings, especially those bleeding-heart woke fuckers who thought differently, was a challenge more to his liking.

His lab bore no resemblance to his father's dark, dirty, smelly, flea- and rodent-infested workshop. The only similarity was the mustard-colored sheet metal exterior that wore a skirt of mud from twenty-five years of rain sheeting off the roof and splashing around the perimeter of the building.

The interior looked much the same as that of a modern research lab. In fact, that's precisely what it was. Color-adjusted LED lighting illuminated rows of stainless steel counter-height benches on which were strewn glass containers of every imaginable size. A wall of warming ovens lined the right side of the cavernous room, while glass-fronted coolers mirrored them on the left. The charred storage cabinet salvaged from the original lab was tucked away in the far corner.

A commercial HVAC system maintained a constant 68 degrees during the coldest winter nights and the hottest summer days, while a security system that rivaled the Pentagon's ensured only one individual's access. A smaller room toward the rear housed five Dell PowerEdge T40 servers and contained its own cooling system.

The entire electrical requirements for the installation were backed up by a Cummins commercial standby generator that automatically powered up in the event of one of the frequent power outages on the island.

The longer he lived on Whidbey Island, the more aware he became of the island's dependency on the aquifer feeding the hundreds and hundreds of drilled wells. Many were individual wells for a single residence, some were for two or three, and many were for small communities ranging from six or seven homes to several hundred or more.

These larger systems required a tank or reservoir to store the water so it could be replenished during periods of lower demand, which was what Harry Hogan was focused on. He had begun concentrating his research on developing a strain of Shiga-producing bacteria that would prove more aggressive and problematic than E. coli 0157.

One requirement was obtaining fecal matter from cows, pigs, and goats for culturing the bacteria. Although Hogan wanted nothing to do with playing nursemaid to any goddamn farm animals, he saw no other option. The necessity of keeping a low profile and remaining anonymous prevented him from relying upon any local farmers to supply him with pig shit and the like.

So, after spending several weeks researching the care and feeding of farm animals, he was ready. First, though, he needed to construct a small barn to house the little fuckers. He was never a handy fellow; more research and study was necessary to build the damn thing.

One of the first requirements was a permit from Island County. After acquiring the necessary paperwork, he could start construction, and an inspector would show up to check his work. *Fuck that*, he thought. *Like I'm letting some asshole bureaucrat on my property.*

The learning curve for barn building was cumbersome for a man lacking any experience in construction. No matter how meticulous his efforts were to follow the instructions and do-it-yourself videos on YouTube, he had twice as many failures as successes. Eventually, though, through sheer persistence, he managed to construct a thirty-by-forty-foot barn of sufficient durability to house his farm animals.

The easy-going nature of South Whidbey, combined with the understaffed building department of Island County, had assured that Harry Hogan's new barn would remain off the books.

A visit to LivestockMarket.com was all it took to locate the animals he needed. It seemed ridiculous to spend thousands of dollars on livestock, build them a place to live, and pay to feed them, plus all the manual labor required, just so he could use their shit to culture bacteria. The money wasn't a problem, but he resented the physical effort he needed to expend to keep the goddamn things alive.

Plus, the bastards stunk up the place so much that he found it necessary to fence in a corral to let the fetid barn air out occasionally. He found that the pigs and cows tolerated each other, but the little pygmy goats wanted their own space. If he put them with the pigs, they'd repeatedly headbutt the little porkers. If they were in with the cows, they wouldn't stop bleating. He was increasingly questioning his decision to produce his own animal feces.

Eventually, he managed to find a way to keep all the animals happy. He wondered, not for the first time, how that Noah fellow had managed things with two of every animal in the world on one boat. He guessed the guy had had some divine intervention that made things a bit easier.

With an endless supply of shit available, he began his research in earnest. He started by identifying the 0157 strain in fecal matter and then began trying ways to influence its genetic makeup. The persistence that had allowed him to complete a barn for his animals also fostered his desire to formulate a unique organism that would be more persistent and virulent than those already identified.

He was confident he had succeeded based on his studies and experiments; the problem was verifying his discovery. The first live experiment was the East Holmes Harbor reservoir, and the results were excellent.

The tricky part was figuring out the dilution factor. There was no way to know how many residences had people in them, how often they took a shower or flushed the toilet, how often they did the laundry or ran the dishwasher, or how often they filled the dog's water bowl. Ideally, the bacteria would be diluted enough by the third or fourth day that the water would test negative. There was always the chance that something unforeseen would occur and very little replacement water would be pumped into the reservoir.

He thought about this possibility for only a minute or two before casting it aside. After a couple more tests, it would no longer be necessary.

A tiny part of him knew that a third of the people infected might also have similar political outlooks on life to his, but he considered that collateral damage.

Twelve

The Cultus Bay community outbreak was six weeks ago. It was front-page news in the *Whidbey News-Times* for a couple of weeks before being nudged from the paper by an aggressive owl terrorizing hikers at South Whidbey State Park. Either wildlife and retirement notices were what the readership craved most, or the possibility of an uncontrolled occurrence of life-threatening diarrhea and nausea was too far-fetched to consider.

Roger Wilkie was occupied once again with the occasional burglary or domestic disturbance that, unfortunately, was a permanent part of the fabric of American life, and the island wasn't immune from it. On the plus side, the frequency of such crimes was considerably less than on the neighboring mainland.

According to her last email, Andie Saunders was still attempting to locate the origin of the unknown Shiga toxin–producing E. coli variant that had infected the residents of the two communities. She suggested that E. coli 0157 could have been cultured and manipulated to create a more virulent strain. But she had no clue how or why the stuff had been introduced into the water systems of the two communities.

Both Jenne and I continued with our life of retirement as the urgency of the outbreaks of illness faded from the top shelf of our consciousness.

We celebrated the election of Jake Early at his log home along with Francis, many of his ex-con buddies, and a house full of neighbors, friends, and Island County government types. All were genuinely happy that the former agoraphobe had been elected, and it appeared the county folks were relieved they didn't have to put up with an outsider.

The next day, the Maxwelton Beach Community residents began showing up at South Whidbey Urgent Care, Whidbey General Hospital, and even the Regional Medical Hospital in Everett.

This outbreak of patients with severe diarrhea and nausea was twice the size of the previous two, and the symptoms appeared more serious. Two of those admitted to Whidbey General were so dehydrated that they arrived with seizures and were close to unconsciousness.

Because the medical facilities in the area had been told to be on the alert for patients with bacterial infections, they immediately notified the sheriff's office. Roger called us at seven a.m. on a Wednesday morning.

"We've got another outbreak, and this one's bad. Two patients admitted to Whidbey General are now in comas, and it's doubtful they'll survive."

"Shit. Have you contacted Andie Saunders?"

"I called her first; she said she'd be over on the next boat. I also spoke with Duke Water, and they told me they tested the water there three days ago. It was clean."

I thought, *Of course it was, just like the others.* "What's your next step?"

"We're going to meet as soon as Dr. Saunders arrives. You two be able to make it?"

"Sure. You thinking nine, nine-thirty?"

"Plan on ten, just in case. See you then."

***

"I've been in touch with Everett. They're getting me samples to culture. They'll be at my lab by the time I get back to UDub. As soon as we break up, I'm going to Maxwelton to take samples from their reservoir tank." Dr. Andie Saunders was all business as we began our ten o'clock meeting.

Besides Jenne and me, there was Andie, Roger, a guy named Edgar Souza representing Island County, and Maria Geddes from the Washington Department of Health. It looked like Roger had been busy. As soon as Roger had made the introductions, Andie took over.

The first question was from Maria Geddes. "Is there any chance this could spread to others on the island or even the mainland?"

"Very doubtful," Andie answered. "This stuff is spread by contaminated water, we think. We're trying to get a handle on how it gets in there."

"You *think*?" Ms. Geddes seemed to feel the need to pressure the only person at the meeting who was doing something about the problem.

Andie hadn't gotten to her elevated status within the epidemiology community by letting bureaucrats control the narrative. She looked directly at the department head and said, "Ms. Geddes, if you have any constructive suggestions on how we should proceed, please tell us. Otherwise, leave us alone to do what we do best, and we'll keep you in the loop."

Geddes chose that moment to study something on her phone while the rest of us looked at each other and raised our eyebrows. After a dozen pregnant seconds, I raised my hand like I was in the third grade.

Andie, now the de facto head of our little get-together, smiled and nodded in my direction. "Kevin, you got something?"

"Just an idea."

"Let's have it."

"By the time we test the water, it's so diluted we get negative results, right?"

"That's what we're assuming." Andie glanced at Ms. Geddes as if challenging her to a duel, but the bait was ignored.

"How about we get samples of water that's three days old and test that?"

Roger spoke for the first time. "How?"

"I don't know for sure, but some of these folks must have water bowls for their dogs or cats that could be a few days old. Or maybe a bird bath or a goldfish bowl. There must be someplace that has three-day-old water in that community."

The Island County rep looked at me as if I was speaking in tongues, the DOH woman offered a sneer, Jenne gave me one of her special smiles, and Roger and Andie looked like I'd found the Rosetta Stone.

"Great idea, Kevin. Why don't you two and Roger get going on this? I'll head back to the lab to get going on the samples from the infected people as soon as I stop by the reservoir."

As Andie gave us instructions, she looked at the other two people in the room. "If you give me your contact info, I'll copy you in on our results, and as soon as we know something for certain, you'll know. Okay?"

Geddes and Souza nodded wordlessly, seemingly assured that the investigation was in exceptionally capable hands.

While Andie collected samples from the huge 45,000-gallon concrete tank, Roger started at one end of the beach community and Jenne and me at the other.

With almost three hundred residents using the Maxwelton water system, it was surprising that those admitted to hospitals only numbered twenty-five. Although it was mid-July, the height of the summer vacation season, it was still mid-week and only 80 percent of the homes were occupied.

We discussed the seeming randomness of the outbreak and eventually chalked it up to several things. Many of the residents used bottled water for drinking. Those who cooked with the community water also boiled it, killing the bacteria. As we knocked on doors, we also found many folks with milder symptoms, probably owing to their robust immune systems.

The third house we visited was occupied by an elderly couple who were physically healthy, but both were depressed at the recent loss of their cat. Apparently, they reported, the little guy had wandered off a few days before and had not returned. I didn't have the heart to tell them he was probably lunch for a coyote or, more likely, one of the many eagles nesting in the nearby trees. It was common knowledge that small pets should be constantly watched lest they become a tasty morsel for some of the more aggressive predators on Whidbey Island.

"Did you keep a water bowl anywhere for your cat?" Jenne asked.

"Yes, we kept one in the garage near his litter box. There's a cat door in the garage entry where he can come and go as he pleases. I guess I should say as he pleased, but ..." It was clear the older woman was upset at the loss of her pet.

"Is it still there?" I asked.

"No, the cat is gone." The husband seemed to have lost the thread.

"He's asking about the bowl, Ralph, not Tommy."

"Oh, the water bowl. I think so. Filled it up the day he left, on Sunday."

"Great. Can we take a sample of it?" Jenne asked.

"I guess so, sure, but we'll put another one down, you know, in case he comes back."

I supposed it was possible that Ralph would see Tommy again, but it was doubtful. We collected the water in one of the empty bottles we'd brought and labeled it with the address as instructed by Andie.

We were successful at two other homes; one was a seldom-used dog bowl, and the other a bird bath filled three days ago. When we met up with Roger, we found that he, too, had several samples gathered from pet water bowls. He put them into a bag designed to carry six bottles of wine, and for a fleeting moment, I thought about the problems that would arise if anyone inadvertently drank the likely poisoned stuff.

"I told Dr. Saunders if we were lucky enough to get any samples, I'd bring them to her. I'll take the next boat over and get these to her lab right away."

"Are you sure we can't do that, Roger?" I thought maybe he'd want to watch over his flock on the island.

"Um, no, that's okay. I'm off now anyway, so it's no problem."

As he closed the door of his Ford Explorer police cruiser, Jenne looked at me, shaking her head.

"What? Did I do something?"

"You're dense."

"Huh? What do you mean, dense?"

"I think, O husband of mine, that Roger might have the hots for the professor."

"Really? How come? Why do you think that?"

"You haven't seen the way he looks at her? Like in the meeting this morning?"

"Um, no. I was paying attention like you should have been." Once again with the head shake ... "What? What?"

"I noticed his interest the first time we met. I don't know about Andie's status, but she's probably available."

It was as if men and women were in separate dimensions much of the time. "And you know this how?"

"When we took that hike several weeks ago, she said she was done with the dating scene. I think she was married long ago and divorced, but since then, nothing long-term."

"I think Roger could be out of his league." As soon as the words were out of my mouth, I knew I was in for a tongue-lashing.

"Why? Because he's a cop on an island?"

"No, no, of course not. I thought that she's this famous epidemiologist, and he's, you know, not as worldly." I thought maybe I'd closed the door on my pigeonholing faux pas, but it was not to be.

"Maybe there's a lot more to Roger than you think. Have you considered that?"

"No, ma'am; please enlighten me."

"Just so you know, Roger was with the LAPD for fifteen years before he took the job here. He worked homicide and was one of their senior detectives."

"You're shitting me! How do *you* know this?"

"When all that stuff with Sharon Waffle and the battery thing happened, we spent a couple of hours waiting for you to show up one day. He told me he'd rather keep it on the low down, so I never said anything."

"So all this time you knew we had a star from the LAPD here on little tiny Whidbey Island? And how come he's here and not in LA anymore?"

"I did, yes. It's not something he likes to talk about, but he was feeling a little down at the time, and he said his wife died unexpectedly. He took some time off and decided he needed a change of scenery. That was five years ago, and now he can't imagine being anywhere else."

"Sheesh, I had no idea. No wonder he never seems flustered about anything."

"After he shared this with me, I did a little checking online. He solved several high-profile crimes, including one with a serial killer that had the city paralyzed for a few months. The guy was a bona fide star."

Hearing this backstory, I felt like a schmuck for assuming that Wilkie was some small-town deputy sheriff who was in over his head when it came to solving serious crimes.

Now sufficiently humbled, I said, "I guess we're lucky to have him involved in this thing, and I'm sorry for thinking otherwise."

I should have known better; it always amazed me the diversity and expertise of the residents of Whidbey Island. From Air Force test pilots to software entrepreneurs to world-renowned artists and writers, the island was home to more than its fair share of accomplished people who preferred to stay under the radar.

Thirteen

Dr. Andie Saunders got back to her lab a little after one o'clock. The situation on Whidbey Island was more concerning to her than she'd let on to anyone at the meeting, especially now that there were likely fatalities. It meant whoever was doing this was now a murderer.

She had been at the University of Washington for a dozen years, teaching one of the advanced classes in their graduate program while traveling extensively to disease and bacterial outbreaks worldwide.

A native of San Diego, she took the job at UDub after spending almost a dozen years at Scripps Research Institute studying bacterial infections, their causes, and treatment methods. It wasn't so much the lure of university life or the desire to spend eight months a year in clouds and drizzle that had caused the move; it was more her failed marriage to one of the senior staff members. They'd dated off and on for a few years, breaking up for a few months, then getting back together for a few more. She accepted his proposal, thinking mistakenly that their relationship would improve if they tied the knot and lived together permanently.

After only a year, she was sure she'd made a mistake, and when she found out he'd been screwing his administrative assistant, she packed her things and moved out. The separation was amicable, but his senior position at the institute made her employment there untenable. It wasn't just the whispers, rumors, and disinformation regarding his infidelity that drove her away; she could no longer stand the sight of the asshole. She gave her notice the week after she signed the divorce papers.

Andie relocated to Seattle three weeks before Christmas, during the darkest, rainiest time of the year, and for three months she questioned her sanity in making such a drastic move. She had been contacted by the University of Washington Medical Center once before and this time, took them up on their offer. She rented a small bungalow in Wallingford and was shocked at the depth of her loneliness and misery during that time.

She found some sense of purpose after committing to a gym membership and showing up seven days a week regardless of her energy level. There, she met Alice DeGroot, and at her suggestion, she started going to therapy and became aware that she wasn't the only person in the world dealing with a breakup. She started running with Alice and eventually worked up to joining her, competing in marathons a few times a year.

In her early forties, Andie was a decade older than Alice, but her gym work and running gave her the appearance of a much younger woman. She dated infrequently, still nursing scars from her previous marriage, never quite finding someone who she felt challenged her while respecting her and earning her trust. Her friends and associates at school offered to set her up, but after several swings and misses, she no longer encouraged their efforts. She was seemingly content to be highly respected by her peers both at UDub and throughout the country, but there were times when she fantasized about meeting someone to settle down with. And now that Alice was living on Whidbey Island, she missed her running buddy.

***

The knock on her lab door startled her. It was almost six, and most staff and students had left for the day. She looked up to see the cop from Whidbey standing there with an armful of water bottles.

"Hi, Dr. Saunders. Here are the samples we collected from what we think is water that came from the reservoir three days before the outbreak."

"It's Roger, right?"

"Yup."

"Call me Andie, please, and thanks for making the trip so quickly." She wasn't exactly sure why, but a slight blush accompanied her unforced smile.

"Not a problem. I figured you'd want them right away—you know, to see if they are contaminated with that Shiggy stuff." Roger, too, was wearing a grin.

"Shiggy stuff?"

"I figured it was easier than Shiga toxin–producing E. coli."

Andie was encouraged that this guy was only pretending to be a dullard. She enjoyed his quiet retreat from the seriousness of the situation. "Let's keep the Shiggy thing between us. If my students heard me say that, they'd laugh me out of the university."

"Works for me. Where do you want these?"

She pushed a mound of paperwork aside and said, "Put them here, and I'll get to them immediately."

Roger placed the samples on the counter, stopped, and looked at his watch. "Hey, Andie ..."

"Yes?"

"The traffic sucks right now, and I'll have to get in line for a boat anyway. You want to grab a bite?"

Andie wasn't sure how she felt. Roger was a good-looking guy, if slightly older than she was, and in their two meetings, he had appeared intelligent and capable, but her experience with the opposite sex was a bumpy road. She hesitated a beat too long.

"Hey, no biggie. If you're swamped, that's cool. I just thought maybe ..."

"That sounds like a great idea, Roger. Let's let the Shiggy thing rest for a little while." She wasn't sure what had tipped the scales, but maybe a diversion was what she needed right now.

At her suggestion, they headed for the University Grille, within walking distance of Andie's lab in the UW Medical Center. During the school year, the casual yet upscale restaurant would be filled with faculty, but in late June, getting a table was no problem.

The 70-degree temperature was perfect for sitting at one of the half-dozen tables in the small courtyard at the rear of the restaurant. The giant potted ferns, rustling in the faint breeze, lent their seating a tropical feel and a measure of privacy. With only one other table in the outdoor dining area occupied, the muffled jazz piano and the tinkling of glassware were all that could be heard.

"Sheesh, this place is nice. I've been on the island so long, I forgot what it's like to eat at a fancy restaurant."

"There must be *some* nice restaurants there," Andie said. "Besides, this place isn't *that* fancy."

"Oh, there are, sure, but most are pretty casual, and frankly, the population is too small in the winter months to support anything of any size. From what I can see, you have your pick of any food imaginable here."

"You're right about that, especially here in the University District. The diversity of cultures lends itself to more ethnic food choices than I've had time to try."

"Yeah, that's one of the few things I miss about LA."

"You used to live there?" Andie was surprised at this.

Roger suddenly looked as though he'd revealed more than he had intended. "I did, but that was a while ago."

Andie wasn't sure why, but his reluctance to comment further caused her to dig deeper. "What did you do when you lived there? Were you a cop?"

With a deep sigh and the look of someone visiting times and places of a past life, he appeared to reach a crossroads. "I was a detective with the LAPD for over a dozen years."

Andie's eyes grew wide, and she was at a loss for words. The county deputy sheriff sitting across from her, the guy she thought might be a little old for her yet could possibly be a comfortable fit, had been a detective with one of the premier police departments in one of the largest cities in the country.

Fortunately, the waiter appeared, asking if they wanted a drink before ordering. They both looked relieved and almost shouted *"yes"* simultaneously.

As if Roger's revelation hadn't happened, they made small talk until their drinks—Roger's scotch rocks and Andie's vodka martini—arrived.

She looked directly at Roger, now seeing him in an entirely different light. He was solidly built with a weathered face and Coke-bottle-green eyes. At a smidge under six feet, she could see why his sympathetic countenance might serve him well in dealing with the public. Right now, wearing jeans, sneakers, and a Tommy Bahama sweatshirt, he could easily have been mistaken for someone years younger.

"Hey, you," he said. "Cheers." At this, she appeared startled, then he offered his glass up, and they toasted, somehow touching fingers instead of drinks.

Still unsure what to say next, she was grateful when Roger rescued the conversation. "Did that surprise you? You know, about the LA thing?"

Finding her voice, she said, "It did. I think when you live on an island, people assume you're not particularly worldly. I'm guilty of that too, I guess."

"No worries. It's not something I talk about very often, and it was another lifetime ago."

"Can I ask why, or would you rather I not go there?"

After a few seconds, Roger seemed to have reached a decision. "I got married out of college and pursued a career in law enforcement ..."

After almost twenty minutes, interrupted only by the waiter taking their dinner order, Roger finished by saying, "And that's my story ..."

Andie was first stunned that this kind and accomplished human being would share his experiences and heartaches with her and, secondly, that she was as attracted to him as she had ever been to anyone.

Both were silent as their dinner was delivered. She reached across the table, squeezed his hand, and said, "Thank you for sharing that. I'm sure it wasn't easy."

"Actually," he said, "the decision was hard, but telling you was easy after that. For some reason, I wanted to ... How's the salmon?"

"Great segue. Are you always this clever?"

"Mostly, yes. Now spill the beans; you weren't born here at UDub, right?"

She chuckled with both enjoyment and nervousness at the same time. "I can see why folks like you, Roger. You have a wonderful way of asking for information, and it doesn't seem like the third degree."

"Just wait until I get you in an interrogation room under the bright lights."

She shared her life experiences with this man, something she hadn't done with anyone but Alice and her therapist. When she was finished, she felt a connection with this stranger that she had never felt with another person.

Neither of them had touched their meal, but fortunately, they had ordered wine with their dinner, which seemed to be all they needed. When the waiter returned, he asked if the food wasn't to their liking.

"I guess we weren't hungry after all," Andie said. "Maybe we'll just finish our wine and stay a little longer."

The waiter nodded, cleared the table except for the wine glasses, and made himself scarce. It appeared he wasn't born yesterday.

As if a mutual understanding had been reached, their conversation flowed easily, almost as if they were old friends. Each new experience or revelation shared now served to build a solid foundation for whatever materialized down the road.

Andie's cheeks were sore; she hadn't smiled this much in years and was grateful to this man for allowing her to do so. Forgotten was the reason they had met until Roger mentioned it.

"I guess we won't get those test results tonight, eh?"

"Shit, I forgot about them, and it's your fault. You ply a woman with charming stories and wine, and it's no wonder they forget about things." She said this with an ear-to-ear grin.

"You're right, my bad, but perhaps the lovely woman also played a role in this."

"Well, maybe so," she said, "but I'll get on it first thing in the morning." She turned serious. "I think I know what I'll find, and it scares me a little."

"Me too, but we *will* get to the bottom of this. I promise."

For maybe the first time, she had complete faith in a man's commitment. "You know, Roger, I believe you will."

"I'd better get going, or I'll never get back to Whidbey. When do you think you'll get the results?"

"If I get the cultures going in the morning, I should have an indication by the following day, on Friday."

"Should we touch base then?"

"Why don't I bring the results up to the island? Alice left me a standing invitation, and it'll be nice to get away for the weekend. Also, maybe we could get together?"

"Geez, I don't know, Andie; I might be busy."

"Huh? What? Seriously? You better not be, or I'll kick your ass."

"Okay, okay, I'm not busy—not when you put it like that ... sheesh!"

They laughed as they stood to leave, then walked back to the Medical Center, often bumping shoulders along the way. When they eventually arrived at Andie's Nissan Leaf, Roger leaned over, gave her a quick kiss on the lips, and squeezed her hand. "See you Friday."

She opened her door and sat behind the wheel as Roger left for his cruiser. She sat quietly for a few minutes, his kiss lingering, thinking it had been a most remarkable evening indeed.

Fourteen

I assumed Roger would let us know whenever he heard back from Andie Saunders about the results of the tests on the three-day-old water samples we submitted.

It was Friday morning, and it was summer on Whidbey Island. Days like this made the seemingly endless periods of drizzle and darkness worth enduring. The high temperature for the day would be 70 degrees, and a cloudless sky was promised. Unlike in the Midwest and on the East Coast, mosquitos and house flies were rarely a nuisance. The only threatening wildlife on the island was the genuine possibility of running into one of the black-tail deer with a vehicle.

It was an idyllic place to live, and we full-time residents did our best to keep it a secret. Unfortunately, the word sometimes got out, and folks occasionally moved here.

Jenne was also a golfer, albeit a fair-weather one. Her interest in other endeavors sometimes took precedence over time on the links, but today she had consented to join me. It was a glorious morning, the fairways lush, the greens speedy, and the traffic light. Whenever she hit a great shot or sunk a lengthy putt, I enjoyed it at least as much as she did. Most of the time, I enjoyed the betting and good-natured ribbing with the guys, but, truth be told, I wouldn't have traded the time on the course with only the two of us for anything.

"Did I tell you Alice asked us to join them for dinner tonight?" We were walking to the sixth tee after both parring the fifth, and Jenne had a spring in her step.

"No, hon, you didn't. Did we respond in the affirmative?" I knew *we* did, of course, but it never hurt to score even a small measure of sympathy from my wife.

"Yes, we did, Kev. I'm sorry, did you have other plans?"

"Of course not, dear; I would have let you know,"—and I'd lost the tiny higher ground I once perched upon in the blink of an eye.

She was laughing now, and her joy was contagious. Even though she had just turned sixty, she had the looks and toned body of a woman ten years younger. Her Irish–Croatian lineage had blessed her with sparkling hazel eyes and an olive complexion, and her gray ponytail thrust out the back of her ballcap made her look like a college student. It was her smile, though, that lit up a room.

Was this ruddy-faced Irish knucklehead ever lucky or what?

By the time we walked up the hill from the eighteenth green, it was mid-afternoon. We stopped in the clubhouse for a lemonade, said hello to those we knew—most of the folks in the bar—and then hopped into my pickup for the trip back home.

We arrived at the Robbinses' residence just before six and were surprised to see Andie greet us at the door. Wearing shorts, flip-flops, and a white linen shirt, she looked nothing like the world-famous microbiologist from the University of Washington.

"Alice told me I could stay here whenever I wanted, so I took her up on it. The two of them are in the back doing something with a smoker. C'mon in."

As we followed Andie to the back patio, I glanced at Jenne, raising my eyebrows. She mouthed the words *I know*, acknowledging that the professor was in great spirits and even had a bit of a skip in her step.

Seth and Alice greeted us as we stepped outside and noticed Roger Wilkie seated in one of the lounge chairs, sipping something with an umbrella in it.

"Hey, Kev, Jenne, nice to see you someplace other than the station." He stood, greeting us.

We shook hands and looked at the Robbinses, whose looks suggested they knew something we didn't.

"When Andie told us she was coming for the night, we thought throwing salmon on the smoker would be fun. She came up to visit with Roger about those test results, so we invited him too."

We nodded, both of us still curious about the social interaction going on. Luckily, I was able to break the feeling of awkwardness. "Hey, cool. How does a guy get a beer here?"

"I got it, Alice. See if you can take care of this one." Seth did something with the smoker while we began with small talk.

Eventually, the conversation turned to the bacterial episodes on the island when Andie offered, "I came to let Roger know my findings. He just got here, and I haven't had a chance to review them with him, so I'll tell all of you now."

The five of us gave her our complete attention as she stood beside the outdoor dining table. "As I suspected, the water samples Roger gave me were contaminated with very high levels of Shiga toxin–producing E. coli. Regrettably, this new strain appears more virulent than E. coli 0157.

"Now that we're certain the water is the source, we can take steps to prevent other reservoirs from being contaminated, and I guess that's going to fall on you, Roger." As she said this, she looked at Roger with what seemed like much more than a professional attitude.

"Going forward, I'll research this strain and determine where it came from. That might help in locating whoever is doing this." She continued looking at Roger while reporting her intentions.

"Thanks, Andie; this helps a lot. I'll contact the DOH and the county and have them put out a notice to every public water system on the island. We'll also let Duke Water know. I'm sure they'll be able to change their testing intervals, so it's not as predictable."

Roger's plan was practical and effective, although his glance never wavered from Andie as he spoke.

"Is there anything we can do, Roger?" Jenne asked.

He turned to us and said, "Maybe you can help get the word out to the communities on the island's south end. I'll let the DOH know you're on the team and make sure they coordinate with you."

Now that my wife had enlisted our services, it felt like the right time to steer the conversation in another direction. "So, Seth, did you plan on feeding us tonight?"

The collective sigh on the patio told me all were happy moving on to subjects that were not life or death. Once we had sat down to eat, I couldn't help but notice that neither Roger nor Andie were ever more than a few feet apart. Score one once again for my wife.

As the evening progressed, Seth and Alice told us what was new in their world, and Roger and Andie grew quiet. The two of them stood up as dessert was about to be served.

"Roger wants to go over some things with the test results, so we thought it made sense to do it now at his place where he has all his notes."

This made little sense to me, so I said, "Now? It's Friday night; can't it wait?"

Instead of an answer, I received stern looks from Alice and Seth and one from Jenne, which told me I was a stupid, stupid man.

It finally dawned on me after Jenne's admonishing glance what was happening. Roger must have seen me wallowing, too, because he threw me a lifeline.

"I think it's important, Kevin. We want to get on it right away."

"Of course, sure ... I don't know what I was thinking. You two should leave right now and get to work on this."

Now Jenne was just shaking her head and looking at the others with a *what can I do with this moron* look.

We said good night to Roger and Andie and sat back down to finish our coffee, and I got right to the point. "They seem to get along well, don't you think?"

Jenne was the first to throw her napkin, and the other two quickly followed.

"I'm really happy for her. She's a great gal and deserves someone like Roger," Alice offered.

"I agree. I know a little about him, and I think Andie is one lucky professor," Jenne replied.

For my part, I was nodding in agreement, confident that keeping my mouth shut was the best course of action. This was confirmed when neither woman saw the tiny little thumbs-up thrown my way by Seth.

***

The following day brought clear skies and mild temperatures—perfect for the links. Regrettably, someone had promised to take Emma to the dog wash for her all too infrequent bath, and there was no escaping the commitment.

The single most significant contribution to residential bathrooms everywhere has to be the self-serve dog wash, and happily, the local pet shop offered two of these marvels of ingenuity. The machine automatically took your money, provided water, shampoo, and conditioner, and we had a clean-smelling, shiny-coated, happy German Shepherd in fifteen minutes. Sure, there was fur and hair from wall to wall in the tub area, and after blow-drying our sweetie with the wind tunnel–like hose provided, the stuff had spread to the entire room. I could recollect past episodes at home when it would take weeks to scrape the damn dog hair from the walls and tile of our bathroom shower and floor, not to mention the mounds of it plugging the drain—progress, for sure.

Exiting the shop and heading for Bagel Haven with a poofed-up GSD still shaking the remaining droplets from her coat, I saw Roger Wilkie and Dr. Andie Saunders seated at one of the sidewalk tables.

"Hey, you two. Did you get everything worked out last night?" I'm sorry, I couldn't help myself. They looked at me and smiled sheepishly but still dared to maintain their handholding.

"Yes, Kevin, we made great progress," Andie said. "Roger helped a great deal."

"I'm sure he did. Not to change the subject, but what are the next steps, Andie? On the cultures, that is ..."

Her expression was much the same as my wife's when she was about to whack me, but she was much more professional about it. "We'll monitor them. By today's end, we'll have sufficient colony growth to study and attempt to determine the origin. My assistant will supervise the process over the weekend."

Roger also delivered an update: "I sent a message to both Souza at the county and Geddes at state to get them going on the alert for the public water systems. It's the government, of course, but they did say this was a high priority, and they'll get it out first thing Monday. The last thing they want is for this to hit the papers and become a national story. I think they'll get it done."

I thought if they could move that fast, it would help, and then I had an idea. "Jenne has a list of all the HOAs on the island south of Coupeville. If you can draft a notice, we can email them this weekend. The comms from state and county will convey the seriousness of this, but if we get ahead of it, we might do some good."

"I think that's a great idea. How about you get me the contact info from Jenne? I'll write something up and then send it from our office. That way, it should carry a little more weight."

"Sounds good. Will you be heading back today, Andie?"

"I was planning on it, but Roger here has convinced me I'm needed on the island." She said this with a coy look at the local lawman.

"Well, if he says he needs help, then I'm sure you'll be perfect for the job." I could have been mistaken, but I thought I saw Roger slide a middle finger alongside his head, but maybe it was just a little itch.

"I'll stop by with the list as soon as I get the details pulled together."

"You do know they have this thing called *email* now, don't you?" Roger apparently thought it unnecessary for me to deliver the information personally.

"I guess I could, but maybe you'll have some questions, and I might be able to help." I should have quit, but where was the fun in that?

"Kevin, email the damn list, and if I can't figure it out, I'll call you—you know, on the phone?"

I knew when to surrender, so I turned to my faithful companion. "C'mon, Emma. It appears these two would prefer not to be bothered by those of us wanting to provide assistance.

"I'm glad you're here, Andie," I said as we turned to head to my truck. "It pains me to say this, but Roger is one of the most responsible guys I know, and I've seen him smile more in the last two days than in the last two years. I'm happy for you both. I'll send you the list in the next hour or so."

Fifteen

The results from the Maxwelton community were excellent. The new E. coli strain he had cultured was far more virulent than the bacteria used at Holmes or Cultus Bay, and soon, he'd have enough to make a lasting impression on the woke pricks who were destroying the real America.

Although Harry had little formal education, his research and study habits—thanks to Christine Raggio of the Multnomah County Library—were exemplary.

Harry had created a strain of Shiga toxin–producing bacteria that was certain, even in small concentrations, to eat away enough of the small intestine lining to produce life-threatening complications.

He started with common E. coli bacteria cultured from the feces of his two Belted Galloway cows. With a simple gene-editing CRISPR kit, he began randomly altering the genome structure of the cultured organism. It was a trial-and-error process using the most aggressive bacterium to produce the next.

After trying waste from the Choctaw pigs individually and in combination with that from the cows with no appreciable success, he moved on to the pygmy goats. While culturing bacteria from these cute little guys' fecal matter, he noticed how easily the genome structure could be altered.

After months of effort and random swings and misses with the goat feces, he stumbled upon a strain that was even more destructive and durable than Escherichia coli 0157. It took another few months to culture sufficient quantities of the stuff to use in his trials, and so far, they had exceeded his expectations.

The Maxwelton event proved that even in minute concentrations, a sufficient percentage of the population was infected to cause panic among the residents. Like everyone in this age of instant awareness, however, once the furor died, some other event would come along for the locals to worry about.

His next target would bring national attention to tiny Whidbey Island, but first, he needed to produce enough of the toxin. Now, the country would see the folly in going down the road of tolerance for bleeding-heart liberals who wanted the government to coddle and babysit those who couldn't make it on their own. Somehow, the fact that his entire wealth resulted from an inheritance failed to register even a toehold in his mind.

Whidbey Island had its share of wealth and also of those less fortunate. Its sense of community, though, resulted in a mutual existence where those with much gave much and rarely did a family or individual fall through the cracks.

Sixteen

It was mid-week before Andie was confident enough in her assessment to issue a full report to the state and county regarding the strain of E. coli found in the Maxwelton community water system.

Roger Wilkie, of course, received the report a day earlier, and he asked us to stop by the office so he could share it. He had successfully gotten a notice to the list of HOAs on South Whidbey, as had the Island County DOH. For now, the state was letting the county take the lead.

"Andie says the colonies cultured from the water we collected produced a strain of Shiga toxin–producing bacteria twice as dangerous as the 0157. She said whoever is producing this stuff—and she's convinced it's here on the island—knows what they're doing."

"How do we track this person down?" Jenne was already thinking ahead.

"I asked her if she had any ideas about that. She said whoever it is either has a substantial laboratory or has access to one. She also said this person is no dummy; there aren't too many people in the country capable of creating this."

Since all of the attacks were on the island's south end, it made sense that the creator of the toxin would be located there, too; it was just that the rural nature of the place suggested otherwise. Almost every resident knew something about their neighbors, and keeping such a secret would have been difficult. I said, "You think someone could keep a secret lab here? It's hard enough keeping who's sleeping with who a secret. Right, Roger?"

A nasty look from my wife and a wave of dismissal from Roger told me my attempt at lightening the mood was a failure. "No, really, you think this makes any sense?" I attempted to get the train back on track.

"As far as I know, there are no scientists working in secret labs here. Maybe at the Navy base in Oak Harbor, but I'm pretty sure we don't need to worry about them. I suppose somebody could hide something away in the forested areas, but still, as you tried to say, it's hard to keep secrets on an island."

"Did she say anything about what raw materials someone would need to develop these bacteria?"

"We talked a little about that, but it wasn't long before she got into something way over my head. Basically, E. coli is found in fecal matter, and, as we know, there's plenty of that around, so it's tough to narrow down the possibilities."

Jenne appeared to be considering this and said, "So, we live on an island with plenty of farms, ranches, and livestock and where almost all of the human waste is handled by on-site sewage systems, *and* this stuff grows in fecal material? Shit, excuse the pun, but the possibilities seem endless."

I shared the same frustrations, and from the looks of Roger, so did he. "For now, let's focus on beefing up security where possible. Most larger communities have responded to my email and are taking steps with cameras or alarms. They've agreed to post watches until they can get the stuff installed. The smaller ones—under twenty or so—are probably not in too much danger, but it wouldn't hurt to remind them. Maybe you two can help with that."

"We'll head back home and start making some calls. Will Andie be coming up again soon?" Jenne's questioning was way more subtle than mine, almost as if she was kind and concerned, which she was.

Roger looked at me with a smirk as if to say, *See, smartass, this is how you're supposed to act.*

"Yes—she's coming up Friday for the weekend. We thought we'd take a trip to Ebey's Landing, then maybe stop at a B&B in Coupeville."

Since my wife's inquiry was so well received, I thought it was time to restrain my sarcasm. "The weather looks great, and Coupeville is a charming spot to visit."

Roger looked at me as if not sure who was speaking. "Yes, it does. We're looking forward to some time away from this crazy shit—sorry, there's that word again."

"Tell her hi from us. Hopefully, things will be quiet while you're gone." I thought I had cleaned up my act, although a glance from my wife suggested I was only rounding second.

Seventeen

The colony growth of the bacteria from the altered genetic material from the goat feces took longer than expected. It was lethal enough, but the quantity needed for his final operation was still too great.

The reservoir he targeted held over 600,000 gallons of water, meaning he'd need 50 gallons of tainted culture to have the desired effect. This was more than he could physically manage by himself. Once again, the only solution was to manipulate the bacterium's structure.

Bringing the livestock to his compound made the breeding material for the bacteria easily accessible. The downside of the goddamn animals was that they required feeding, watering, and cleaning up after.

The cows were easy. He'd leave them in the pasture he'd fenced in, make sure their water trough was full, and that was enough. The pigs were even easier. They hung out in a smaller section of the pasture and ate anything. The goats were another story altogether.

They were cute little animals with long beards and stubby little horns, but they were high maintenance. They would eat anything that grew, so if he left them in with the cows, the cows wouldn't have anything to graze on. They couldn't hang with the pigs either because of the headbutting thing.

They mostly hung out in the barn and a small side yard for which he had to build yet *another* goddamn fence. To make them even more annoying, the little bastards were constantly bleating. If a bird landed on the fence, they'd bleat. If a cow or pig came too close, they'd bleat. Even when he came to feed them, it was as if they wanted to have a conversation. He'd have had them for dinner if it hadn't been for their unique shit.

He'd only hold on to the cows and pigs until he was through with his campaign. He entertained thoughts of having them butchered and stuffing his freezer for the long winter, but if he were honest, he would have acknowledged that when he was finished with his mission, *he* likely would be as well.

He set these thoughts aside and began the intensive process of altering the new strain of bacteria harvested from the waste material of the very talkative pygmy goats.

Eighteen

It had been almost three months since the Maxwelton outbreak, and there were no reports of any other infections. There had been an E. coli outbreak in Oak Harbor, but that was traced to a bad batch of hamburger that was immediately removed from the shelves.

It was now the end of September. Each passing week reinforced the notion that either whoever had contaminated the water systems had given up the campaign or moved from the island, or the security measures taken by the communities were enough to discourage any further sabotage.

Our official meetings with Roger became less frequent, as did his with the county Board of Health. The state DOH official hadn't been heard from since the last meeting over the Maxwelton outbreak.

Andie Saunders became a frequent visitor to the island, and several times we had gotten together with her, Roger, and the Robbinses. All of us were happy for the couple, and the further removed we got from the bacterial outbreaks, the more the mundane aspects of life were welcome. A current-day philosopher once said, "Comfortably boring is the sweet spot of life." I think she may have had a point.

"You really think we're done with this?" I was looking back and forth from Roger to Andie, but it was understood my question was directed at the microbiologist. We had joined them for coffee at the Braeburn, one of the fine eateries in the small town of Langley, which sits on the shores of the Saratoga Passage.

"I'd like to think so, but probably not. We're trying to figure out where this stuff comes from."

"It's from shit, though, right?"

"Nicely articulated, Kevin."

Sadly, Andie Saunders had adopted a somewhat sarcastic tone when addressing yours truly. Not only did I enjoy it, I welcomed her to the dark side. If there was any uncertainty about her intention, it was dispelled when Jenne offered her a healthy fist bump.

The adult that I am, I chose to ignore them and continued, "No, really. You said before that the bacteria comes from fecal material."

"I did, but this stuff has been altered genetically to produce a more virulent strain—one that is resistant to common water treatment practices. The university is so interested in locating the source, they have me working on it full time."

"I'll say. You should see the books and notes at my house. They're strewn all over." Roger confirmed her diligence.

A feigned pout from Andie was enough for the deputy to backpedal quickly. "Of course, I wouldn't have it any other way."

The occasional weekend visits by Andie had progressed to every weekend, and most of them stretched to include Fridays and Mondays. That they were smitten with each other was an understatement.

"Have you made any progress, Andie?" Jenne asked.

"So far, all we've been able to do is exclude groups of animals. The bacteria aren't from bovine or porcine fecal material, or human either, for that matter. Considering the number and variety of domestic and wild animals on the island, the list of candidates is endless.

"We're working through the groups with the highest populations first. We're currently looking at dogs, horses, chickens, and deer. The only bright spot in all this is if we find the origin is from an animal smaller in number, it may be easier to locate the source."

I thought the task in front of Andie was monumental and that there had to be another way. "Has there been any activity at all on the cameras?"

Roger slurped some coffee and shook his head before saying, "None. But there's no way this fucker's getting away, and you can bank on it. He—I'm guessing it's a guy—has made people seriously sick and killed two of them."

There was a few seconds of silence before Roger realized that his outburst may have been more intense than intended. I could see why his determination had made him a legend at the LAPD.

"Sorry ... I'm sorry. I guess this thing's getting under my skin. Here we live in this idyllic location with wonderful, interesting folks, and some asshole is poisoning the water. It pisses me off."

Andie reached over and squeezed his hand. "We'll get him, Roger."

"I know, I know. It just feels like we're waiting for something awful to happen, and we can't do anything about it."

I felt his frustration, and one look at Jenne confirmed she was of like mind. "Is there anything at all we can do?"

"Short of driving aimlessly around the island and stumbling upon a laboratory producing dangerously toxic bacteria, I can't think of a thing."

We all chuckled at Andie's articulation of the difficulty of what we were trying to accomplish, but there may have been a sliver of daylight in her conclusion.

"Hey, you two are the pros, and we're just the helpers, so if extending our sightseeing drives from thirty minutes every Sunday to an hour or two might turn up something, we're your men ... and woman ... man and woman." Sheesh, that was close.

Jenne was rolling her eyes and shaking her head, but at least she was smiling. "I think he means if we come across something that's even a possibility, we'll let you know."

When she said it that way, it seemed so much simpler.

***

As we stood to leave, a shiny black van pulled into the accessible parking space in front of the Braeburn. Roger was the first to announce the arrival of the new county commissioner. "Well, if it isn't Jake Early, our brand-new representative."

We watched as the side door slid open and the hydraulic lift lowered Jake to the pavement.

"Hi, everyone. I can't tell you how rewarding it is to mix with the little people." His broad grin confirmed he was happy to see us.

"You keep saying shit like that, and you'll be in for a recall. You'll have served the shortest term in the history of Island County. What brings you to these parts?"

"Kevin, Kevin, Kevin ... I thought you'd welcome the chance to be seen with a county official, you know, you can tell all your friends and—"

"I think we've had enough of this drivel, Jake. How's the new gig?" I could always count on my wife to cut through the bullshit guys often use to hide their genuine affection for each other.

"Thanks, Jenne; you know how annoying your husband can be."

"Um ... you *too*, eh?"

"Yup, sorry—I get around him, and he brings out the worst in me. I saw you here and wanted to tell you the news. One of the duties of the commissioners is to sit on the Board of Health and, as the commissioner for South Whidbey, I'm your man. On a serious note, any progress on the E. coli thing?"

Before answering, Andie asked, "Does that mean we won't be seeing Edgar Souza?"

"You're Dr. Andie Saunders, right? I'm Jake Early. I've heard great things about you, but I gotta say, you hanging with Roger here gives me cause for concern.'

"Funny, Roger said the same about our new county commissioner."

Jake laughed loudly at this; he knew when he'd met his match. "Edgar's still on the board, but I wanted to be the liaison because I live in the area and, frankly, because I knew you were involved. Besides, I'll get to see even more of all of you. So, any news?"

Roger took the lead. "We were just now talking about it. We're concerned folks will let down their guard because there have been no new outbreaks, and we're worried what comes next could be worse."

"Shit."

"We're doing everything we can at UDub, trying to get a handle on the origin of the stuff, but it's slow going."

"Edgar said you knew your stuff. He got a kick out of the lady from the state trying to assert herself. He said after that, he was afraid to ask you anything."

"Geez, come on! What's wrong with you, big, strong men? If I came across too sternly, I apologize. Over the years, I've found that when the bureaucrats get involved, everything takes longer, and often the results are finessed so much that they don't tell the entire story. Tell Edgar he can ask me anything. He seemed like a good guy."

"I will. Meanwhile, I'd like to stay on top of this. When's the next meeting of the team?"

Roger answered, "We don't have anything scheduled because there hasn't been much to discuss. Mostly, we're updating whatever progress there is—and there isn't much—via email. I'll make sure you're on the list. Andie's trying to isolate the source of the fecal material used to culture the bacteria, but it's going to take some time. Otherwise, we're in reactive mode."

"I may be the newbie at the county, but I can still pull some strings if necessary. Let me know if you need anything—people, money, whatever; please let me know if I can help."

As Jake was wrapping up, the driver's side door slammed, and out jumped Francis. His brutish looks and tattooed face often led to folks misjudging the man. Hell, the first time *I* met him, I feared for my life. I could tell by the look on Andie's face that his initial impression was still startling.

"You gonna introduce me, Jake, or do I have to do it myself?"

"Sorry, Francis, I got carried away—you know, now that I'm so important."

Francis shook his shaved head and walked up to Andie. "Hi, I'm Francis, this one's brother and, most of the time, his driver. I'm starting to regret suggesting he run for office. I think it was easier when he never left the house." He delivered this with a smiling face and an extended hand.

Still uncertain, Andie shook the proffered hand, which swallowed hers whole. "I'm Andie; nice to meet you."

"I was listening to the football game and saw that my brother was beginning to annoy everyone. I figured a rescue was necessary."

Roger laughed loudly, and the rest of us followed suit—even Andie, although she appeared to be inspecting her hand to make sure all the fingers were still attached.

From his wheelchair, Jake was almost able to reach his brother's shoulder to give him a loving pat.

"Sorry, Francis, the conversation threw me off. Andie, this is my brother and one of the kindest men I know." The sincerity of his tone left all of us silent.

Eventually, Francis shook off his brother's hand and said, "I heard what Jake said about offering to help at the county level. I just wanted to say that if you need anything, when the shit hits the fan, call me. I still know some folks."

Francis's *folks* were some ex-cons he had served time with. They proved invaluable when we had to locate an embezzler a few years ago. Roger, although not personally involved, knew the whole story. He nodded in agreement and said, "If we get in a bind, Francis, we'll call you, and thanks for the offer."

Francis punched the air for emphasis and said, "Sure thing. Let me get Jake out of here before he becomes too much of a pest."

Jake said his goodbyes, and the two brothers loaded themselves into the van and departed.

As it backed out of the parking space, Andie looked to be still processing what she had just witnessed. "Those two are interesting ..."

"I'll fill you in on all the details on our way home. Jake and Francis are among the best people I know, and I'm sure Kevin and Jenne will agree. They sometimes pretend to kibbitz with each other, but it's all in good fun."

We nodded our approval and departed the Braeburn, still processing where we were at this ambiguous stage in the investigation.

Nineteen

Manipulating the genetic structure of the existing bacteria was time-consuming. Harry Hogan had an idea of what he was doing based on his research, but it was mostly a trial-and-error process.

Often, after he'd altered a bacterium, it would fail to reproduce, and he had to start over. It was frustrating, and, as always, his menagerie of animals got on his nerves—especially the bleating little goats. Even in his lab, he could hear the little shits expressing annoyance or displeasure at something; he never knew what.

It was almost as if they were laughing at him while he studied the microscopic bacteria living in the small dark brown pellets of their feces. The stuff reminded him of the Raisinets he used to eat as a youngster. The only blessing was that he no longer needed to screw around with the waste from the larger animals; it was too big and smelly.

Eventually his dedication bore fruit. After months of failed experiments, he finally produced an incredibly virulent bacterium. More importantly, it could reproduce rapidly into colonies of sufficient quantity to wreak havoc on the population he was targeting.

He knew almost all of the private water systems used some chlorination, so it was essential this new strain could tolerate the levels used in the reservoirs. To be certain, though, he needed to test the microbes on a smaller scale. He looked at many of the reservoir tanks on South Whidbey to see which community would be easiest to pursue.

In many instances he saw people parked in cars at the tanks, and in others, upon close inspection, he could see cameras had been installed.

Considering the previous three attacks, it shouldn't have surprised him, but just knowing that people were looking for him created more angst than he was comfortable with. It was less the fear of being caught and more the thought of failing at his prime objective that was the cause of this distress.

It was early October, and Harry still needed to find a water system to meet his requirements. Even following the Duke Water vehicles around proved fruitless because they no longer seemed to be on any fixed schedule. He was growing impatient, and then one night, while in the little barn sweeping up the Raisinets, he had an idea.

Who says the trials need to be on Whidbey? There are plenty of other water tanks in small communities throughout the state.

He hurried back to his lab and studied the map of Island County he'd posted on the wall. The county was comprised of just two islands, Whidbey and Camano. The difference between the two was that Camano Island was connected to the mainland at Stanwood, Washington, via the Camano Gateway Bridge.

Camano Island lies between Whidbey and the mainland and has approximately 16,000 people. Although no ferry is needed to access the island, it lies considerably farther north of Seattle than the ferry terminal to Whidbey Island.

Hogan had only been there once, fifteen years ago, when he had picked up a seriously inebriated young woman from a bar in Mukilteo. He had stopped for a beer while waiting for the ferry after spending the day searching for lab equipment in Seattle.

Harry was asexual. In his teens, his interest in girls was no more significant than that in his own sex. Although inexperienced in same-sex encounters, he'd had enough with the opposite sex to know it didn't interest him. Even self-serve release wasn't something he cared about.

Why Holly from Camano attracted him, he still couldn't put his finger on. She might have reminded him of his mother, or maybe she had a little of the Portland librarian in her. For whatever reason, looking at her in her intoxicated state, something long ago stowed in the sub-basement of Harry's mind stirred.

He sat beside her, initiated a conversation, and eventually fed her enough coffee and water to allow her to speak without slurring her words. She had broken up with her boyfriend earlier and never left her seat. She'd vowed to get stupid drunk and succeeded admirably.

Still hesitant about what was driving him, he volunteered to take her home. Had he known she lived on Camano Island and, worse, the island's south end, he surely would not have offered.

The drive took over an hour, and Holly snored and drooled the entire trip. Upon arriving at her small cabin, he shook her awake and told her she was home.

"Would you like to come in?"

Whatever had caused young Harry's attraction to the woman was but a distant memory. "Nope."

He left her at the end of her drive and began the journey back to Mukilteo to catch the late boat back to the island, still kicking himself for wasting his time with the woman.

His recollection of that trip was of a place similar to Whidbey but slightly more suburban. After some research, he discovered that most of the communities on Camano had similar water systems to those he had already targeted.

Now that people on Whidbey had been alerted to the possibility of someone infecting their water tank with dangerous bacteria, there was no need to disguise where the infection originated. He couldn't care less when they tested the system.

He packed his supplies and drove north through Oak Harbor, over Deception Pass, and through Anacortes. The drive to the bridge at Stanwood was fifteen or twenty miles longer this way, but it eliminated the necessity of waiting for the ferry.

***

It was late afternoon when Harry crossed the Camano Gateway Bridge. The mid-October sky was clear and cold, and the daylight was quickly receding.

It still amazed him the level of detail that could be found on the web. The Island County website displayed maps showing the location of all the wells and all the small public water systems on the island. He'd selected a small seventy-household association located mid-island.

As he drove south on Camano Hill Road, he recalled his trip to the island many years ago. A more evolved individual might have briefly wondered what had happened to Holly, but such considerate thoughts found no space to inhabit the recesses of Harry Hogan's twisted mind. A fleeting familiarity with the place was all he could muster.

He passed the reservoir tank for the Camano Mid-Island Homeowners Association just as the sun disappeared. The tank was fifty yards from the road, in a small clearing surrounded by blackberry bushes, alders, and firs. His research had noted the tank's capacity was 28,000 gallons, perfect for his needs.

Making his way to the top of the tank with barely enough daylight remaining, he cut off the vent pipe as before and emptied a single quart of liquid into the reservoir. He had upgraded his protection to a full-face organic vapor mask, and his face dripped with sweat even in the cool temperature.

He hurried back down the access ladder and returned to his pickup; with only a short sprint to the finish line, he wanted no chance of discovery. The drive back to his home was long, but a feeling of accomplishment washed over him as he listened to Marley's comforting words: *Don't worry about a thing, cos every little thing gonna be all right!*

Twenty

Most Saturday mornings I'd be on the links with my buddies at MBGC, but today I found myself approaching Roger Wilkie's residence on the west side of Lone Lake.

It was my first visit to his home, so I was surprised to see only a mailbox with his number on a post by the side of a narrow gravel two-track. I drove by the east side of the lake almost daily on my way to the golf course or the grocery or hardware store, but I never thought about it other than the serene views it offered and had never been to this side of the hundred-acre lake.

I took Lone Lake Road south to Murdock and then to Ribbit Road to a dead end. He had warned me that his home might be tricky to find, but, like all men everywhere, I assured him my keen sense of direction would never let me down. Looking at the narrow entrance between the blackberry canes now, I wasn't so sure.

I slowly proceeded, the gravel snapping and crunching under my tires for what seemed like forever. According to my odometer, though, it was less than a half mile until the brush disappeared, delivering me into a small meadow with a vintage white farmhouse smack in the middle.

A wrap-around porch highlighted the two-story white structure that sported Kelly green shutters and a river-rock chimney. I knew it was Roger's home because he was sitting in one of two Adirondack chairs, clasping a mug of coffee in both hands and grinning. Andie sat in the other, she too holding a mug. They were both bundled up in poofy parkas.

As I opened my door, he stood to greet me and said, "Any problem finding us?"

"Of course not. Never even made a wrong turn. What are you two doing outside in 40-degree weather?"

He lifted his mug and gestured for me to look in the other direction. I hadn't realized it, but the road to his house sloped gently uphill, and the view from his porch was spectacular. Facing east, the sun broke through the layer of fog camped over the lake. The light off the water was dazzling, and the reflection on his porch was enough to add a few degrees of warmth to the setting.

"Geez, you guys, this is stunning. You never told me you were a rich landowner and had a view to die for."

"Hah, good one. You should have seen this when I bought it years ago. The house was falling apart and had been on the market for a year. Something weird in the CC&Rs prohibited any new construction, and nobody wanted a project of this magnitude. I figured I had plenty of time when I wasn't working, and the deal included septic and well, so I bought it. What you see is half a dozen years of sweat equity."

"Nice, huh?" Andie looked as if she was born to live here and stood to give my arm a friendly squeeze.

"It's beautiful. Now I'll have to forgive Jenne for volunteering me to give you a hand with your bathroom remodel."

"Oh, you were volunteered, were you?"

"Nah, I was looking forward to it, but I can't tell my wife. Let's take a look and see what you're thinking."

We went inside, and I was pleased to see that Roger had done excellent work and his design sense was spot on.

"Nice job, Roger—really well put together."

"Thanks. My wife was an interior designer, and I guess some of it rubbed off. She was always a proponent of keeping the structure classic and simple and letting the furniture, rugs, and art do the decorating."

"What's the story on the bathroom?"

"I pulled out the old cast iron tub, and we're putting in a walk-in shower." I couldn't help but notice the "we" in his comment, but the adult in me let it go.

"Okay, what's the conundrum?"

"I'm ready to rough in the plumbing, and we're not sure what height to put the shower head. I'm six feet and Andie's only five-six, so where do we put it?"

Once again, I was mildly surprised at the direction the discussion had taken. This was Roger's house, but it sorta looked like it was going to be someone else's too. *Man, I wish Jenne were here to tell me what to say.*

I figured there was nobody but the three of us, so how badly could I screw this up? So I dove in. "Um, no offense, and remember, I'm just helping here, but it sounds like we need to accommodate the two of you, right?"

They looked at each other as though I had spoken a foreign language, then Roger said, "That's correct."

"Like, you're both living here? Together? At the same time?"

"Yes, Kevin, you've got that right," Andie replied. "There's a smaller cottage in the back that I'm turning into my office. I'll still go into UDub once a week for a day or two, but I'm an island gal as of last week. Roger asked me to marry him."

"Yikes! No shit? Really? That's fantastic! I'm so happy for both of you." I hugged them both and meant every word. "Who else knows?"

"Only you, but we figured if we told you, then everyone would know soon enough." He chuckled. "We've seen each other constantly since last spring, and we both assumed we'd be together forever. We wanted to iron out a few logistical issues first, so we haven't broadcast anything. Feel free to, though."

"I'll put out the word. Jenne will be thrilled. And the shower thing?"

"Yeah?"

"Is that a real question?"

"You bet your ass. I'm not gonna be able to reach the damn showerhead if it's seven feet high." I appreciated Andie's straight talk.

"Simple. Shower head goes to seven feet, and you install a diverter and a hand-held shower on a vertical bar to the right. You can adjust the height to anything you want. The diverter lets you switch from one to the other or have them both on simultaneously. As far as the rough-in goes, the diverter and shower valve come with a layout diagram. Easy peasy."

"I suppose I should have been able to figure that out."

"I'm sure you could have, Roger, but it seems you've had other things on your mind."

The heavy lifting done, I joined them for coffee and sat in front of the fireplace that still had enough glowing embers to supply some warmth. We made small talk for a while, and then, as I got up to leave, Roger's cell phone buzzed. He looked at the number and raised a finger, asking for a moment.

***

"When?" I could only hear Roger's side of the conversation, but the look on his face was enough for me to get the gist of things.

"How many ... Jesus ... What about the rest of the residents? I'll get things moving here, and I'm sure Andie—Dr. Saunders—will want to be there ... Yeah, sure, I'll call you."

After disconnecting, he looked up to see Andie and me staring at him. "Where and how many?" I asked.

"It's Camano Island this time. We should have warned them. I was so focused on us here that I never considered them at risk."

"No way you could have known." Andie put her hand on his shoulder.

"What's the situation?"

"It's a small community, mid-island, about sixty-five or seventy homes. Unlike here, most of the residents are full time. Fifty residents have been admitted to the hospital, most in Everett, and some less serious ones went to Cascade Valley in Marysville. Whatever this is, it's lethal. Three of those admitted were DOA, and it seems another dozen could be headed that way.

"That was Wally Turpin, the deputy sheriff that oversees the Camano office. People started getting sick last night, and when the EMTs became overwhelmed, they started using police vehicles to transport them. The Life Flight choppers made runs all night. They've cordoned off the entire community and told the remaining folks not to use water, not even for toilet purposes."

"I need to get over there right away," Andie said. "We've got to get samples and culture this stuff. I want to know what we're dealing with."

"What can I do?" I felt like I was in the way, but if I could help, I wanted to.

"Get in touch with Jake Early and fill him in on what's happening. He probably already knows, but if not, he needs to. We'll need him on our side when the news goes national."

I departed immediately and left my two friends to attend to their duties. The cell service is spotty on the island, so I had to wait a few miles before connecting with Jake. After several attempts, the call finally went through but went to voicemail. "Jake, call me right away," was my message to him.

It took ten minutes before Jake got back to me. He was *not* aware of the situation and was all business when I told him what I'd learned.

"I was outside with Francis and left my phone in the study here. Let me put you on speaker so I can see what's in my email."

He was silent for a moment, and I could picture him sitting in his wheelchair, scrolling through his messages. Then I heard, "Shit, just fucking perfect ... that'll be a big help."

"Jake ... Jake, talk to me. What's going on?"

"Looks like some of the press got wind of all the folks going to the hospitals. Also, because of the number of those admitted, the hospitals had to report it to the state DOH, and they passed it up to the CDC.

"We've got more people showing up than we can handle. It's a weekend, which helps, but it'll be a shitshow very soon. We'll be overwhelmed with official-looking people, most with their heads up their asses. There's something on CNN right now ... hold on a minute."

I could hear the volume rise on the TV in Jake's home office. He kept it on CNN for background noise and the occasional interesting breaking news alert. I was afraid this was one of them.

"Goddamn it ... oh no ..."

"*What?* What's going on?"

"They're calling this a terrorist attack, and Homeland Security is getting involved. It's domestic, they say, so the FBI will also be here."

"Son of a bitch, this is gonna be awful."

Twenty-One

There was no quick way to get from Lone Lake to Camano Island by car, and the Island County Sheriff's Department didn't have a helicopter. Driving north through Anacortes would take well over an hour, and taking the ferry was out of the question.

However, the department had a patrol boat, and its current location at the South Whidbey Harbor in Langley proved fortuitous. With very few places to dock on Camano Island, Roger made arrangements with Wally Turpin to be picked up at a mooring buoy owned by the small community of Pebble Beach on the island's south end. Kevin had managed a quick conversation with Roger during the crossing and related the gist of his conversation with Jake Early.

In less than fifteen minutes they were speeding to the sandy beach in a rubber inflatable owned by a waterfront resident who ordinarily used it to check his crab pots. The blustery southerly wind made the 50-degree temperature feel more like the mid-30s. Turpin was a muscular man whose weathered complexion resulted from many years out of doors, both on land and at sea.

Once ashore and inside the warmth of the patrol car, Roger relayed the blossoming scope of the event to Turpin and suggested he be prepared for the onslaught. It was a ten-minute drive to the Camano Mid Island HOA reservoir tank site, where two deputies were standing guard, their yellow crime scene tape having been draped over the entire area.

"I think it's best if you take your samples quickly and get outta here before the hordes show up. There's a spigot on the back of the tank they use for routine testing."

Andie went to fill the testing bottles while the two lawmen conferred. "Thanks, Wally. What can I do to help?" Although Roger was the senior deputy, this was still Wally's patch, so he allowed him to control the situation.

"I'm guessing once the Feds get here, they'll be taking over, so anything you can do to help me keep the folks on the island from freaking out would be welcome."

"Sure thing. Let me get Jake on this. Maybe he'll be able to get in touch with the governor's office and she can stop the Federales from completely running the show. Let's have him ask her if she can send a few of the state cops here to give us a hand too."

"Good idea. Maybe I'm out of line here, Rog, but are you two an item?" He nodded in Andie's direction. "I'm only asking because she's a looker, and, you know, well ... you're not."

It was very much in character for Turpin to interject a moment of levity in the middle of a crisis. It was one of his qualities that endeared him to both supervisors and subordinates alike.

"Wally, what the fuck? We're working here. And ... why do you ask?"

"Cuz it looks like you are, you know, the way you two look at each other."

"That obvious, huh?"

"Yup."

"Yeah, we are ... now can we get back to work?"

"Sure. What are you thinking?"

"I'm thinking whoever is doing this saw the heightened security at the reservoir tanks on Whidbey, so they decided to attack someplace with less chance of being seen. Andie's trying to narrow down the origin of the bacteria, but it's slow going."

"Do you think if or when the Feds get here, they can help do that?" Wally asked.

"Andie is one of the most respected microbiologists in the world, so they might end up going to her anyway. Let's see how things shake out over the next twenty-four hours. Your big problem is going to be with the press. Until this is over, say nothing to them and tell your deputies the same thing. Refer all questions to the sheriff's office in Coupeville."

"Got it. You think Sheriff Mosley can handle this?"

"I think he's a politician and up for reelection next year. He'll love talking to them if things are going well, but if the shit's hitting the fan, he'll duck and cover and turn them over to me."

"You think?"

"I know. Take us back to the boat so we can get to work. I'm confident this guy's on Whidbey Island. Keep me posted on any developments and make sure the rest of Camano is alert for anybody screwing with their tanks."

***

"I know Roger's got his hands full, so if it's okay, I'll fill you in and you can let him know the particulars when he gets back." Jake had called me as soon as I'd returned home.

"Sure thing. What's happening?"

"Once I saw this thing exploding, I called Governor Whitney. The other two commissioners are with me on this, and because the thing started on South Whidbey, I'm leading the parade. She got right back to me when she saw what was happening.

"When Homeland Security gets involved, she loses some of her authority, but she successfully got Roger and me a seat at the table. Tomorrow afternoon is the first meeting, and it'll be at the county offices in Coupeville."

"What about the sheriff?"

"She knows the guy's an opportunist and prefers he's not involved. She called him and told him she wanted the investigating officer—Wilkie—there and one of the three commissioners; that would be me. She also offered to lean on the state patrol for help with the press and the circus that's bound to happen."

"I'll update him, but I'm sure he'll need to talk to you."

"Of course. For the next few hours, though, I'll contact the hospitals to see how the residents are doing. For the unfortunate ones who didn't make it, I'll call the families and offer whatever assistance they need with arrangements."

"Okay, Jake. Good luck, and I'll follow up with Roger."

Twenty-Two

The death toll reached eight before the symptoms of the most seriously ill began to subside. They were similar to E. coli but exponentially more severe. Those who died did so because of their internal organs shutting down. They were mostly elderly, but a thirty-year-old father and a teenage girl were among them.

CNN, Fox, and MSNBC, along with the three major broadcast networks, were all on the scene. Most of their reporters had to endure a lengthy commute from the Seattle suburbs because of the lack of lodging in and around Camano, and their grumpiness was reflected in their on-air reporting.

All but Fox reported the event as a tragedy in a small community with no progress to date on the culprit or the reasons behind the sabotage. Fox, on the other hand, felt the need to remind its viewers that this, indeed, was a terrorist attack on domestic soil, and it was important now more than ever to protect one's homestead by any means possible.

There were interviews with the families of the deceased, the residents of the small HOA, and the patrons of the independent coffee shop on the island.

The task force's first meeting occurred on Sunday afternoon in Coupeville on Whidbey Island, the Island County seat. Attending were Roger Wilkie—the sheriff suggested he take his place—Jake Early, Maria Geddes from the state and Souza from the county, Dr.

Liam Mallory from the CDC, Dale Olmsted from Homeland Security, and Matt Steele, SAC from the Seattle office of the FBI.

Also seated at the table was an attractive, slender woman with striking blue eyes. Olmsted had yet to meet Andie and seemed perplexed that the rest of the group looked at her to start things off; he was the head poobah from Homeland, after all.

Matt Steele, a good friend of Bill Owens from Bellevue and a casual acquaintance of Wilkie's, hadn't been introduced, but he'd heard of her. Several years before, he'd led an investigation into a white supremacist cult determined to murder the members of a private golf club in Bellevue. It was then that he had the pleasure of becoming involved with the O'Malleys. Steele was smart enough to sit back and see how things played out.

"Thanks for getting together at such short notice. I know Matt here, and I've met most of you, but I haven't had the pleasure ..." Olmsted nodded at Andie as he spoke.

"I'm Andie Saunders from UDub."

"And you're here because?"

"I asked her to be. She's been helping us attempt to locate where the toxin is being produced," Roger explained.

"I understand that. It was okay for you to do that when this was a local issue, but now it's a mass killing. That's why we've been brought in. We have the best and the brightest in the country at our disposal, and we will use them. It's why we've got the CDC here, and the FBI, and it's why we're going to solve this thing quickly."

"That's what I told the governor," piped up Geddes.

Olmsted turned to the director of environmental health for the CDC. "Dr. Mallory, how do you suggest we determine where this stuff is coming from?"

"As soon as I received the call, I discussed this with my staff members. They all suggested we get the leading microbiologist in the country to work with us, and that's what I hope to do."

"And have you?"

Mallory turned to face Andie. "Dr. Saunders, will you work with us on this?"

"Of course. I'll be happy to."

Geddes once again found something important on her phone while Olmsted's puffy face turned a brighter shade of red.

"Well ... okay, good ... um, what do you suggest, Dr. Saunders?"

Once again, the assembly turned to face Andie. Before she spoke, she caught a glimpse of a wry smile from the FBI guy.

"We've determined that whoever is doing this has taken E. coli bacteria from an unknown source of fecal material and has manipulated the genome structure to produce a startlingly virulent bacterium. The strain used in the Maxwelton community was probably used to create this latest batch. I'm still running tests on the tank's water and fecal material from the victims, so I'll have more to say after seeing those results."

"How bad is this bacteria, Dr. Saunders?" Matt Steele asked.

"Please, everyone, call me Andie. If this strain of bacterium infects a person, they will have viciously painful abdominal cramps, nausea, and very quickly will have bloody diarrhea. The loss of fluids will dehydrate the individual rapidly, and unless they are put on IV fluids immediately, their internal organs will shut down, and they will die."

The only sound in the conference room was the ticking of the clock.

"Jesus ... that bad?" Steele was looking pale.

"Excuse my language, but it's fucking awful. It's a terribly painful infection." Andie's intensity shocked the room, and everyone, including Olmsted, now looked to her for direction.

Jake Early, quiet until now, asked her, "Any ideas on how to proceed?"

Olmsted looked as though he wanted to respond but wisely held his tongue.

"We understand why everyone is here, and while it's a mass killing and could be considered terrorism, it's still restricted to Island County and these small association water systems. We think this attack was made on Camano because most Whidbey systems have increased security measures. Seeing how staffing is no longer a problem, I suggest we increase the security on Camano and maybe even on some of the rural systems on the mainland.

"I think whoever is behind this is still experimenting with the bacteria, and it's got to be why each one has been slightly different and more dangerous than before. I keep thinking there's a bigger plan at work with this guy—we think it's a guy. If this last attack was a test, then we've got trouble.

"Roger and I are pretty sure this stuff is being produced on Whidbey Island and in some lab. We think it's on the south end, too, because that's where the first attacks occurred. Maybe we can get some detailed aerial shots to review and see if any structures could be used as a lab. It's a long shot, but ..."

"I can help there," Matt Steele said. "We've got access to current satellite images that are remarkably detailed. If we see *anything*, we'll contact you, Roger, and we can send a team immediately."

"What do you need from us?" It appeared even Olmsted was content to let Andie take the lead.

"I could use a couple more lab assistants. We know fecal material harbors the basic E. coli that is then manipulated, but we don't know from what animal. The testing takes time and people, so that will be a big help. We've got plenty of room at UDub for them."

Olmsted turned to the CDC official. "Dr. Mallory, is that doable?"

"We'll get some folks from Atlanta here on the next plane. I'm guessing you can steer them in the right direction, Andie?"

"Yes. It's basic lab work, but it'll help if they have experience with E. coli."

"I'll make sure of it."

After agreeing to meet daily via Zoom, they broke into smaller groups to plan their next steps.

Twenty-Three

I t took over a week, but with no further developments and the supply of people to interview dwindling, the national press drifted on to other tragedies and stories of note around the country.

Roger and Matt Steele were now working closely together, poring over satellite images, looking for a building that might be the lab they were searching for. They even looked at older images and overlayed the newer ones to see if something new had been built without being permitted.

A Florida uprising by a group called the Exterminators had required Olmsted to visit the Sunshine State to intervene. The group, spawned by the feud between Governor DeSantis and Disney, vowed to sabotage the huge theme park by placing oversized mouse traps throughout the property. The things were custom made and measured two feet long by one foot wide. When a curious youngster went for the stuffed Mickey used as bait, the industrial-strength spring would snap with tremendous force, causing broken limbs and mangled fingers throughout the Magic Kingdom. The resulting carnage forced Disney to close the park until all the traps could be found. Because children and their parents worldwide blamed DeSantis for inspiring the group, he insisted it was Olmsted's job to find and arrest the perpetrators.

Jake Early was now in direct communication with Governor Whitney, and Maria Geddes was tasked with ensuring childhood immunizations throughout the state stayed the same. Souza was working with the local hospitals to develop a protocol for treating any patients that might show up in the future.

Andie Saunders, her lab assistant, and two additional microbiologists with extensive bacterial research spent twelve hours a day eliminating animal species as a source for the original fecal material. Her three helpers suggested she return to Whidbey for the weekend to perhaps get inspired by some animal she hadn't yet considered. It had been a grueling week, and the thought of spending time with her fiancé immediately brightened her spirits.

Twenty-Four

Jake and Roger had filled me in on their progress, or lack of it, and I did my best to stay out of their hair. I knew Matt well because of our previous encounter and was happy he and Roger were leading the investigation into the terrorist who had the people of Island County so unnerved.

"Kevin, Andie's here for the weekend because we both need a break. How about you and Jenne coming over for dinner tonight?"

While on my way to the golf course, I answered the phone and was surprised it was Roger.

"You sure you're not too tired? Really, you both have to be exhausted."

"Nah, it'll help us get our minds off things. Besides, I'll call it payback for your advice on the shower."

"You can't be done with it yet?"

"We are. I did the rough plumbing the day you were here, the tile guy was here all week, and I finished the trim work today."

"Sheesh, you move fast."

"Andie forced me to hurry."

I heard an insult by a woman's voice in the background and marveled at the comradery between the couple. "Okay, okay, we'll be there."

"Think you can find it again?"

"Bye, Roger; see you and Andie tonight."

I had forgotten how dark it was at six p.m. during the waning days of October on Whidbey Island. There was no moon, no streetlights, and no other vehicles on Murdock Road.

"Hey, Kev, you think they named this road after the frogs?"

"Huh?" We had just turned onto Ribbit Road when Jenne thought to ask the obvious question—one that had totally bypassed me.

"I bet they did. Just like Fox Spit and Moonraker and Little Dirt Road, the road-naming folks on the island had a subtle sense of humor. Damn, it's dark out here."

"You sure you know where you're going?"

As men everywhere would respond, I shrugged and said, "Don't be ridiculous. Of course, I do. At least, I'm pretty sure I do ... there it is."

Luckily his mailbox post had reflectors on it, so I managed to avoid hitting the damn thing. I turned onto the gravel drive and nudged along, glancing at Jenne, who was less confident of my navigational skills.

Roger had texted me to make sure to bring Emma, who was peacefully snoring in the back. At least *she* was confident in my abilities.

As we entered the clearing, the porch sconces and subtle landscape lighting confirmed we had arrived at the Wilkie residence. Jenne breathed a sigh of relief while Emma barked, excited for new smells and old acquaintances.

Roger and Andie greeted us on the porch and ushered us into the warm and inviting great room, where the fire was ablaze and crackling, the smell reminding me of camping as a kid.

We settled into the cozy leather lounge chairs, Emma curled up in front of the fireplace, and we chatted with Andie while Roger poured us a glass of wine. "You must be exhausted with all this," Jenne told her.

"It *has* been a grueling week, but the two scientists from the CDC have been very helpful, so that's allowed me to make at least *some* progress."

"How about you, Roger? How are things going with you and Matt?"

He handed us our drinks and grabbed the remaining chair beside the fireplace. "I'm glad he's working with us. He's been helpful and cooperative without stepping all over us the way some agents tried when I was in LA. He also gave me the lowdown on that white supremacist attack a few years ago; said it was pretty scary there for a while."

I flashed back to that time, thankful that Shelly Owens hadn't been killed, but it had been touch and go. "Yeah, I'm glad it's behind us, but Matt was aces. Things might have been drastically different if he hadn't been in the mix."

"He said you and Jenne somehow manage to get involved with investigations totally unrelated to interior design." His smile gave away the subtle message he was delivering.

Jenne looked a little unsure, but our host quickly covered by saying, "He said he doesn't know how it happened, but if it weren't for you two, the death toll would have been far worse."

"I'm glad that's behind us, and rest assured, we won't be sticking our noses where they don't belong. By the way, any progress with Matt this week?"

"Hah, glad to see you're keeping your nose out. The satellite photos are very detailed, much better than what we've been working with, but it's still like a needle in a haystack. When you see the island from above, it's stunning how many small sheds and farm buildings are scattered all over. I doubt that many are permitted. It's now a process of highlighting the most likely ones, then sending agents or deputies to check them out physically."

"Is there some way to find out which residents might have the background to produce something like this toxin?" Jenne asked.

"I wish," said Roger. "There are almost nine thousand homes on South Whidbey alone. We can determine who lives where, but searching each person's background would take forever."

"What about something in the paper? You could say the suspect might be some scientist or researcher, and if anyone knows someone like that, they could send an anonymous tip." She wasn't letting go.

Roger paused momentarily, twirling his wine glass as he thought. "I suppose we could try something like that. We don't want neighbors thinking other neighbors are terrorists, though. Let me give it some thought. Anything we can do to generate more leads will help."

"Are you still working on eliminating animal feces, Andie?" Just the sound of my question was distasteful.

"Yup. We've got shit from almost anything that moves on Whidbey Island. Rabbits, raccoons, squirrels, bobcats, coyotes, foxes—we even got some buffalo shit from one of the ranches. Not to mention llamas, alpacas, sheep, and all the geese, gulls, eagles, and every other goddamn bird in the world. The candidates are endless, and the culturing takes time."

I looked at my wife, thinking the professor's exhaustion was evident. I could tell she, too, looked uncomfortable.

Roger reached over and squeezed Andie's shoulder.

"Ah, shit, sorry, you guys, and excuse the pun. When I'm in the lab working, it's almost a Zen thing; I get lost in the process. Then I get away from it up here and think about the futility of what we're trying to do. I go from weary and tired to pissed off and determined. I'm sorry it bubbled over."

"Yeah, well ... how about those M's?"

By Jenne's punch in the arm, I suspected my efforts at subject-changing fell a bit flat. It did get Andie laughing, though, so maybe I was successful.

Roger suddenly stood and took over. "Let me show you the new shower my interior designer helped me with. Then, after the grand tour, we've got a huge pot of Bolognese that needs attention."

The mood sufficiently lightened, we dutifully followed the deputy to view his latest project.

***

After the weekend had passed, Andie returned to her lab while Roger and Agent Steele assembled a team of deputies and federal investigators. It would be their responsibility to visit any property where a building could house the equipment needed to produce the toxin.

They knew that a small outbuilding, a garage, or even a basement could be a candidate, making their search that much more difficult. Andie had suggested that because of the equipment needed and the requirement for precise temperature control, it was more likely that the facility being used would be free-standing, so those properties would be tackled first.

The rural nature of South Whidbey Island, as far as the investigators were concerned, was both a blessing and a curse. The locals were friendly and welcoming, which was understood by the deputies but unfamiliar to the FBI agents, who were used to working in crowded metropolitan areas.

The sheer number of farms and ranches was the problem. On the island's south end alone, there were more than several hundred such places, ranging in size from over fifty acres to as small as one acre. The number of structures was daunting, even if single homes, garages, and basements were excluded.

The farms growing crops for local restaurants and farm stands were well known, and the chances of them sabotaging their own marketplace were absurd, so they were quickly discarded. That still left almost 150 properties that produced crops for their own use and that of friends and neighbors. Of these, most had ancillary structures that could possibly house equipment capable of producing the poison that had sickened and killed the small community on Camano Island. And that was where the team started.

Roger had difficulty imagining someone who grew crops or raised livestock would be warped enough to develop a bacterium capable of sickening and killing their neighbor. They had to start somewhere, though, and so they did. The six-person squad broke into three teams, with Matt Steele and Roger coordinating their efforts.

Because every site visit required the team to physically view each building on the property, making more than five or six stops in a single day wasn't easy. Still, at this rate, they'd be done in a week or two, assuming they didn't locate the source. If that were the case, the teams would have to start anew with individual garages.

It was agreed that the *Whidbey News Tribune* would carry the story and suggest that the perpetrator lived on the island and that they were possibly producing the toxin locally. It was hoped this would spur a concerned neighbor into reporting any suspicious activity.

Twenty-Five

The results of the Camano Island test were exhilarating. It had taken only a small concentration of the bacteria to infect the water supply, and the outcome was exactly what he'd been hoping for. The modest amount of chlorine in the system was nowhere near enough to destroy his creation.

What Harry Hogan hadn't expected was the rapid response of law enforcement and the degree to which they were pursuing him. The story in the paper was dead-on accurate about his possible location, and he'd heard at the grocery store that FBI agents were visiting all the farms and ranches.

Not knowing if his small menagerie of animals was considered a farm or a ranch, he hurriedly took steps to disguise anything that might suggest he was the one they were looking for.

In a matter of days, the building he used as his lab was transformed. The incubators were hurriedly stored in a rented self-storage facility, as was his supply of engineered bacteria and the old Mossberg shotgun. The outside temperature was now in the 40s and 50s, so the only necessary addition was some tables and a small space heater. As long as he received cash, the owner of the run-down storage complex didn't care if Mussolini was the renter, and three months in advance was enough to seal the deal.

The cooling units and other large lab equipment were picked up by an off-island moving company and were stored in a warehouse in Anacortes.

Once he had moved everything from the pole building, he took delivery of enough two-string hay bales to fill up half the building to eight feet high. He filled the remainder of the space with various used farm implements and tools that he cobbled together from two of the local equipment rental yards.

He did his best to clean up after his pigs, cows, and goats and got the corral and pasture ready for inspection.

Sure enough, on the sixth day of the task force's campaign, he received a call from the remote phone outside his driveway entrance gate.

"Mr. Hogan?"

"Yes?"

"This is Special Agent Lovvorn and Deputy Turpin. We're investigating the source of a recent terrorist attack, and we'd like to look at your property and buildings."

"Don't you guys need a warrant or something to do that?"

"We can get one if you'd like, sir, but everyone else is letting us take a look without one. It might take us a day or so, but we can come back if that's what you wish."

Harry figured if he protested too much, it would raise a red flag with the law enforcement officers, so he buzzed open the heavy iron and cedar gate.

They drove up to his house, where he met them on the porch. "What can I do for you folks?"

"Sorry for the inconvenience, sir, but we're checking every farm building on the island's south end."

"Well, not sure what you're looking for, but be my guest—look around. Do you need me?"

"No, sir, as long as we can get in the barn and that yellow building over there."

"They're both open; just be careful of the little goats. They like to headbutt anything they see."

They nodded their understanding and had just turned to begin their search when Lovvorn turned back. "Mr. Hogan, if you don't mind me asking, why the big fence and gate? Why all the security?"

"I'll tell you why; I like my privacy, and I don't care much for strangers, especially all these woke assholes here on the island. Is that a problem?"

The investigators looked at each other, then Lovvorn looked back at him. "No, no problem, sir. We'll be on our way."

***

"I guess you get all kinds here, Wally, but that guy gives me the creeps." Special Agent Jim Lovvorn spoke to Wally Turpin as soon as they were out of earshot of Hogan.

"We do, but I can't argue with you. Maybe it's best the guy is all by his lonesome out here. I guess everybody's entitled to their own opinion, even if it is a little extreme. Let's look at the barn first, then tackle the other building."

The barn was relatively new but poorly maintained, and other than three tiny goats, the structure was empty.

"Cute little guys, eh?" said Wally.

"Yeah, they are, but ... ouch, the little bastard butted me in the knee."

Wally thought it was funny but wisely held his laughter, even when the three animals started bleating their little heads off. "Hey, I've got a question."

"Yeah?"

"What's a right-wing recluse doing with these cute little things?"

"I don't know. Maybe for milk or just for pets. Maybe he's got a softer side we haven't seen."

"Right, sure ..."

"Hell, I don't know; he's got pigs and cows too. Maybe he's a survivalist, and he wants to be self-contained. It's not our problem, anyway. Let's check out the other building."

They walked a hundred yards to the single door that allowed entry into the large, dirty yellow, steel pole building, opened it, and flipped the light switch.

"Holy shit, it's like the goddamn sun in here," Wally shouted as they shielded their eyes from the thousands of lumens emitted by the modern LED lighting.

The interior smelled of fresh hay, and as their eyes adjusted to the brightness, they saw what appeared to be a storage facility for the kind of supplies found on any farm or ranch.

"Why such a strange building out here?" asked Lovvorn. "You'd think they'd keep the hay in the barn where it would be nearer the animals."

"Yeah, and what's the deal with all the bright lights? You think they installed them to see the hay more easily?"

"It seems screwy for sure. Let's have a few words with Hogan."

They arrived back at the house and were ready to knock on the door when Harry Hogan stepped out.

"You two finished?"

"Actually, sir, we had a few questions." Lovvorn let Wally take the lead because he was considered a local and seemed to put most folks at ease.

"Yes?"

"That building over there." He nodded in the direction they had just come from. "It seems a little odd to use for a storage facility."

"I inherited this place from my old man, and he built that thing. I always thought it was strange, and I never knew what he used it for. The place caught fire, and he died in it. I cleaned it up, installed new lighting, and now I keep feed and equipment there."

"Why such bright lighting?" asked the FBI agent.

"My eyes aren't so good; I can't see shit, so I made sure it was well lit in there."

The two law officers looked at each other, seeming to arrive at the same conclusion, and Wally said, "Thanks for talking to us, Mr. Hogan. We'll be on our way."

Once inside the sheriff's vehicle, Jim Lovvorn asked his partner, "What do you think, Wally?"

"I think the guy is fucking weird, that's what."

"Yeah, me too, but do you think he could be the guy we're looking for?"

"I don't know. Something off about him for sure, but I have trouble seeing him as a scientific mastermind who developed some new bacteria that's killing folks in Island County."

"I agree. A recluse, absolutely, and that building could be used for a lab, I guess, but there was no evidence of anything, and we can check the aerial shots to see when it was built. Let's also check with the fire department to see if he's telling the truth about his father dying in it."

"Makes sense to me. We've got one more to do before we call it a day. Let's get it done so we can meet with Matt and Roger and get their take on it."

Twenty-Six

I t was late Friday afternoon when I showed up at the sheriff's office with four pizzas and two six-packs of one of the local IPAs. Tired of seeing me mope around the house on this drizzly day, Jenne suggested I take refreshments to the task force, who were meeting to discuss their findings before the weekend.

When I walked through the door, it was five-thirty, and the only remaining members were Roger and Matt and the team of Wally Turpin and another agent whom I had not met.

"What? Am I late? I brought food and drink for the team, and only four of you are left?"

Wally chuckled, Roger and Matt shook their heads, and the unnamed agent looked on curiously.

"Sorry, Jim—this knucklehead is Kevin O'Malley, the famous interior designer slash detective."

"Hey, Matt, I'm standing right here."

"Oh yeah, sorry, I forgot. Kevin, say hi to Jim; he's been with the Seattle office for five or six years."

I feigned injury and shook hands with Lovvorn. "Good to meet you, and pay no attention to these guys. They'd be lost without me."

He smiled, still a little uncertain, but it appeared that the beer and pizza were more important regardless of who I was. He popped a can and grabbed a slice of the pepperoni.

"So, fellas, how's it going?"

"We should tell you why?" This from Roger.

"Because I'm your friend, and maybe I can help. Lotsa scuttlebutt going on around here, you know. Maybe I'll hear something."

"At the risk of regretting this, okay ... but you gotta promise me that anything you hear from us stays between you and Jenne. We know she's the brains of your little detective agency anyway."

"This hurts me, Roger."

"We were just starting to hear about the day from these two. They were the last to finish, and everyone else was gone. Suffice it to say that nobody has found the secret lab yet."

Matt took over from Roger. "Anything exciting from your travels today, Jim, Wally?"

There was a questioning glance between the two partners, and since Lovvorn's mouth was full of pizza and beer, Wally answered.

"We didn't see any hidden labs anywhere, but our next-to-last stop was interesting."

Roger and Matt turned from their pizza hunt to give him their undivided attention. "Talk to me, Wally; how interesting?" Matt showed the intensity that made him one of the agency's finest.

"We went to this property owned by a Harry Hogan. The damn place was surrounded by a high fence, and the only way in was through a huge, locked gate. The guy was one of those far-right assholes who like their seclusion."

"There are probably a few more like that here. Why did this guy pique your interest?"

"Well, first, he didn't seem like any farmer or rancher I've ever known. He had some livestock, but they weren't particularly well cared for. Also, he had this strange storage building, right, Jim?"

Lovvorn swallowed, then took over. "It was a steel pole building, maybe fifteen or twenty feet high, and the only windows were up high. There was one entry door and one overhead garage door, and that was it. The odd thing was the lighting in the place."

"How so?"

"It was the brightest hay barn I've ever seen. Hogan said he did it after there was a fire. He said he couldn't see very well."

I hesitated to interrupt, but I couldn't help myself. "Why does someone need to see very well in a hay storage barn?"

"Exactly. It made no sense to us either, but besides some gardening tools and miscellaneous crap, there was nothing there but hay," Wally said.

Matt asked if Hogan could have moved everything, and Lovvorn responded, "I guess so, but we didn't see any signs of anything, and ... I don't know, the guy seemed off, but maybe not smart enough to pull this. Also, there was a lot of hay for the amount of livestock the guy has."

Roger asked, "What now?"

"We want to look over the satellite shots to see if we can figure out when the building was built, and we'd like to check with the fire department to verify the details about the supposed fire."

"Makes sense to me. Why don't Roger and I look at the aerials, and you can check with South Whidbey Fire. Do you think it makes sense to put a tail on him, Jim?"

"Ahh, maybe not just now; I'm not sure how we'd do it anyway. Whatever we tried would be easy to spot; remember, we're on an island."

After listening to the four law officers discuss the strange but questionable suspect, I had a brilliant thought. "Would it help to circulate a picture of this guy to see if anyone recognizes him?"

"It would if we had one, but we don't," Roger explained.

"Where is his place? Maybe I can start asking around to see if any of the locals know him."

Wally answered, "It's in the woods, east of Smuggler's Cove Road and southwest of Greenbank. Must be at least twenty-five acres there, and a good portion is fenced. Good luck finding somebody who knows him."

"He's got to buy feed for his livestock, and he has to eat sometime, so he has to go out occasionally." I wouldn't give up.

"Do what you want, Kevin, just stay out of trouble. For the rest of you, let's call it a day. Matt's staying on the island this weekend, so we'll check out those overhead shots, and maybe you two can talk to the fire department on Monday. Right now, I'm meeting my soon-to-be wife for dinner. See you Monday." Even with all that was going on, Roger seemed in good spirits.

Twenty-Seven

Harry Hogan knew that the outbreak of bacterial infections on little Whidbey Island and neighboring Camano was a big story. All the major networks and streaming channels had covered the tragedy, and although other earth-shattering events had taken over top billing, the unsolved nature of the attacks had kept them in the news.

Even though he'd taken steps to evade any suspicion, the visit by the two cops had unnerved him. It might not have been front-page material at the national level anymore, but these island yokels were a pain in the ass.

He had checked on the progress of his bacteria cultures the previous day and found that he was almost halfway to the amount needed for his final assault, and now he needed another week before he'd be ready. Although he hadn't thought much about the future after his consummate victory, he now considered it.

If his calculations were correct, the next attack would produce hundreds of deaths and seriously compromise the lives of over one thousand souls. Once that happened, law enforcement would move heaven and earth to bring the perpetrator to justice, which meant his home on Whidbey Island would have to be abandoned.

Even though he despised most of the inhabitants, he had found a sense of contentment living on the island, the only real home he'd ever known. Whether it was the exposure to nature, the solitude, or the calmness of the environment, he would miss living there.

With the culmination of his campaign so close, he'd be damned if he let the local task force be his undoing. He searched online and discovered the officials trying to thwart his efforts. It appeared the leading players in the investigation were the local deputy, Roger Wilkie, and Special Agent Steele from the FBI. Homeland Security had left those two in charge, even to the exclusion of the Island County duly elected sheriff.

The news releases also mentioned that a famous microbiologist from the University of Washington was also on the team and that she had first discovered how the bacteria was being spread. It cited the ongoing testing and the efforts of the research team to isolate and identify the origin of the bacteria.

There was nothing Hogan could do to hurry the growth of the new, more lethal bacteria, but perhaps he could find a way to throw his pursuers off his trail long enough to allow him to finish what he'd started. Among the equipment and bacterium cultures he had in storage were several liters of the material from his initial attack on the East Holmes Harbor water system that might be useful in accomplishing this task.

Twenty-Eight

It was Monday morning, and I found myself at a conference table in the Island County office building in Coupeville. Roger Wilkie and Matt Steele were presiding, with Turpin and Lovvorn and the other two teams of agents and deputies in attendance. At Roger's invitation, I was there along with Jenne, and Jake Early represented Island County.

Also at the table was Dr. Andie Saunders, who many hoped might shed some light on the origins of the bacteria.

Lovvorn and Turpin had just reported on their visit to Harry Hogan's property on Friday, and Turpin was now relating his conversation with the South Whidbey fire chief. "Hogan was telling us the truth about the fire that killed his father, and it happened when he said it did."

"That still doesn't explain the lighting in there or why he's got so much hay for so few animals," Lovvorn added.

"He was telling the truth, too, about when the structure was built. The aerial shots confirm that it was built a few years after Ivan Hogan inherited the property," added Matt Steele.

"So, how do we proceed with this guy?" asked Wally Turpin.

"For now, I think we have to keep looking. We'll keep an eye on Hogan, but his story pans out even if he comes across as odd. I'll grant you that the lighting and the hay things are strange, but this *is* Whidbey Island, and we have our share of quirky folks. Let's keep moving forward." Roger appeared frustrated at the slow progress being made.

He turned to his fiancé and said, "Andie, would you please bring the rest of the group up to date on your progress?"

"I'm sorry to say that whatever progress we've made has only been in eliminating species that could have been used as a source for the fecal material used in culturing the Shiga-producing toxin that we've identified. To date, we've eliminated more than fifty animals native to Whidbey Island, and by week's end, we hope to have excluded another twenty or so. It's slow work, and I fear it could even be some exotic animal not found here."

I could sense the doubt in Andie's voice and demeanor, and it was clear to me that the seeming lack of progress by the task force was wearing on them. All these professionals were working twelve-hour days and still getting nowhere.

Roger brought me out of my reverie. "You hear anything out there, Kevin, Jenne?"

"No—just folks talking about what happens next. There's still a lot of fear of the unknown and how it could be them next. The grocery stores are out of bottled water now that that's all people are drinking."

"The governor has promised to keep the stores stocked with water and has even had the National Guard set up distribution points on both Camano and Whidbey. She said she'd expedite whatever we needed." Jake was doing what he could, but even *he* seemed to feel his hands were tied, waiting for the terrorist's next step.

Twenty-Nine

Since his move to Whidbey Island twenty-something years ago, Hogan's trips to the mainland had only been for equipment and materials unavailable on the island or too suspicious to have shipped there. When he did venture off, he made it a point to spend as little time as possible among the traffic, the noise, and the crowds of people who were part of the vibrant Puget Sound communities that made up the Seattle metropolitan area.

Even so, he was well aware of the wealth of many of its inhabitants created by the likes of Microsoft, Starbucks, Boeing, and numerous other hi-tech companies that seemed to spring up every other week. In less time than it took to tie his shoes, his internet search promised that the wealthiest suburbs of the Queen City were the tiny towns of Medina, Clyde Hill, and Hunts and Yarrow Points, all in West Bellevue.

The Cedar and Tolt Rivers, originating from snowmelt from the Cascade mountain range, provided the water for the entire Seattle metropolitan area, including the east side. The system was of a size that would be impossible to sabotage, so Hogan devised a scheme that would both buy him some time and also take a few of the rich woke fuckers out of the game.

Most West Bellevue inhabitants purchased their provisions at the local grocery store near the Bel-Square Mall. It was one of hundreds in a large chain but catered to the whims and fancies of the local community and was well known for its exotic offerings. Its website proudly displayed its wares, including photos of the store's interior.

Hogan's reclusive lifestyle required very little wardrobe diversity. He found a pair of tan slacks stuffed away, hanging in the back of his closet. After dusting the crease off, he ironed them, wondering if pleats were still in style.

With no other option than his Brunt work boots, he figured he could get by with them without garnering much attention. A sweatshirt over his wife-beater, then covered by his fleece-lined Carhartt, completed his outfit and offered enough room to accommodate what he needed. The final touch was a wide-brimmed fishing hat that obscured a good portion of his face.

After stopping by the Ace Hardware store in Freeland, Hogan proceeded to the ferry dock in Clinton in time to catch the three o'clock boat. Once on board for the twenty-minute trip, he had time to assemble his equipment.

First he transferred the E. coli solution from his initial batch into the soft plastic quart container he had just purchased. The squeeze bottle came with a sprayer attached, which he discarded. He screwed on another cap with a simple squeeze spout much the same as a ketchup or mustard container. He secured a three-foot length of flexible plastic tubing to the top of the cap and put the contraption aside until he arrived at the grocery store.

One of the few upscale grocers still having an open salad bar, the Bellevue store prided itself on its fresh produce and soups, constantly refreshed throughout the day. The rush would be on just after four, and the staff would have to hustle to keep up.

Harry arrived at the parking lot and pulled into a far corner, where he would be less likely to be noticed. Taking off his three-quarter-length jacket, he fastened the plastic bottle around his chest with a Velcro strap, ensuring it was positioned just under his left arm. He pulled the tubing through his right sleeve, making sure not to kink it, and shrugged back into his coat.

He now plugged the tiny irrigation drip spray nozzle he'd bought into the tubing sticking out several inches from his sleeve. After two quick wraps of adhesive tape around his wrist to stabilize the tubing, now in the palm of his hand, he exited his truck and walked briskly to the store's entrance.

The salad bar was toward the front of the store on the right side of the entrance, where it would be seen immediately by those looking for a quick solution for their evening meal.

Hogan picked up a clear plastic clamshell and began selecting from the vast varieties of lettuces and greens on display. With the tongs provided, he reached his right arm under the sneeze guard and began to grasp a small portion of each one. As he did so, he squeezed his left arm against his body, forcing a minute spray of the toxin through the tubing and misting through the spray nozzle.

He replicated this procedure over most of the choices on display until a small elderly woman interrupted him. "Are you going to be all day, or will I have a chance to get some food here?"

Startled from his concentration, he looked up and said, "Oh, um, sorry, I'm finished."

"I should hope so," she replied. "You've taken enough to feed an army."

Still rattled, Hogan took his provisions to the self-serve checkout and swiped his card. He grabbed a handful of sanitary wipes from the dispenser near the entrance, thoroughly wiped his hands, then headed back to the safety of his vehicle. He removed his coat, then the apparatus, and carefully wiped it down before stuffing it and the wipes into a plastic trash bag.

After driving around to the rear of the building, he tossed the bag into a giant blue refuse container, then negotiated his way through the annoying traffic back to I-405 and began the slog to the ferry terminal in Mukilteo. *How the fuck do these people do this every day?* he thought; he couldn't wait to get back to the solitude of his island sanctuary.

Thirty

Detective Bill Owens was interviewing a suspect in a string of car thefts on Thursday afternoon when he was interrupted by Detective Julie Houser. Although a junior detective with only a few years of service on the squad, she knew to bother her boss only if it was vital.

With two sharp raps on the door, she opened it to the expected look of disdain from Owens but still plowed ahead. "Sir, call your wife right away."

His look immediately turned to concern; he knew his subordinate wouldn't have bothered him unless it was important. "What is it? Has she been in an accident?"

"No, not that. She's at the hospital ER; she said there are another dozen people with similar symptoms."

"Take over here, Julie. Replay the video first and pick up where I left off. He says he doesn't want a lawyer, but be careful with him and read him his rights again on video. I think he's about to rat on his associates, so make sure he does."

He attempted to call Shelly several times on the short drive to the hospital without success but arrived at the triage desk in less than fifteen minutes. The waiting area was packed; most people were doubled over in obvious pain.

"I'm Bill Owens. My wife, Shelly, called me twenty minutes ago, but I haven't been able to reach her."

The attendant scrolled down her computer screen and asked for his ID before offering any information. Then she said, "Your wife is in with the doctor. You can go back there if you like."

After hurrying through the large swing doors, he gave the nurse his name, and she directed him to a curtained-off treatment area at the end of the corridor.

As he slipped through the opening to his wife's bedside, he was shocked at her appearance. An academic-looking thirty-something woman wearing a stethoscope around her neck looked up immediately. "You're her husband?"

"Yes."

"She'll be out for a while; we've given her something for her pain. She should improve once we get enough fluids into her, although she'll still be sick for a few days. She's lucky she's in good shape; this could have killed someone with a compromised immune system."

"What is it?"

"It's E. coli but more serious than I've seen before. We've had two elderly folks die from the outbreak and a roomful of patients still waiting for treatment."

"Where did it come from?"

The doctor looked at her notes before answering. "They're still trying to locate the source. The common thread here is that everyone is from the same general area and shopped at the same grocery store. The DOH has already started investigating, so hopefully they can find it fast. The King County official said something about getting help from the local police too."

"That would be me. I'm the chief of detectives for Bellevue Police, but all this is news to me. If you give me the name of the county rep, I'll contact them immediately. Can I wait here until Shelly comes around?"

"Why don't you return to the waiting area until we can get her in a room? I'll make sure we get you as soon as that's done."

As Owens walked back down the corridor to the admitting area, he knew what had happened. Whoever masterminded the E. coli outbreaks in Island County had now decided to expand his wave of misery into *his* city.

He found a quiet corner, away from the poor souls groaning from the agony induced by the Shiga toxin, and immediately called Roger Wilkie.

***

"The son of a bitch poisoned a bunch of folks here in town, Roger, including Shelly. I'm at the hospital right now. Why? What the fuck is his plan?"

"Geez, Bill, is she okay? Are we sure it's the same thing? Couldn't it be just an outbreak—some bad food?"

"Possible, but something tells me it's the same thing. The doc says she'll be okay, but she's in rough shape right now."

"Matt Steele is working with us up here on this. I'll have him get in touch right away. Also, Dr. Andie Saunders can tell you for sure if it's the same guy."

"Who?" Although Andie and Roger had been a couple for many months, their contact with those on the mainland had been minimal, and Bill Owens had his hands full fighting crime in Bellevue.

"Andie is the microbiologist at UDub working with us on this. She's in direct communication with the CDC and knows more about this thing than anyone."

"How do I reach her?"

"Um ... she's right here. Also, Bill, we're engaged."

"What? Huh?"

"Long story, but later. She's telling me she'll be there in a couple of hours. Meet you at your office?"

"Yeah, that'll be great."

"Tell Shelly we're thinking of her."

"I will. I'm going to see her now, and I'll be at the office when Andie gets there."

When Owens walked into her room, Shelly was awake. With IV tubes and monitors seemingly attached to every appendage, she looked like something from a grade B science fiction movie. But she *was* smiling.

"Hey, baby, you scared the shit out of me." He bent down to hug the parts of her that weren't attached to something.

"Well, there's none of *that* left."

"Huh?"

"The shit; I've had diarrhea so bad it was bloody. Geez, Bill, I've never felt so sick. It's better now, but I'm wasted." At only five-two, she was a small woman with a vibrant personality, but now her skin was pale and appeared even more diminished.

"I'm sorry, hon. Do you know how you got it? I think this is the same thing that's happened on Whidbey."

"While you were working late yesterday, I stopped by the store and bought some things from the salad bar for dinner. That's all I had to eat."

"That *has* to be it, then. Did the doctor say when you might be able to leave?"

"She said if I continue to improve, maybe later this afternoon."

"That's great news. Listen, I've got to get going on this, and I'd like to get over to that grocery store before I meet with this microbiologist from UDub."

Even as he was speaking, Shelly started to doze off. He kissed her forehead and left to find out what the hell was going on.

Anything that remained from the previous day's salad bar had already been bagged and taken by the county official from the DOH. When Owens arrived in the parking lot, she was packing the evidence into the rear of her government hatchback.

"Is that from the salad bar?" His tires chirped as he pulled in next to her.

Startled, the woman assumed a defensive posture. "And you are?"

"Sorry—I'm Detective Bill Owens from Bellevue PD. My wife is one of those infected, and from what she told me, the contaminated food came from here." As he said this, he displayed his shield.

Relaxing a little, the fifty-ish investigator said, "I'm Linda Jeppesen from the DOH. The hospital contacted us as soon as this outbreak happened, and we interviewed those admitted. All of them had food from this store, and this salad bar, and we suspect many more folks with less severe symptoms are also out there."

"Can you spare any of the evidence? I'm meeting with a microbiologist shortly, an authority on this stuff."

"That wouldn't happen to be at an office in the Bellevue Police Department, would it?"

"Uh, yes. Why?"

"Because Andie Saunders is *our* expert on this. She's heading the task force for the CDC, and she knows more about E. coli than any other human being. I'm supposed to get this stuff to her there."

It wasn't often that another agency, especially one from King County, got out ahead of him on a case, but he was grateful for it this time. "That's terrific, Linda. I'll see you there. I'm glad we're on the same team."

He didn't know much about this Saunders, but if Wilkie was engaged to her *and* everyone who came into contact with her was impressed, she had to be impressive.

Thirty-One

“I’m going to spend the next couple of days at Shelly’s,” Jenne said, stuffing some clothes into a small backpack.

I had just walked into the house after spending the last half hour with Wilkie, getting filled in on the outbreak in Bellevue. I’d reached Bill on my way home, and he’d told me how Shelly was doing. I passed the information on to Jenne, who was visibly upset at what had befallen her best friend.

“That’s probably a good idea. Bill’s hands are full, and she’ll be weak when she gets home. Do you think maybe you should let her know?” As soon as the words left my mouth, I regretted them, and the glare I got confirmed my fears.

“Kevin?”

“What?”

“You know Shelly’s my best friend, don’t you?”

“Um, yes, I do.”

“And you know how she cared for me when I broke my ankle?”

“I do.”

“So what makes you think she won’t welcome my help?”

“Nothing. You’re right; I should know better.” I knew groveling and apologizing were required, and the sooner I got it out there, the better off I’d be.

"Besides, I'll call her as soon as I get on the boat. You don't think I'd show up without letting her know, do you?"

"No, honey, of course not. You're the most considerate person I know."

"Kevin?"

"Yes?"

"Shut up and help me carry this stuff to the car."

With Jenne off to help out at the Owens household, it was just Emma and me holding down the fort. I would have offered my detecting services to Bill, but even *I* knew when to stay out of such a volatile situation. We were great friends, but unlike Roger Wilkie, he sometimes resented my intrusion into police business. I think this has more to do with a big city force than the understaffed Island County Sheriff's Department.

I puttered around the house for a few hours while Emma pursued her favorite activity in her senior years—sleeping—and then my phone buzzed. It was Roger.

"Kevin, you busy?"

"Nothing I can't put on the back burner. What's up?"

"Andie's in Bellevue and Matt's here with me. Would you mind stopping by? We're brainstorming this new development, and it might help to have your perspective on this."

I was surprised I was included but did my best to hide it. "Sure. I'll be there in just a bit."

It took fifteen minutes to get to the sheriff's office. When I walked in, Matt Steele and Roger were studying something, and Jim Lovvorn and Wally Turpin were throwing wads of paper across the room into a wastebasket.

The four of them looked at me and stopped what they were doing. "What's up?"

"We're trying to figure out why this guy targeted Bellevue," Roger answered.

"Are we certain it's the same guy and not just contaminated food?"

"Andie's at her lab working on it now. She said the bacteria from the fecal samples suggest it's the same as that used in the first attack here on Whidbey. She won't know for certain for about twelve hours."

Matt added, "So we're operating under the assumption that it is the same person."

They were probably right, since, as a coincidence, it was too far-fetched.

"Have your teams looked at everything on the south end?"

"We have," Lovvorn answered. "Nothing suspect except for that farm with the building with the bright lights."

Matt looked up from his studying. "Have we checked this Hogan guy out yet? You know, his background, etcetera, etcetera. Roger and I were looking at the overhead shots and agreed that his place was the only one that raised any suspicion. We were also wondering what this is." He pointed to a small rectangle at the rear of Hogan's storage building.

"It's a generator. We must have missed it since it was on the back side of the structure," Lovvorn answered.

"Why have a generator for a hay storage barn?" I asked.

"Exactly," said Matt.

"I did a little digging after our visit there," Wally Turpin said. "There's no record of any crime with him, and I went back to his teenage years. Nothing."

"Any parents or siblings?" Matt was in full FBI mode.

"His old man owned the farm; he got it from *his* father. His mother still lives in Portland, but nobody's interviewed her. It took us a while to find her because her last name is Rogers, not Hogan."

"We're not making a whole lot of progress here, Wally, so how about you and Jim taking a trip to the Rose City and looking Ms. Rogers up?"

"On it, boss."

The two partners left the office, leaving only the three of us. I tried to see the situation from the perpetrator's perspective and could only come up with one answer as to why the Bellevue attack had happened: *Maybe the team was getting close and didn't realize it.* When I offered my take on things, both Roger and Matt stared at me with a look of something I was unfamiliar with. Respect.

"Matt, could it be?" Roger asked.

"If that's the case, Hogan is the only person we're looking at. If he's our guy, then let's start running everything about him through a magnifying glass. We need the video from the Bellevue store, and we need to scour every available database to find out what purchases he's made over the last few years."

"The local stores are easy because we know all of them, and they're pretty good about giving us information. But what if he buys his supplies online like most of the island population?"

Matt grimaced as he answered Roger. "We can get the information from the online sellers, but first we need a subpoena. Because this is a national story, we shouldn't have any trouble, but it will delay things."

I hated to rain on my own parade, but the last thing I wanted was for the team to spend time on a wild goose chase. "Hey, you two, it was just a thought. Maybe I'm wrong."

"You *could* be, Kevin, but I think you could be right too. It's the only thing that makes sense. We'll know for certain if he's the guy by tonight. Right now, though, we can start the wheels turning to investigate Mr. Hogan. I'll speak to Andie and let her know what we're thinking." Roger's enthusiasm for finally having a target to focus his energy on was contagious.

Thirty-Two

Two days after Hogan had visited the former Seattle bedroom community, the Bellevue attack became front-page news. As intended, the TV and print journalists made the event the lead story for the subsequent two news cycles, temporarily putting little Whidbey Island's problems on the back burner.

What he hadn't counted on was some goddamn scientist at UDub figuring out so quickly that the E. coli toxin was from the same batch as the first incident on Whidbey. Rather than deflect attention, he had succeeded in ensuring another entire police force was on the lookout for him.

He still needed more time to culture enough of the new and improved toxin for his final play, and he needed to come up with something.

Although he hated to leave the island, Harry Hogan could see no other alternative. He felt sure he had used enough of a disguise to avoid being seen at the grocery store, and he was confident he had done enough to allay the suspicions of the two investigators. It was the scientist at the university who might be his undoing, but he wasn't about to let that happen.

The article on the internet identified the person as a Dr. Andie Saunders, and he intended to take this particular piece off the board until his poison concoction reached critical mass.

Getting in line for the four o'clock ferry, he tried to contain his angst; he hadn't come this far to let some woman be his undoing. He was driving the 1985 GMC Sierra pickup with the tattered cab-over camper he'd had since moving to Whidbey. Although seldom used, the mechanics were sound and belied its weather-beaten and moss-covered appearance.

Cursing the late afternoon traffic, he made his way to the University of Washington's sprawling 500-plus-acre campus on the western shores of Lake Washington. The information he'd obtained via his internet search showed the woman's picture and even identified the location of her lab.

Hundreds of people, mostly students, crowded the streets and sidewalks, making his journey to the parking garage hazardous. The last thing he needed now was an accident thwarting his plans. Posing as a newsperson, he had called her office while on the ferry and was told she would be tied up for the rest of the afternoon.

He found a spot on the first floor of the garage adjacent to the complex, the camper top almost scraping the low overhang at the entrance. After parking, he walked the short distance to the Science Building and sat in its lobby. With the microbiologist's online photo still on his phone, he studied it, ensuring he wouldn't miss her.

Shortly after seven, the diminutive Dr. Andie Saunders exited the elevator into the lobby of the world-famous medical center, her exhaustion after a grueling twelve-hour day clearly showing on her face. It was understandable that she never noticed the slightly built man sitting in the corner, who rose to follow her as soon as she reached the door.

The staff parking on the second floor was accessed by the elevator in the small enclosure at the rear corner of the nearly empty garage. Passing a lone shabby-looking camper, Andie reached for the door just as she felt a sharp stab in the back of her neck.

Hogan was confident the carfentanyl would knock her out in seconds, and he was correct. He caught her as she collapsed and got to his camper before anyone else entered the concrete structure. From his wildlife experiments, he was sure she'd be unconscious until he returned to his compound. Although the deer hadn't complained when they'd regained consciousness, he suspected she'd have a hell of a hangover when she awoke.

***

The smell was the first thing she noticed, followed by the recognition of a skull-pounding headache. It was damp and musty with the unmistakable tinge of ammonia off-gassing, most assuredly from animal feces.

With her eyes still closed, and her head slumped over, she took inventory of her additional aches and pains. Her shoulders hurt and her wrists burned. She felt zip-ties bite into them when she tried to move. She was sitting in a wooden chair, and the tightness at her ankles confirmed that they were fastened with additional ties to the legs of the chair.

Then she heard a sound she'd never before encountered. The solitary *meh-eh-eh, meh-eh-eh* had the timbre of a young child crying for her mother—a young child who was a heavy smoker.

Opening her eyes, she found three bearded little horned creatures looking up at her. The pygmy goats were being forced to share their quarters with this human and were not happy about it.

Now that they saw she was awake, all three started bleating; none of this was helping the throbbing behind her eyes. Andie, unaccustomed to farm animals, tried talking in soothing tones to quiet down the cacophony produced by the tiny herd. Her parched throat seemed to produce a sound unheard of before by the horned trio as all three turned their heads in question while abruptly ceasing their noisemaking.

She began shivering in the damp cold of the barn and tried to remember how she'd ended up there. Her last recollection was reaching for the elevator, feeling a pain in her neck, and then nothing.

She heard footsteps approaching in the silence, but she pretended to be still unconscious rather than saying anything. Someone slid the door aside, walked up to her, and shooed the goats away.

"Shit, I hope I didn't get the dosage wrong," she heard.

The sound of water splashing, followed immediately by cold water being thrown in her face, startled her, and she gasped.

"Howdy there, Professor. I'm guessing you've got one hell of a hangover."

She said nothing, hoping to find out where she was and why she was there.

"No comment, eh? I'll give you a hint: I'm the guy you're looking for. I'm the one who made all those people sick. What do you have to say *now*?"

The tumblers began clicking into place. *This is Hogan, the guy Roger told me about, and I'm probably at his house. And what's he doing with these cute little goats? That's it—the goats!*

"It's the goats, right? The goat feces, it's what you're using to develop the E. coli variation, right?"

"The articles said you were smart, and I guess they were right. Yeah, that's what I used to culture the original batch. Of course, since then, I've made some minor adjustments, so I won't need these noisy little fuckers any longer." As he said this, he kicked the smallest goat in the rump, which caused all three of them to start screaming.

"Goddamn, these things are annoying." He opened a smaller side door and clapped his hands to move them into the corral. As he did so, a blast of cold November air huffed in, making her shiver even more.

"Why am I here? What do you need me for?" She said this through chattering teeth.

"I've got one more project ahead of me, and I can't have you screwing anything up. I haven't decided what I'm going to do with you yet, so I need you out of circulation for a few more days."

"Are you going to kill me?" She was afraid to ask but wanted to see who she was dealing with.

"I don't know yet. Just don't give me a reason to." It appeared Hogan had no qualms about killing scores of people from a distance, but doing it up close and personal was another story.

"Can I have some water? And I'm cold ..."

"Tough shit. I need to check on some things. If you behave, maybe I'll give you some later."

He left the barn, sliding the door closed as he did so. She was freezing. Her pullover rain jacket did little to keep out the dampness, and although it was afternoon, it was still November in the northwest, which meant 50 degrees and drizzle. Within minutes, she heard him drive off.

She needed to find a way out, to warn Roger and his team, but her situation was grim. As she considered her options, she noticed the smallest goat had returned to the barn through the door leading to the corral. Its two buddies closely followed it, and soon she was being serenaded by the bleating of all three. Hogan was right about one thing: they *were* annoying, but they were also adorable.

She spoke soothingly to them, and soon they quieted down. The little one went behind her chair and started butting it with the top of its head. It stopped for some reason, and began licking her hands with a tongue that felt like sandpaper. Soon the other two joined their pal, and she felt them chewing at her zip-ties. She'd heard they would eat anything ... but plastic zip-ties?

One would nip her wrists occasionally, but they seemed more interested in the tough plastic than her soft skin. In five minutes, she snapped what remained of the ties and was able to stand stiffly and lift the chair through those binding her ankles.

While the goats busied themselves with the plastic, Andie rubbed the circulation back into her wrists. From what Roger had told her about the suspect, she knew he lived alone, so she wasn't concerned about being seen by anyone else.

She slid the door aside, and although it was overcast, she squinted as her eyes adjusted to the daylight. While remnants of her headache persisted, she could at least function without feeling nauseous. She saw several other farm animals in a fenced pasture, what looked like a small cottage, and the large mustard-colored building she'd heard about.

A dilapidated camper sitting on an old pickup was stationed at the side of the house. She wasn't sure exactly where she was, but Whidbey Island has a peculiar, narrow shape, and driving in a constant direction would eventually lead to either the main highway or the shores of Puget Sound.

Opening the door of the old truck delivered smells of dirt and body odor, but the keys were in the ignition. The truck was an old one with a stick shift on the column; luckily, her college years driving a stick-shift Chevy Nova had embedded the "H" pattern into her memory.

The steering was sloppy, and the shocks were shot, but the old V8 engine responded instantly when Andie stepped on the gas and eased off the clutch. As she approached the entry gate, the infrared sensor slowly swung it open. The top-heavy camper, combined with the inefficient shock absorbers, made the turns and curves more exciting than she preferred, but at least she was free from captivity.

The vehicle swayed and glided down the winding gravel drive until it ended abruptly at a well-traveled two-lane road. She'd ridden on many South Whidbey roads with Roger during the past year, and this one looked familiar. If she was right, it was Smuggler's Cove Road, and either direction would take her back to the main highway.

She turned left and, traveling as fast as she dared, she began to notice familiar landmarks. She'd be passing South Whidbey State Park very soon if she was correct.

Because it was the off-season, most of the population of the beach communities was either on the mainland working or retired in snowbird country. Traffic was nonexistent, and daylight was fading. A Toyota pickup truck passed in the opposite direction and slammed on its brakes. Hearing the screech, Andie looked in the left rearview mirror in time to see the driver do a 180, then head back her way.

She was sure it was Hogan. She gave the big rig as much gas as she dared as she passed the park entrance, aware that this section of road was heavily wooded and utterly devoid of additional traffic. If her recollection were accurate, she'd reach Lagoon Point Road in less than two miles and hoped there would be other vehicles around.

The dust-covered gray pickup was now on her tail, and she could see the look of fury on Hogan's ferret-like face. He slammed into the back of the camper, causing Andie to fishtail back and forth over the two-lane road. Giving the engine a little more gas, she righted her direction of travel and sped ahead on the straightaway section.

Passing the yellow crossroads sign for Lagoon Point Road, she tapped the squeaky brakes, aware that Hogan might ram her again at any second. She slowed to take the right turn and saw Hogan's truck almost touching her. Afraid to slow anymore, she turned right abruptly, feeling the top-heavy contraption she was driving list dangerously in the opposite direction.

The tiny correction she attempted wasn't nearly enough to stem the vehicle's momentum as it tipped violently left, then crashed onto its side before slamming into a 300-year-old cedar standing silent watch on the roadside. The last thing she saw was a tiny chipmunk scurrying madly away as the road rushed to meet her, then ... only blackness.

Thirty-Three

"Andie's missing."

"*What?*" I hadn't heard from Roger, so I stopped by the office after picking up a latte at the Crabby Coffee in Freeland. He was pacing in front of a worried-looking Matt Steele.

"She's not answering her phone and hasn't shown up at her lab. I tried reaching her last night but figured she was working late, and we'd check in this morning.

"I just got off the phone with your buddy Bill Owens. He said he'd personally get on it right away. He's headed to UDub now and then to her place."

I already felt better knowing Bill was on the job, but Roger was a mess, and Matt was more concerned than I would have thought.

"Are you going to the mainland?"

"Not yet. I'm going to give Bill a couple of hours to see what he finds out. Considering the Bellevue attack, Matt thinks this has something to do with the case."

Rather than get in the way, I told the two lawmen I'd check back with them later, then headed home to update my wife, who had returned from nursing Shelly Owens back to health. I called on the way and managed to deliver the disturbing news through several dropped calls.

"There must be something we can do." Jenne was always about action.

"Bill's on it, so let's wait to see what he finds out before we do anything that might get in the way." I knew that even if I could convince her to wait, it wouldn't be for long.

We puttered around the house and garden until noon when I suggested we drive to Ebey's Landing to take Emma for a stroll. Although reluctant to leave, Jenne agreed it would be a welcome distraction.

We strolled the magnificent cliffs in the drizzle until the three of us were soaked, and my phone buzzed. It was Matt Steele.

"Hey, Kev, Roger told me to fill you in. Andie was nowhere to be found at the university, but her car was still in the garage building next to the medical center. Owens is afraid she might have been kidnapped, so he put out an APB and her picture."

"Shit, this isn't good. Where's Roger?"

"He just left the office. Said he was going to pay Hogan a visit. I told him I'd stay here in case of any further developments."

"Thanks for the call, Matt. I know you're busy, but if you hear of anything, drop us a note if you can."

We returned to the truck and headed south on Highway 525, the main thoroughfare on the island.

"Turn here." Twenty minutes into the return trip, Jenne started giving orders. Naturally, I was obliged to do so, having a good idea of what was going on in her mind.

We took Smuggler's Cove Road south just as dusk settled in, where the rain-slicked road was like a black ribbon through the tall Doug firs. The murkiness was pierced by flashing red and blue lights up ahead as we approached Lagoon Point Road, where an old camper was lying on its side up against a giant cedar.

"Kevin, it's Roger over there." Jenne was pointing to a uniformed man at the rear of the ambulance.

I pulled off onto the shoulder, making sure I was out of the way of the EMT vehicles and the sheriff's patrol car, and a uniformed deputy immediately jogged up and told us to leave.

"Tell Roger it's Kevin O'Malley and ask if we can do anything." At the mention of Roger's name, the deputy relaxed and walked back to where Wilkie was standing. Roger looked over, nodding with a worried look on his face. He said a few more things to the EMT before making it over to us.

"It's Andie. I was on my way to Hogan's when a call from a family heading home from the park reported an accident; they're still parked up ahead. They said a camper had rolled over, and another vehicle had fled the scene. When I arrived—I was first on the scene—I checked the driver and saw it was Andie. She was unconscious."

"How is she? Is she okay?"

"She started to come around after I got to her, but it took the techs to pry her out of there. They had to get her out of the passenger side door. Nothing appears to be broken, but they're pretty sure she's concussed. They're taking her to Coupeville right now."

"How did all this happen? Was it Hogan?" Jenne asked.

"She was pretty foggy, but she said something about being tied up at Hogan's and something kinda wacky about little goats. I called Matt before you arrived and had him take a couple of agents to Hogan's place. I'm going to follow her up to Coupeville."

"Will you text us and tell us how she's doing? We'll get the word to Alice and Seth and the rest of her friends. In the meantime, if you need anything, make sure to let us know."

Thirty-Four

Hogan was shocked to see his old camper lumbering toward him on his return home. *How did that bitch manage to get free?*

He stomped on the brakes, slid into a turn, and headed after her on the deserted rural street. Catching up quickly and accelerating into the back end of the old GMC, he could see her work to steady the vehicle and finally get it under control.

She made a right turn faster than the unstable vehicle could take, and the damn thing tipped over and skidded into a tree. He hoped she was dead, but when he pulled off the road to take a look, a Subaru Outback coming from the opposite direction also moved to the side of the road.

He saw the looks of dread on the faces of the entire young family when the dad got out to lend assistance and then the concern in his expression when he pulled his Tacoma back onto the road and sped away.

Things were unraveling quickly, but he was still committed to his plan. The cultures were proceeding nicely in his rented storage unit, but the last time he checked, he was still short of the quantity needed. According to his calculations, he was still several days away from being ready.

The problem now was staying hidden until then. If the scientist was still alive or if somehow the owner of the Subaru could give a description, he would be arrested very soon. He'd miss his compound and the quiet comfort it provided, but he'd be thrilled not to have to deal with those fucking goats anymore. He wasn't sure what would happen to them or the rest of the animals, but he didn't care.

He'd never understood why his father had kept a good portion of his funds in a numbered account, but now he was glad he had. He suspected his old man's lifestyle was of such a nature that conventional banks were not fond of him. He'd always kept a generous supply of cash on hand, eschewing the risk associated with credit cards, and had stuffed the glove box full of Benjamins when he'd left his home.

Driving back to the main arterial, he headed north. He wasn't sure how much time he had, but he needed to find a place to hunker down until his stash of misery-producing organisms was ready for prime time.

As a first step, he needed to do something about his truck. If the cops were looking for him, they knew there were only two ways off the island, and one required a ferry trip. The other was over the Deception Pass bridge that connected Whidbey Island to Fidalgo Island. The bridge, only two lanes and easy to monitor, would be the logical place to pick him up, and the ferry was an even worse choice.

Passing the town of Coupeville, he made the decision to ditch his ride. With almost a thousand acres of forest land west of Route 20, finding a remote location would be easy. In complete darkness save for his headlights, he passed several dirt and gravel roads leading into the woods until he found a parking area for the Kettles Recreation Area.

He pulled into the small gravel lot, then got out and removed the license plates. Choosing a downhill walking path, he drove haltingly; all the while branches and small trees scraped the mid-size truck's sides. Slipping and skidding, he drove until the opening narrowed to only a few feet. He backed up the hill a hundred feet, grabbed the money, and got out; he turned the lights and ignition off, put it in neutral, and sent the old truck down into the brush.

He stood there in complete darkness and silence, realizing he needed to climb the muddy path back to the park entrance, back to where he could find a ride to someplace he could hide. Using the flash on his cell phone, he negotiated the half-mile uphill trek, finally arriving at the trail entrance.

After three tries, he found an Oak Harbor Uber driver willing to make the trip to his location.

Thirty-Five

"Roger, hey ... where am I? No ... wait, wait ... it's the goats, it's the goddamn goats."

"Easy, Andie, easy. You've been in and out of consciousness for over an hour." Roger was standing by her bedside, undoubtedly thinking his fiancée was delirious.

"My head hurts like hell, but I'm okay. Hogan drugged me last night when I was going to my car. He tied me up in his barn, but I got away thanks to the goats ... I'm sure it's the goats. It's the one domestic animal I haven't looked at yet."

"Whoa there, slow down. Let's take these things one at a time. How did he drug you so quickly?"

She reached up to her neck and rubbed the spot where the needle had struck her. "He must have used a strong opiate. I had a brutal headache and was nauseous when I woke up. It still itches a little."

"What's all this about goats?"

"He's got three of these tiny goats. They're very cute—very loud but cute. Anyway, when I came to, I told him I knew it just *had* to be the goat feces, and he confirmed it. They're the source of the original E. coli bacteria. We can culture their waste to confirm it, but that's probably unnecessary now."

"Not essential right now, but we'll need to document it in case we ever get this guy to trial." Roger paused briefly, taking her hand. "I'm glad you'll be okay, Andie. The doc said they want to keep you overnight for observation. I've got to get back to the office to try and locate Hogan before he does any more damage."

Andie was beginning to nod once again, but then she snapped awake. "He said something about one more thing to finish. I think he's planning something big."

"I was afraid of that. I'll pick you up tomorrow when they decide you're clear to go." He squeezed her hand and kissed her forehead. It was time to go to work.

It was approaching nine-thirty by the time he got back to the office. Expecting only the dispatcher to be there, he was surprised to see Matt Steele, Jim Lovvorn, and Wally Turpin seated in the conference room, slurping mugs of coffee.

"How's Andie?" Matt was the first to ask.

"She's okay—a little banged up, but the docs say she should be ready to leave in twenty-four hours. From what she said, she was lucky."

Roger continued to tell her story. "The son of a bitch drugged her and tied her up at his place. Somehow, she got away in his camper and crashed the thing when she tried to get away from him. If that family hadn't come by, I hate to think what could have happened.

"It's Hogan for sure too. She said he confirmed it. Said the original strain came from some pygmy goats."

"Hey, when we were there, one of 'em butted me in the knee." It seemed Jim still held a grudge.

Wally chuckled at the memory, then said, "We're here to talk about our visit to Portland."

"Shit, sorry, I forgot. What did you find out?" They had Roger's attention now.

Turpin began the report. "We found Hogan's mother, Ms. Rogers; she lives in a retirement community in Lake Oswego. She hasn't heard from Hogan since he left home as a teenager, but we discovered a few things."

Matt looked as though he wanted Wally to move the tale along and said so. "C'mon, Wally, just tell Roger what you know."

"Okay, sorry. The kid was fucked up and used to torture animals and shit. They kicked him out of school, and he stayed with his grandma, who was a card-carrying right-wing nut job. He worked at the library, where I guess he picked up some knowledge.

"We found the librarian who was there too. She remembers him as very intelligent but thought he was strange. She kept him away from any patrons."

Roger's eyes narrowed as he absorbed the narrative. "So there's no doubt he's our man, and he hates people who aren't like him, which is just about everybody; that about it?"

Turpin and Lovvorn looked at each other, shrugged their shoulders, and simultaneously answered, "Yup."

Matt picked up the conversation. "I've got agents at the ferry terminal and the Deception Pass bridge. It's possible he got across the bridge ahead of us, but it's doubtful. We know what he was driving, so we'll get him if he tries to get off the island."

"Do we have any photos or a good description of him?" Roger asked.

"We've got an old driver's license photo, but that's about it. The guy does a good job of staying out of sight. Maybe Andie can help us with a description when she's up to it." Matt sounded hopeful.

"Maybe ... look, it's getting late. I appreciate all of you for staying, but let's get some sleep. We'll meet at nine tomorrow and try to figure out our next steps." The team was exhausted, and Roger needed to recharge for whatever tomorrow would bring.

***

Roger told us about Andie's condition the previous evening, and we got a much-needed night's rest. I was sure the team now searching for Harry Hogan was swamped, so I moped around the house complaining to Jenne that I felt left out.

She told me to grow up and take Emma for a walk; she needed to focus on her HOA duties. When she uses that tone, I've always found it best to vacate the premises, so I grabbed the leash and proceeded to the beach even though the blustery, overcast skies were less than inviting.

The best thing about the beach in mid-November is the utter solitude. Except for soaring, chattering eagles and the occasional seal barking, it was as if I were the only soul in the world.

I wondered how any rational human being could do the things that Harry Hogan had done and what demons would drive such a person. I supposed it resulted from faulty wiring at the start and a devastating dose of inadequate environmental nurturing throughout his formative years. It was a shame the human race was destined to accept those who fell through the cracks of a civilized society in such a way, but, for now, that was where we were.

Now that Andie was safe and the professionals were on his trail, I felt better about Hogan getting apprehended before he could do further damage. Still, the guy was resourceful and had a knack for keeping a low profile.

We spent a few minutes playing fetch the stick in the water until Emma tired of it and found something disgusting to sniff and inspect. When she decided to taste whatever it was, I put her leash back on and headed back to my truck. We'd had enough experience to know that dogs will eat absolutely anything and that the cleanup from ingesting such delicious morsels was to be avoided at all costs.

Jenne was still working on something or other when I got back to the house, so I dropped Emma off and headed into Freeland to see if the task force had made any progress. I knew I wasn't officially part of the team, but I *had* contributed during the early stages, hadn't I?

"Kevin, hey, good to see you." It was a little before noon when I arrived at the sheriff's office, and Matt Steele was the only one there. At least he *seemed* happy to see me.

"Hey, Matt. I'm guessing the troops are out looking for Hogan, right?"

"Correct—all but Roger. He's picking up Andie from the hospital in Coupeville. They should be back soon. She was one lucky lady to escape from this nutjob."

"Any progress on finding him?"

"No, not so far. We got a team up to Deception Pass quickly, so we think he likely didn't get off the island that way. As you know, it's much more difficult to escape via the ferry system since everyone is screened before getting on the boat. We're assuming he's hiding out on the island somewhere."

"How about a private boat?"

"Yeah, we considered that, but with the small craft and gale warnings lately, it's difficult for a small boat to get across, and the larger ones we'd know about. We've got a team at his place in case he returns, but we think that isn't very likely.

"We also sent a forensic tech with them, and she confirms that there's evidence of feces, chemicals, and all sorts of bacteria in that building he was using to store his hay. He had to be using it for his bacteria production, but there's none there now."

I tried to put myself in Hogan's place. If I knew the FBI *and* the locals suspected me, I'd move everything and get away as fast as possible. It was odd that he hadn't been apprehended and even stranger that there had been no reports of sightings. I said this to Matt.

"We talked about that this morning. According to Andie, he said something about another attack—something on a larger scale."

"But he doesn't have access to his lab or any place to develop the bacteria."

"Yeah, we discussed that. If he's still on Whidbey, he has to have another place to keep his equipment. Our best approach is to develop a good description, a rendering anyway, and get it all over the island. This place is too small to hide for very long."

I thought Hogan had done a pretty good job of staying out of sight for two decades, so maybe he knew something about hiding in plain sight, but I kept those thoughts to myself.

Thirty-Six

Just as I walked into the house, my cell phone buzzed. It was Roger.

"Kevin, I need a favor."

"Name it; what can we do to help?"

"I'm on the way back with Andie, but I don't want to leave her alone, and I need to be at work right now."

"Bring her here. We've got the lower guest suite. She can rest until she feels ready to return to work."

"You sure? I hate to be a pain in the ass."

"Shut up, Roger. See you when you get here."

I disconnected and told Jenne we'd be having a house guest for a while. As expected, she was thrilled to be able to lend a hand.

When they arrived, Andie looked a little tired, but besides a few scratches, she was uninjured. We hugged her gently, and even Emma seemed to know better and curtailed her usual exuberant greeting. As soon as we got her into the house and had made her comfortable, Roger took off to manage the hunt for Hogan.

"Would you like to lie down and rest for a bit?" Jenne was already assuming nursing responsibilities.

"If you don't mind, I'd like to sit for a little while and regroup; I'm not sure I've had time to do that."

"How about coffee?" I looked at Jenne, letting her know that I, too, could offer assistance. She shook her head at my feeble attempt, but Andie surprised me by saying, "That sounds wonderful. I'd love some."

I went to the kitchen and brewed a pot for the three of us. When I returned, bringing sugar, milk, spoons, and napkins—Jenne had trained me well—the two women were discussing ways of tracking down Andie's assailant.

"Roger thinks he's still on the island, that he couldn't have made it to the bridge before they got a team there." Jenne filled me in on their conversation.

"They have a driver's license picture of him, and that's all. Roger said he'd get a sketch artist to me so I could try to come up with a likeness. I'm probably the only one who's seen him up close." As tired as she was, Andie was still trying to help.

I wondered if Lovvorn and Turpin could have done the same and said so.

"Roger said that when they were at his place, he wore a floppy sun hat and glasses. At the time, they were more concerned about his barn."

"Do you remember what he looks like?"

"I can't forget ... remember, the asshole kidnapped me and tied me up with his animals."

One of Jenne's many talents was her ability to sketch and draw almost anything. It was one of the things I loved watching when we made a sales presentation during our interior design days. We'd be sitting at a table, and while she was telling the client what it would look like, she'd also be sketching it in great detail. The clients were mesmerized by her ability and fascinated that what she was drawing could be the design they were hoping for. Although reluctant to acknowledge her incredible talent, she always convinced the clients they were in good hands with our firm.

"Hey, Jenne, why don't you try while Andie's right here?"

"I don't know, Kev; I haven't drawn anything for some time."

Andie's face perked up when she realized she could help. "Jenne, could you try?"

After a few seconds, she relented. "Okay, but don't be upset if it doesn't work out."

I retreated to our office area and retrieved Jenne's sketch pad and a handful of her many hundreds of pencils.

It took an hour and maybe twenty sheets of paper before Andie was satisfied with the rendering. "That's him ... that's him for sure."

Jenne looked less sure about what she'd come up with and said, "He seems like just an average Joe, nothing remarkable about him."

"I think that's what makes him hard to identify," I replied. "Except for those beady eyes and that smirk, he could be anyone. Let me get this to Roger so he can put it out to the field teams. At least they'll have something to go on."

I scanned it, emailed it to Roger, and then called him. "Andie and Jenne worked out this sketch. Andie says this is exactly what he looks like—says she couldn't forget that face."

"Good work, Kev. Tell them both thanks for the fine job. I'll get this out right away."

"I'm guessing no progress ..."

"It's early, but there is something. Couple of hikers reported an old Toyota pickup ditched in the woods west of Coupeville. No plates on it, but they use the trail frequently, and they said the truck wasn't there two days ago. We're sending Jim and Turp over there to check it out."

"If it's his, that means he's still on the island, right?"

"Probably, or it means he's driving something else, has a disguise, and is already in the wind." It sounded like Roger was getting overwhelmed, but I couldn't blame him.

"You think?"

"Nah ... I'm just pissed that we can't nail this asshole. I *do* think he's still here, and I do think he has plans to do something else. Matt and his crew are a big help, but Whidbey Island is *my* home, and these are my people, *and* he fucking kidnapped my future wife. It's personal, Kevin."

There wasn't much I could say, so I told him we'd be around if there were anything we could do. He thanked me and said he'd stop by later to see how Andie was getting along.

Thirty-Seven

George Weber had recently returned from a year-long cruise in the Mediterranean courtesy of the US Navy. He'd completed his four-year obligation, and with no other place to call home, he settled right where he was in Oak Harbor.

The Whidbey Island town, home of the Whidbey Naval Air Station, existed primarily to support the 10,000 service members and civilian contractors who inhabited the base.

Weber had served on a carrier based in Everett, Washington, for twelve months. He had moved to Oak Harbor, hoping to be one of those contractors who were paid handsomely for providing technical and mechanical support for the many EA-18G Growlers housed there.

Alas, the requirements for providing such services were above Weber's intellectual and motivational capabilities, and he now found himself providing Uber services to those who held the jobs he coveted.

The population of Oak Harbor could only support a small fleet of Uber drivers, and often company rules were ignored when the potential passenger pool dwindled.

On this night, a call came in from a remote location south of town. Usually, the app was used, and drivers were discouraged from accepting any questionable fares. Business had been sluggish, though, and he needed the money, so Weber accepted the customer, ignoring his better instincts.

It was dark when he pulled into the gravel parking area at the trailhead, and as he turned 360 to face back to the road, his headlights illuminated a smallish fellow with copious amounts of mud smeared on his jeans and jacket.

Still suspicious, Weber rolled the window down partway and addressed the man.

"You the one who called for a lift?"

"Yes, I am."

"How come you're out here without a ride?"

"I was driving up to the pass with my girlfriend. She's a shitty driver, so I always tell her to keep her eyes on the road. She got pissed off, we fought, and she dumped me off here. When she took off, I ran after her and fell in the mud ... fucking women."

George Weber wasn't sure if the guy was telling the truth, but he'd had women problems himself, and frankly, he didn't give a shit. "This is way out of my area, so it's gonna cost you."

"How much?"

"Fifty bucks."

The guy peeled off some bills and handed them through the window. "Here's thirty bucks; you'll get the rest when we get to town."

Thinking he probably should have asked for more, Weber handed the guy a newspaper, told him to put it on the seat so he wouldn't get mud on it, and took off for Oak Harbor.

***

With his ball cap pulled down low and a three-day-old unshaven face, Hogan felt he was safe. The pimply-faced kid behind the desk never looked at him anyway.

He had the Uber driver drop him off at the Home Depot parking lot and walked the half mile to the motel. Like many military towns, there were plenty of inexpensive places to stay, and with a couple of swipes of his phone, he found a fifties-style motel that fit his needs. The Growler Motel was L-shaped, one level, and the rooms' entrances were off the parking area. He could park in front of his door when he found suitable transportation.

The kid had no problem taking cash, and as long as the guest left a $150 deposit, there was no need for a credit card. Hogan suspected he'd never see the deposit again but didn't care; he had more pressing things to do.

The following morning, his immediate concern was finding transportation. With thousands of temporary residents, primarily military and many off on maneuvers, an ample supply of used cars was always available in Oak Harbor. The trick was finding one without going through the formality of registration and insurance.

The Home Depot parking lot was the local hotspot for temporary labor and the favored location for private sellers to park vehicles with posted "for sale" window signs. Hogan meandered through the half-dozen cars and pickups, looking for something that would suit his needs.

Several were wrecks eventually to be towed away, and a few were too new for his liking. A dark green 2005 F-150 with a dented rear quarter panel and a sign that boasted "RUNS GREAT" and a phone number caught his attention.

He thumbed the number into his cell phone and was answered by a scratchy elderly voice. "What is it?"

"Calling about your truck for sale. How much do you want for it?"

"It's not mine; it's my daughter's. She's out of the country for a while and wanted me to sell it for her."

"Okay, how much does *she* want for it?"

"Not sure exactly. She just told me to get the best price."

Hogan didn't know how much anything was worth, but there were posted prices in some of the other vehicles, so he took a chance.

"How does five grand sound?"

"Don't know, really ..."

"Have you had any other offers?"

"Nope."

"How about four grand then?"

"Five sounds better ..."

"Okay. I'll give you five grand for it. Can you meet me here?"

"Can't do that. Just got a new hip and can't drive yet."

"Then how can I give you the money?"

"Just drive the truck over to my place. It's not far, and you can see how it runs."

Hogan was becoming impatient with the old geezer. "And just how am I going to get the keys?"

"Truck's open; keys are on the passenger side visor."

"What if I just steal the truck?"

"You could do that, but a couple of those guys hanging out looking for work are my daughter's friends. They're the two big guys with the cowboy hats. I have to call 'em and tell 'em it's okay that you're taking the truck. Then they'll follow you over here."

Hogan hadn't done much negotiating in his life, but he was glad he hadn't if this was standard procedure. He agreed to the old man's terms, climbed into his new rig, and found the keys. The engine turned over immediately and rumbled rather than purred, but it seemed capable enough, and he proceeded to the address he'd been given. Sure enough, a couple of heavyweights in cowboy hats got into an old Buick station wagon and followed closely behind.

The house was a small cottage south of town on a tree-lined street. His two escorts parked on the roadside and chatted between themselves while he made his way to the front porch and pushed the doorbell. An eternity passed before a white-bearded Santa Claus lookalike hobbled to the door using a walker.

"Howdy there, Mr. ...?"

"Smith—it's John Smith."

The old man's eyes narrowed, but he said nothing.

Hogan thought it best to get things over with, and he produced the roll of fifty hundreds that he'd put together on the drive over.

"Will this take care of it?"

"Yup, it sure will. I think there's a title in the glove box that you've gotta do something with, and then you gotta get new plates, right?"

"Sure, of course. I'll take care of that stuff right away."

Santa's smirk suggested he thought otherwise, but he said nothing as he closed the door and shuffled away. Hogan noticed one of the guys in the Buick talking on his cell phone as they pulled away. He wondered if the old man would be of any help to the authorities who would be searching for him but decided to dismiss the thought.

Thirty-Eight

It was nearly dark when Roger came by to see Andie. She had been restless most of the afternoon, which we took as a sign that her concussed condition was a thing of the past.

As soon as Jenne opened the door to let him in, I asked, "Any news?"

His tired face brightened as soon as he saw Andie's improved condition, and I had to wait until he'd finished hugging her before I got an answer.

"The truck turned out to be his, so we think he's still here. We've got the sketch Jenne did out to all the TV stations and law enforcement entities across the country, but I'm guessing he's still local."

"How did he get anywhere if he ditched his truck where they found it? Could he have an accomplice?"

"I don't think so. The guy's been a loner his entire life, so we have to assume that's still the case. Either he walked somewhere, hitchhiked, or had a vehicle waiting there."

I tried to put myself in the place of someone on the run on an island where I still had something to finish. "It seems a stretch to have a vehicle waiting there, since he fled almost in a panic. If he walked, then where? He was close to Coupeville, but that town is too small to hide in, and Oak Harbor is almost ten miles away. That's a tough walk in the middle of the night."

As Roger considered this momentarily, Andie spoke up. "With all the publicity about this guy, who the hell would pick up a hitchhiker at night?"

"If you're right, then how does he get anywhere?"

"He could call for a ride—a taxi or Uber or something." Jenne chipped in.

"Yeah ... I guess." Roger didn't seem convinced but didn't see any other options.

"On another subject, I'm going to be pretty busy for a while, and I'd rather you weren't alone, Andie." Roger turned to us. "Would you mind terribly if she stayed here?"

"I think we can tolerate her for a little longer." I was always prepared to lighten the mood, even at the expense of a disapproving look from my wife.

After a long hug from Andie, we said our goodbyes to Roger. Jenne and Andie left for town to pick up groceries, which meant Emma and I could relax and watch Monday Night Football.

Either she wasn't a Seahawks fan or she thought the game was dull, because the old girl was asleep in five minutes, leaving me to enjoy the game uninterrupted. Fifteen minutes later the phone vibrated. It was Jake Early.

"Don't you have important government work to do? There's a game on, you know."

"Hi, Kev. Good to hear your voice."

"Yes, I'm sure, me too. To what do I owe the pleasure?"

"You know I'm copied from Wilkie on the updates of the search for Hogan, right?"

"Yup, I do. That's so you can keep the state bureaucracy on top of things, yes?"

"Correct. Well ... Francis sees all that stuff too, and he thinks he can help."

I knew that Francis had resources of the ex-con variety, and they'd been of great help in identifying a drug kingpin who'd threatened our lives several years ago. I didn't see how they could help with this situation, but that wasn't my call; it was Roger's, and I couldn't see him working with a bunch of formerly jailed hackers.

Not wanting to get in the middle of something, I did my best, waffling, "Geez, that's good to hear, Jake, but maybe you should be talking to Wilkie about this."

"Yeah, I guess, but I'm thinking he would disapprove. It might be better if we run this through you."

Uh-oh, it sounded as though Francis was already on the move. "Jake, are you telling me your brother is working on this *now*?"

"You know how he gets when he thinks he can fix something."

I did. The man had single-handedly kidnapped an embezzler from British Columbia and smuggled him back into the US to make restitution. Francis was one resourceful dude.

"Jake, tell me what he's up to."

"He called his buddy Mickey in Denver and told him what was happening. Remember him?"

"I do." Mickey was one of a trio of hackers who had become friends with Francis while in prison. They were all in on drug possession charges resulting from unfortunate lifestyle choices. Because of overpopulation in the prison system, they were housed with violent felons and relied upon each other for safety and social interaction until they were released.

"Mick knows people in Oak Harbor. He had his associate there hack into the cell activity—don't ask me how—and discovered a conversation between an Uber driver and a customer the night before last."

"How is that possible?"

"Don't ask me. Francis thought Hogan had to be in Oak Harbor because it's the biggest town on the island, and he figured he needed to get a ride from someone. He told Mick to concentrate on the drivers in that area."

It looked as though Francis was a step ahead of the task force, perhaps because he could sidestep those pesky little nuisances called search warrants, which required probable cause.

"Tell me about this conversation."

"It was an Uber driver, and the call was from the Kettles Recreation Area. The caller said he needed a ride into Oak Harbor, and that was it."

"Any way to identify this driver?" I was afraid of the answer.

"Um, yeah, there was."

"*Was?*"

"Mickey was able to trace the driver's phone and got his name. He gave it to Francis."

"And?"

"And Francis is up there right now, interviewing the guy, showing him the sketch."

"Jake, Roger and his team need to know about this."

"I know; that's why I'm telling *you*."

This was perfect—now I had to be the bad guy. This was the kind of thing that always pissed Bill Owens off. I'd somehow get in the middle of things, and it wasn't always my fault. I guess I *was* a shit magnet.

"Will you get ahold of Francis and have him call me? I need to know what he finds out before I talk to Roger. I don't want Francis in trouble."

"Got it. I'll text him and tell him we talked and that he should call you."

"Thanks for the call, Jake."

"Sure thing. Always happy to help one of my people."

Thirty-Nine

The steering on the old truck was a little shaky, but the 5.4-liter V8 under the hood performed as advertised. It took forty minutes to get to his storage unit in Freeland, where he found his cultures progressing nicely. At this rate, he figured he would have sufficient volume to accomplish his goal in three days.

Uncertain of what the next few days would bring, he was glad he had left the shotgun in with the incubators. He put it in the truck with him and was encouraged by the feeling of security it provided.

Considering the typical late November weather, he thought the chances of anyone recognizing him were remote. The constant drizzle and cold temperatures had forced most people inside, and those driving were too occupied with streaky wipers and fogged-up windows to notice a mass murderer driving a battered old pickup.

He hadn't shaved for several weeks and used enough Just for Men Beard Coloring to take ten years off his appearance. He correctly assumed that any photo they had of him would be ambiguous, either from some unnoticed CCTV camera or even from his driver's license.

While returning to his temporary lodging, he tried to picture his life beyond his final act. He had been so obsessed with the mission that he had difficulty imagining what it might look like. He guessed there would be no hiding place even if he managed to escape. He supposed he could go to Russia or Belarus or one of those places if he could somehow manage to get there, but he couldn't be bothered making an effort. He settled for discarding those thoughts and focused on preparations for the upcoming Sunday. What happened after that would take care of itself.

Forty

"Hey, Kev, Jake told me to call you."

It was six-thirty, and Francis interrupted my first cup of coffee. "Hi, Francis. Good to hear from you."

"So, I talked to the Uber guy. His name is Weber—George Weber."

"You know, Francis, the cops and the FBI aren't going to be happy about this."

"Yeah, well, I call this island home too, you know. I can't sit around waiting for something bad to happen. Want to know what I found out?"

I knew better than to try to convince him otherwise, so I listened to what he had to say. "Sure I do. Go ahead."

"I showed Weber the sketch that Jenne did, and he thought it coulda been Hogan. He said it was dark, and the guy looked like he had fallen in the mud. He said he wasn't very big and hadn't shaved in a while."

"The mud thing makes sense if they found his truck where Weber picked him up. Where did he take him?"

"He said he dropped him off in the Home Depot parking lot."

"That's great work, Francis. How about coming to the sheriff's office in Freeland and you can brief the task force?"

"Nah, I think I'm gonna knock on doors around here and see what I can find out."

"They won't be happy about this." Just as the words left my lips, I realized my mistake.

"Fuck 'em, you tell them."

And so I did. Rather than call Roger, I drove fifteen minutes to the sheriff's office, arriving at eight-thirty. I was surprised to see the entire team and an additional guest, my good friend Bill Owens from Bellevue.

When I entered, they stopped talking and looked up at me. "Hi there" was all I could muster.

I was lucky that Roger was running the show, because the look from my buddy was anything but friendly. "Hey, Kev, we're kind of in the middle of things here. We all agreed to get together and come up with a plan to catch this son of a bitch; even Bill came up."

"Hey, Bill." I tried to be cordial, but it was brushed aside.

"Kevin?" Roger seemed eager for me to leave.

"I'm sorry to interrupt, but I have news to report."

"Wow, color me surprised. O'Malley's stirring the shit once again."

I ignored the comment from the Bellevue detective and addressed Roger and Matt Steele by his side. "I'm pretty sure you're not going to like this, but Jake's brother, Francis, is ... um ... doing some investigating on his own, and he's ... um ... made some progress."

Roger sat down, Matt shook his head, Bill grumbled, and the two-person teams just looked at each other with puzzled expressions.

"Okay, okay, let's let Kevin talk, and we can scold him later."

I nodded my thanks and proceeded. "You all know Jake, and some of you know his brother, Francis. Those who know him are aware he's been in prison before."

"Yeah, in McNeil." This comment was from one of the FBI agents on the team. McNeil Island was a notorious prison for the worst of society until its closure in 2011. Still, to this day, it is a detention center for violent sex offenders.

"Yes, he was in McNeil, but his offense was only possession of a controlled substance. He was there with three others convicted of the same offense and was only there because of overcrowding in some other prisons."

"Can we get to the point?" I was momentarily happy with Bill's notorious impatience.

"Okay, here's the deal." I relayed Francis's suspicion that Hogan was in Oak Harbor and told them that he had got one of his buddies to hack into the cell conversations on the night Hogan had ditched his truck. There was more grumbling and head shaking around the room at this apparent breach of ethics.

"Anyway," I continued, "he found the Uber driver who picked Hogan up and knows where he dropped him off." At this point, everyone in the room began talking at once.

Roger stood and walked over to me. "What's he doing now?"

When the rest of the task force saw the adult in the room focusing on practical matters, they quieted down.

"He told me he was going to knock on some doors and snoop around."

At this, Roger turned to those assembled. "Everyone, let's get to Oak Harbor. Bill, I'd appreciate it if you could come with me and Matt; we can use the help.

"Kevin, I need you to get in touch with Francis and tell him he's going to have a lot of company very soon. Tell him I'll be there and ask him if he'll meet with us."

"*Ask him?*" Matt was surprised that Roger hadn't brought the hammer down on Francis.

To my surprise, Bill said, "In my experience, Matt, Francis knows what he's doing. He saved our lives a few years ago. He may come across as a little rough, but he's one of the good guys."

Bill walked over to me, shaking his head. "You're amazing, Kevin—simply amazing." He slapped me on the back as he left the room, and I wondered if I was the only one who detected the sarcasm in his voice.

***

I returned home to find Jenne and Andie gone. A note said they had gone to Langley for breakfast and they'd be home later in the morning. I let Emma out to sniff around and take care of necessary activities and sat down to call Francis.

I got his voicemail, but knowing him, I didn't bother leaving a message. He'd call when he saw my number. I felt useless hanging around the house while all the activity was in Oak Harbor, so I sat down with pencil in hand and tried to put myself in Hogan's mind. From what Andie said, he had another act of sabotage planned, and she thought it would be much worse than his others.

Since he was on the run and didn't have access to his home or farm or whatever it was, and his plans included some sort of biological attack, he still needed access to the bacteria he had developed. If the attack was going to be on Whidbey Island, then his stash of lethal microbes would still be nearby.

I took some deep breaths, closed my eyes, and thought about the possibility of hiding something on the island. The truth was that there were many places. About a third of the summer population on South Whidbey were part-timers, meaning they had boats, crab pots, and miscellaneous summer gear to put into storage during the winter months. This probably explained the proliferation of self-storage facilities on the island. There were also dozens on the north end due to the transient population at Whidbey Naval Air Station.

A few of these facilities were owned and operated by large corporate outfits, but most were locally owned and unconstrained by company philosophies, employee handbooks, and the like. Many were family enterprises that the owners ran.

Hogan had done his best to stay off the radar so far, so it made sense that he would choose a location where he would go unnoticed. Most of these operations had hundreds of units and were accessible anytime.

Because it was apparent that Hogan had moved his equipment quickly, it made sense that if he had used a self-storage unit for his gear, it would have to have been on the island's south end.

I had just started listing the places I thought were the most likely candidates when my phone buzzed. It was Francis.

"You called, Kev?"

"Yes, and I told Wilkie and the task force what you've been up to."

"Okay, and?"

Not much fazed Francis. I guessed spending time housed with miscreants and evildoers would have that effect on someone.

"And they're headed up that way. They said they'd like to meet with you so you could fill them in."

I wasn't sure if I'd lost the connection. "Francis? You there?"

"Yeah. I was trying to think why I should see them."

"Francis, Bill and Roger know you and respect what you've done. All they want to do is find this guy, and you might be able to help them. Just meet with them for a few minutes, please?"

"Okay, but I'm gonna keep at this until I find the son of a bitch. I don't care what they say."

I was pretty sure those in charge knew Francis would only do what Francis wanted to do. "I think they'll be fine with that. I'm going to give Roger your number. He'll call when they get there, and you can arrange a meet, okay?"

"Okay, bye, Kev." The call ended abruptly—no surprise on my part.

After going back to what I was doing, I came up with dozens of possible self-storage locations that I thought could be candidates, but I managed to narrow them down to six.

One of these was a national moving and storage outfit that boasted uniformed employees and spotless units. I immediately crossed it off the list.

Now, I had five to choose from, and I'd begun prioritizing them when Jenne and Andie walked in the door. They looked surprised to see me.

"How come you're home? We thought you'd be out helping the cops find Hogan." Jenne said this with just a touch of humor.

"I guess they think they can get along without me. Feeling better, Andie?"

"Much, thanks to you two. What *are* you doing?"

I explained my thinking and was heartened when both of them nodded enthusiastically. Jenne said, "That's a great idea, Kev. Who do you have it narrowed down to?"

When I showed them my shortlist, Jenne said she knew the places and agreed they were the most likely choices.

"How did you plan to investigate these?"

"I thought I'd find the managers or owners and show them the sketch you came up with. Everybody on the island wants this guy caught, so it's not like we'll run into any resistance."

"Can we help?" Andie asked.

"Sure. How about you two take the ones in Freeland, and I'll take the other three. Call if you get anywhere, and if not, we'll meet back here when we're done."

With the balance of our day now planned, we headed out the door—to catch a killer.

Forty-One

Since his appearance hinted strongly that he wasn't a cop or an immigration officer, Francis mixed easily with the struggling souls waiting to be hired as day laborers who were milling about the Home Depot parking lot.

He had received a call from Roger Wilkie saying they would be arriving in thirty minutes and would he meet with them. He'd rather have been trying to find Hogan, but Roger and Bill were good guys, and the FBI agent, Steele, seemed okay as well.

While he waited—he told them it would be in the parking lot or nowhere—he began showing Jenne's sketch to those looking for work, hoping to catch a break.

With plenty of time on his hands at McNeil Island, he had learned enough Spanish to speak the language reasonably well and understand it a little better. Many of those he approached were Hispanic, and when he made an effort to speak their language, it at least *seemed* they were listening. A few turned and walked the other way, but Francis chalked that up to his unflattering countenance more than his lack of mastery of their language.

A small, disheveled man, somewhere in his forties, started walking away when Francis approached him. "*Esperar*, please ... stop."

The man hesitated for a moment, then turned to face him. "What do you want? I speak English, by the way."

"Sorry, it seems most of the guys here don't."

"I guess ... Again, what do you want? I have places to go."

Francis opened the folded sketch of Harry Hogan and showed it to him. "I'm looking for this person. He's the guy who's been poisoning people, and he's already killed at least a dozen folks."

The man's face took on a sympathetic air, and he leaned closer to get a better look. "This the one who's been spreading that E. coli stuff around?"

"It is."

"I can't be positive ... but maybe I saw him yesterday."

"Where? Here?"

"If it's him, he was walking around the other end of the lot where those cars for sale are parked. The guy looked the same, but he had more of a beard—sorta grayish and short."

"Do you know where he went?"

"Nope, but maybe you should ask those two guys with the cowboy hats by that Buick wagon over there. The big ones ... and I'm not talking about the hats."

Francis thought his witness had a bit of a sense of humor, and he wondered for an instant what had happened in his life that had led him to seek out daily jobs from a Home Depot parking lot.

He asked him, "I'm Francis Early. If I want to talk to you again, how can I get ahold of you?"

The man shrugged and turned away. He spoke over his shoulder. "I'm usually here in the mornings unless I get picked up right away; then I'm not."

"What's your name?"

By now, the man was forty yards away, but Francis heard him clearly as he told him his name. "I'm Mikee—two e's, no y. See you ..."

Interesting, thought Francis; he wondered if he'd seen the last of Mikee with two e's. As he headed across the lot to visit the cowboys—the big ones—a sheriff's SUV pulled up next to him, and three law officers exited.

"Francis, thanks for meeting us. You know Bill, of course, and this is Matt Steele with the FBI." Roger indicated the federal agent, and they shook hands. It seemed Steele was checking his hand after the action to make sure it was still intact.

"What have you found out?" Bill Owens got straight to the point.

"I'm pretty sure the guy was here. The Uber driver said he dropped him off here, and that guy over there"—he pointed to where he'd last seen Mikee, but only a few shoppers could be seen returning to their vehicles—"well, I just talked to this guy who said he'd seen him yesterday. I was just about to question a couple of folks who Mikee said talked to Hogan."

"Mikee?" Steele asked.

"Yeah, he's the one I just talked to."

"Where is he?"

"He took off, I guess."

Matt Steele looked as though he was uncertain of the integrity of Francis Early's reporting. "Anything else?"

"Yeah, those two big fellas over there." He nodded to where the cowboys had been standing.

"Where?" Steele was looking but not seeing.

"Well, they were just over there." As Francis scanned the parking lot, he only saw shoppers—no daily workers.

It suddenly dawned on him. "When they saw three cops pull up and get out, they must have split. I should have known better."

Steele appeared frustrated, and Bill seemed impatient. Roger, who knew Francis best, took over the conversation. "You're probably right. I'm sure most of these guys have crossed the law at one time or another, and many might even be in this country illegally. How about we get a coffee somewhere and we can chat about this? I'll get the other teams knocking on doors."

Forty-Two

He left the motel late in the morning, thinking fewer folks would be around during the noon hour. It probably wasn't necessary to check on his cultures this often, but he wanted no glitches with the end now in sight. His trip completed, he pulled into the gravel drive leading to his unit.

Many of the newer complexes had video surveillance cameras and fancy automatic gates opened with a fob, allowing renters to access their belongings anytime, night or day. Whidbey Self Storage was not one of these. It was owned by the son of its founder, who was more concerned with the money he could pocket from the business rather than keeping up its infrastructure.

Each leased single-bay garage was secured with a padlock supplied by the renter, or if need be, the renter could purchase a nifty Masterlock combination lock from the office at double the retail cost.

Hogan had seen the owner/manager only once, and that was when he initially rented the space. The dilapidated one-room office appeared unoccupied, which was just fine with him. He parked in front of the peeling garage door, twirled the dial on his lock, and slid it out of the hasp. Glancing around to ensure there were no observers, he lifted the squeaky door to its halfway point, then ducked under it and switched the single overhead bulb on.

He quickly closed the eight-foot door and was alone with his multiplying lethal menagerie of microbes.

The dingy space featured a concrete floor and two electrical receptacles, and that was all. Hogan had set up two cheap banquet tables on either side and placed his incubators on them. The electric space heater was in the center and provided enough heat for him to be comfortable. At the same time, the incubators maintained the more critical temperature range necessary for bacterial growth.

After verifying that the current growth rate would provide sufficient bacteria, he carefully checked each of the eight chambers, ensuring the environmental conditions were optimal. The damn things were expensive, but they were worth it. There was still a tiny chance that a storm could knock out power during the next few days, but the incubators' temperature would remain adequate to keep the stuff viable.

He would not return to this place until the day of his assault. During that time, his microscopic associates would multiply, then multiply again and again, until they were ready to be transported to a place that would deliver them to over a thousand unsuspecting souls whose lives would be extinguished or changed forever.

Forty-Three

I t was four o'clock when I turned into our driveway. The managers of the storage facilities I'd contacted were eager to help find public enemy number one on the island, but none of the three had seen anyone that looked anything like the sketch.

I hadn't heard from Jenne, so I assumed she and Andie had similar outcomes. Sure enough, I saw her car as I rounded the curve into our courtyard.

They looked up expectantly when I entered the house, and I shook my head. "And you?"

"Same. They were happy to talk to us, but nada," Jenne said.

"I still think his stuff has to be somewhere nearby."

Andie had been quiet since I came in, but then she asked, "How come there are only five places to store things?"

"There are lots more," I answered. "But I thought it made sense to go with the bigger independent ones. Anyone with a barn or an outbuilding can offer storage, but it would take months if we had to check them all out."

"So, what's the next logical step after the ones we visited today?" Jenne was rarely one to give up without a fight.

"I guess we'd need to look at the smaller places. There's gotta be dozens of them."

"Suppose we say a minimum of thirty units; that would still offer some anonymity. If we look within a ten-mile radius, how many places would we be looking at?" Andie's analytical side was showing.

I looked at the list I had compiled initially and began checking those with thirty or more units. In a few minutes I had another fourteen storage concerns that met our new criteria. These included those we'd already visited, meaning there were nine possibilities for us to check out. I supposed it was possible Hogan had used a smaller operation, but I felt confident in our assumptions and said as much to my associate sleuths.

"After expanding our criteria, we've got another nine potential concerns to visit. It's getting a little late, and we'd probably miss the managers, so let's start first thing tomorrow. We can split up and should be able to finish by noon. Good for you two?"

The following day brought the overcast, drizzly skies that were all too common in November in the Pacific Northwest. I took four storage companies we had shortlisted, and Jenne and Andie took another four. We agreed to meet at the ninth place, since it was a little farther north than the others.

While the businesses I called on were mom-and-pop operations, they all appeared well-run, and the folks in charge were more than willing to help. Unfortunately, all of them were positive they'd seen nobody even remotely like the sketch.

I reached Jenne on her cell and let her know I was on my way to Whidbey Self Storage, the last place on our list. She said they were also on their way.

The puddled and rutted gravel drive led to a collection of dilapidated storage buildings that made me wonder why anyone would choose to store their belongings in such a shitpile. I parked in front of a small single-windowed structure with a shed roof. Within seconds, Jenne and Andie pulled in alongside me.

"Lovely place, eh?" Jenne was the first to voice what we were all thinking. The drizzle had let up, but the temperature had yet to rise above 45 degrees.

"Looks like this is the office, but it's dark inside."

"Yeah. Methinks the proprietor is elsewhere."

"Methinks?" Jenne had been putting up with my sense of humor for so long that she had now resorted to single-word responses with barely a headshake, but it did get a smile from Andie.

"Okay, okay, the place looks empty. Maybe they're closed. Better?"

"Mmm-hmm, much. What do you want to do?"

"I'll try to call that number in the window while you two look around. Maybe whoever runs the place is somewhere on the property."

Andie and Jenne walked toward one of the half-dozen small buildings, each housing about ten individual garages, while I called the posted phone number. Standing next to the office entrance, I could hear the phone ringing inside shortly before the recording commenced: *You've reached Whidbey Self Storage. Leave a message and we'll get back to you.*

I left my name and number and said why I was calling. Hopefully, the manager or owner would check soon, and we could also cross this off the list. I hurried to catch up with Sherlock and Watson before they got out of sight.

"Any luck?" Jenne asked.

"Nah, just a recording. I'd be surprised if someone *were* here from the looks of this place. We can't see what's inside these garages, but let's loop around, and maybe we'll come up with something."

It took all of fifteen minutes to walk around the rectangle made by the four long structures. Other than vehicle tracks in the gravel and the occasional candy wrapper or cigarette butt, there was nada.

"This dump doesn't look very promising. Hell, even if I was a mass murderer, I don't think I could be bothered renting something here."

"I agree; let's get going. I'll leave the sketch with a note under the door just in case." We got into our vehicles and headed home to regroup.

Forty-Four

Francis was pissed off. He had tracked the killer to Oak Harbor, found out where the son of a bitch had been dropped off, and was about to discover where he'd gone when the cavalry had shown up and scared off anyone who could help him. He knew they had a job to do, but they played by the rules, and sometimes, it was more productive to ignore them.

He left the law officers and returned to the Home Depot parking lot. Although it was just past noon, he hoped the absence of Roger and his pals and the possibility of picking up a few bucks might lure some of the day workers back.

He noticed a few men huddled around a hibachi at the north end of the lot, but that was about it. Resigned, he was heading back to his truck when he noticed his buddy Mikee emerging from between two pickups and heading toward him.

"Hi, Francis. Looks like those pals of yours scared a bunch of the regulars away. They're cops, right?"

"They are, but I know a couple of them well, and they're good guys."

"But?"

"Well, they don't always take the most direct path when gathering information. And ... sometimes the folks they need to get information from have had problems with the law."

"So they don't always get what they need, right?"

"Right. By the way, you made yourself scarce when they showed up."

Mikee looked down and kicked at some loose pebbles. "I had some issues back in the day."

"Were you inside?"

"I was."

"What for?"

"Why should I tell you?"

"Look at me. Where do you think I got these tats from?"

Mikee looked at Francis, more interested, and the big man continued, "I was in for possession. They seemed to think I had enough to charge me with dealing, so I spent six years at McNeil Island."

"McNeil? Thought that was for the real bad guys."

"Overcrowding. Me and a few others ended up there because there was no place else to put us. What about you?"

"I was in Monroe for a nickel. Same thing for me—drugs. At least I was able to kick them while I was in there. A lot of good it did me, though. While I was in, my wife left me for greener pastures, and since I got out, I've found it's tough finding work as an ex-con."

"So you come here and pick up whatever you can?"

"Yup. I learned some carpentry skills in the clink, so some local contractors use me when their regulars don't show. One or two said they'll put me on full-time if and when things pick up."

"That's good. I was lucky enough to have a rich brother. He's stuck in a wheelchair, so I help him and take care of his place, and he takes care of me."

Francis, now sensing a kindred spirit, tried again to find something—anything—out. "Mikee, this asshole has killed a lot of folks, and we think he's planning something big. Can you tell me anything that might help me find him?"

"Like I said before, if he's the guy I saw, you should talk to Vaso and Taito. They're the brothers who sorta watch out for those of us who use this place to hang out."

"The big guys?"

"Yeah, they're brothers. I think they're Samoan or something. They were coming here way before me, and they sit in their car with their big hats and make sure nobody takes advantage of any of the guys looking for work. They pretend to be trying to find work but never do; they just sit in that old Buick and keep their eyes open. None of the regulars know them very well, but they've helped all of us at one time or another. They're kinda like guardian angels or something."

Francis wasn't sure what to make of the brothers' reputation, but if they could help find Hogan, he didn't care. "Why did they take off when the law showed up?"

"Don't know—maybe a bad experience?"

"Yeah, maybe. You know where they are?"

"Nope. Just hang around; they'll be back."

"Will you introduce me?"

"Sure, if I'm still here."

Francis nodded, then scanned the lot but didn't find what he was looking for. "Mikee?"

"Yeah?"

"Feel like a tube steak?"

"Of course."

Francis escorted his new pal to the hot dog kiosk adjacent to the main entrance, where they lined up to partake in the gastronomic delights.

They found an empty picnic table and sat, quietly enjoying the company of another with like experiences. When finished, they collected their wrappers and soft drink cups and placed them in the trash receptacle when Mikee pointed to the far end of the lot. "The brothers are back. C'mon, I'll introduce you."

As they approached the '96 Buick Roadmaster Estate station wagon, the two occupants' gazes followed their every step. The passenger side window whirred down when the two ex-cons approached.

"Hey, Mikee, what you doin' here this time of day?"

"Hey, Vaso, no work for me today, and I ran into this guy looking for help."

"He the one was talkin' to the law?"

"He was, but a couple of them are friends of his. No worries here; Francis did time at McNeil."

Both brothers raised their eyebrows, and Mikee quickly added, "He's not like that. It was a possession thing, and the other houses were full. Bad luck on his part."

This seemed to settle the brothers somewhat, and the driver asked, "What help are you lookin' for?"

Francis unfolded the copy of Jenne's sketch and handed it to Vaso, who passed it to Taito. "This is the asshole who's been poisoning the folks on the island's south end. I'm trying to find him before he can do any more damage."

The huge—Francis thought they tipped the scales at three hundred minimum—brothers looked at each other and nodded simultaneously.

"Yeah, we seen him," Taito confirmed, "and we know where he went."

Mikee said, "Can you tell us?"

Some measure of understanding seemed to pass between the brothers as they looked at each other and now acknowledged their responsibility to help this ferocious-looking bald man with teardrop tattoos.

"Yep. He bought a pickup that one of our friends was selling. We followed him to her dad's place to make sure he didn't take off without paying. After he did, we took off and came back here."

Francis had to tell himself to slow down and gather as much information as possible. At some point he'd have to brief the task force. "What kind of truck was it?"

"It was an old Ford, dark green."

"Do you know where he was headed afterward?"

"No, but maybe the old man does."

"What old man?"

"Our friend is overseas, and her dad handled the deal. We can take you there if you want."

Francis was reasonably sure these two were good guys, but that didn't mean he was getting in the car with them. "I'll follow you."

It was barely a ten-minute drive, and the men in the Buick departed as soon as they'd pointed out the house belonging to the Santa lookalike.

After climbing the three steps to the porch, Francis rang the doorbell. He could hear the shuffling of feet and a walker as the occupant approached the door.

The old man's reaction was the one Francis had come to expect from those seeing him for the first time. He let out a gasp and started to close the door.

"No, wait ... Vaso and Taito sent me. It's about the truck you sold for your daughter."

Opening the door several inches wider, the man seemed to relax but was still wary. "What about it?"

Slowly unfolding the sketch, he held it up so the old guy could see it. "Is this the one?"

After studying the likeness for several seconds, he nodded and said, "Pretty sure that's him. Why?"

"He's the person who's poisoning the water supply on the island. I'm trying to catch him before he does anything else."

"Thought the cops were on it."

"They are; I'm helping. Do you know where he went?"

"Nah, he just paid me and took off. The guy did seem a little fishy, though. Said his name was John Smith."

"Can you give me any other information that might help?"

Santa looked down at his slippers and thought for a minute. "No, but I can give you the plate number. I told him he'd need to change it, but I don't think that's gonna be a priority for him."

Francis took down the number, thanked the man, and returned to his vehicle. Now, it was time to bring in the team.

Forty-Five

Langley, Washington, is the quintessential Hallmark Channel town. On the shores of the Saratoga Passage, facing a panorama of the Cascade Mountains, the small town is a favorite tourist attraction for Seattleites and visitors worldwide.

While the bed and breakfasts and small inns are sold out during the summer months when the town is flooded with visitors, those who call this special place home are content with the quiet drizzle and cloudiness prevalent during the winter months.

It's a tight-knit community of nearly twelve hundred souls with incredibly diverse backgrounds. From titans of commerce and tech to famous and not-so-famous artists, musicians, and authors to teachers, social workers, and retired octogenarians, the residents' dedication to their little town and their support of each other regardless of status, income, or fortune is legendary.

The town has its own water system and sewage treatment plant, setting it apart from many of the smaller residential areas on South Whidbey, where individual or community wells and on-site septic systems are the norm. The city reservoir is a 618,000-gallon concrete tank that sits on a small hill on the south edge of town. It is surrounded by a chain-link fence and secured by a ten-foot-wide gate stretching across a gravel access road.

The residents of Langley tend to be thoughtful, progressive, and active stewards of the earth. They were just the type of people Harry Hogan despised, and the time had come to show them who was in control.

His plan wasn't entirely focused from the outset, but the more success he achieved with the smaller reservoirs, the grander his scheme became. He had done the research online and was sure he'd have no difficulty accessing the enormous concrete tank that housed the storybook town's water supply. The only problem would be lugging the two five-gallon containers of misery up the ladder to the top of the structure, but he'd find a way to do it.

Forty-Six

After returning home from our self-storage investigation and letting Emma out for a romp, we sat down and tried to come up with some idea of where Hogan might have set up his temporary lab. Then my phone buzzed. It was Francis.

About the time he got to the part about the old man, I interrupted him. "Francis, you need to talk to Roger about this, not me."

"Nah, I'll keep working on this. They'll want me to bow out if I talk to them. You should tell them."

I knew better than to argue, so after taking down the pertinent information, I immediately called Wilkie.

"Where is he now?" After I delivered the info, he, of course, wanted to know where my bald ex-con buddy was.

"He said he was going to keep at it, so I guess he's somewhere around Oak Harbor."

"Shit ... well ... we'll verify what you've given us and put out an APB for a truck with that plate. Maybe we'll get lucky."

I told him what we were up to with the storage places and that, so far, we'd struck out.

"It was good thinking, Kevin; keep turning over stones. We need to get this guy before he does something truly awful."

Since the speaker was on during my call, Andie and Jenne were aware of the conversation. "It seems like this guy always finds a way to escape." Jenne voiced what all of us were thinking.

"I still think there's someplace we're missing. Those incubators he's using aren't something he can lug around in the back of a truck. They need power, and they're not very portable."

Andie's point made sense, so I said, "I guess we expand our search to the next smaller group of candidates, excluding those who don't have power in the units. Make sense?"

"It does," Jenne agreed. "We should be able to eliminate those by phone, then personally visit the others. Let's hit the search engines and see if our suspects match."

I was beginning to feel helpless about our part in the investigation, but I kept those thoughts to myself.

Forty-Seven

With still two days to kill before he mounted his attack on the lovely town of Langley, Harry Hogan had had his fill of daytime television. He was about to turn off a slimmer Drew Carey, and *The Price Is Right* when a news ticker scrolling across the bottom of the screen caught his eye.

It seemed cops everywhere were now looking for a dark green Ford pickup with a license plate precisely like those on his recently purchased truck.

He'd chosen the run-down motel for its obscurity and the overgrown laurel hedge surrounding the parking area. He was sure the kid watching the front desk hadn't seen his ride, but he needed to remedy the situation quickly.

Waiting until dark, he removed the plates from his truck using the screwdriver on his Swiss Army knife. The next occupied room was several doors away, and he was careful not to be seen.

The massive Home Depot parking lot was a short walk away, and even at the dinner hour, the thing was three-quarters full. Making sure no one saw him, he quickly swapped his plates with the ones on a Ram pickup and returned to the motel unseen.

The F-150 couldn't be seen from the street, so as long as he ordered food by delivery, he was confident he would remain unseen. If someone happened to suspect it, at least the license tabs would be different.

He settled in to review his plans for Saturday night.

Forty-Eight

Feeling like her old self but very tired, Andie returned to the house on Lone Lake to get some much-needed sleep. With all the excitement now stilled, Jenne and I were looking forward to a quiet evening of cooking and cuddling with our faithful companion. Emma, too, seemed appreciative of spending time with just her pack.

Our thoughts were with the team at Oak Harbor, but we did our best to put them aside. Hogan was on the minds of everyone on the island and wouldn't disappear until he was apprehended.

With the TV off and a quiet slack-string guitar performance by George Kahumoku in the background, we sipped a delicious unoaked chardonnay by Larc Hill Vineyard while munching on a chicken and asparagus pasta salad. After more than a dozen years of marriage to the woman across from me, I still couldn't get over my good fortune.

Although we were partners long before tying the knot, she was the only person I'd ever known who *got* me. My frequent sarcasm and disposition to instantly prejudge a person or situation often had me wishing for more patience than I had been given. Jenne had seen through my foibles within seconds of our first meeting, but rather than challenge or find fault, her approach was to play out as much line as necessary for me to realize that I'd stepped in shit once again.

She had been understanding and kind for over two decades but never shy about challenging me when the situation dictated. On the other hand, I was still trying to figure out what she saw in me. With any luck, it would be many years before she realized I'd hoodwinked her.

"Penny for your thoughts, Kev."

"Just thinking how happy I am to be married to you."

"Cut the shit, Kevin. Really, what *were* you thinking?"

See how she does this? She pretends to boss me around, but *she* knows that *I* know she's doing it.

"I really *was* thinking about us and how lucky I am, but I guess it's because of all this nasty stuff going on with Hogan juxtaposed with this little slice of heaven we have right this second."

"Yeah, me too." She reached over, squeezed my hand, and asked if I wanted to dance.

Well, duhuh, I wasn't born yesterday, and I had a sneaking suspicion this could lead to something else.

"You bet." I stood up so fast I nearly knocked the chair over while she snickered and shook her head like I was a teenager on his first date.

***

Friday morning brought rain and small craft warnings. It was common to see heavy rain and winds smacking Whidbey Island as these late fall storms barreled through the Strait of Juan de Fuca. Watching the local morning news, we were informed of heavy winds in the evening and possible power outages. The warnings were increased to gale warnings for the late afternoon and evening, lasting until after midnight.

Whidbey Island natives were used to these weather events, and many had standby generators for such occasions. Losing power for a few hours or even a day wasn't uncommon. While the island's south end was dotted with meadows, farms, and ranches, there were also many forested areas. The north end, where the power supplying the island was routed through Deception Pass, was heavily forested. When winds gusted high enough, they felled mighty Doug firs, tearing through the power lines like they were mere strands of string.

Andie kept in touch with Roger via text and was kind enough to keep us posted on the team's activities in and around Oak Harbor. No one knew precisely what Francis was up to, but I suspected he'd let me or Roger know if he got anywhere.

"Roger and the crew are returning this afternoon; Bill's returning to Bellevue. This storm is supposed to be rough, and he'd rather the task force be back in Freeland until they see what the power outages look like." Jenne updated me on her latest text from Andie. If they were returning, then this weather event promised to be a doozy.

I wondered what was happening with Francis, but it was more curiosity than worry. The man was a rock, and I'd never seen a situation he couldn't handle.

Forty-Nine

While Harry Hogan finalized his plans for the following day, the TV on the crappy dresser droned on about the threatening weather targeting Whidbey and the San Juan Islands. Regardless of the artificial nature of its company, it was better than sitting alone at the scratched-up Formica desk listening to the hum of the tiny refrigerator, considered a significant motel room amenity.

Had he been paying even the slightest bit of attention to the squawk box, he might have taken a different approach to his preparation for his assault on the reservoir for the postcard town of Langley, Washington.

Based on the information available online—and there was plenty of it—he was confident in his ability to access the vent on top of the enormous concrete tank. It was a forty-year-old structure, but the manufacturer was still in business and had posted the specifications online.

There was the matter of finding something to transport the super-charged Shiga-producing bacteria from the incubators to the reservoir, and he was thankful for his proximity to the Oak Harbor Home Depot.

By noon, the gusts were up to thirty miles per hour with steady winds of twenty. Hogan walked to the giant box store, holding his work coat closed against nature's onslaught with his ball cap clamped tightly on his head. When he arrived at the parking lot, he was surprised to see several day laborers looking for jobs and even more shocked to see the lot almost full.

Upon entering the store, he was stunned at the furious activity. Customers had carts loaded with gas cans, chainsaws, cases of water, and batteries of every size and shape. He'd have been shocked if a blue tarp remained on a shelf.

He recalled seeing lots of weather maps on his TV but had paid little attention. Hogan had lived on the island for years and had seen most of what Mother Nature could deliver without skipping a beat. Surely these morons were overreacting.

Bumping into folks from seemingly every country on Earth and dodging the orange trolleys and carts, he finally managed his way to the landscape department. There were pesticide spray tanks of every size and shape, but they wouldn't do.

As he was looking, two short fellows with dark skin, speaking a language unknown to him and not watching where they were going, slammed their cart into him.

"Hey, assholes, watch where the fuck you're going," Harry said but immediately realized drawing attention to himself was not wise.

"Sorry, sorry, sorry …" It seemed to be the only word of English the two gentlemen knew as they patted Harry on the arms and back, perhaps to make him feel better.

"I'm okay … okay, leave me alone." He swatted their arms away, and apparently, "okay" was also familiar to them because they started to leave.

"Wait, wait …" They stopped and turned, looking fearful. "Where did you get that?"

He pointed to a five-gallon plastic gas container with a built-in handle that appeared to have a concealed spout with a securely sealed cap covering it.

The two shoppers looked at each other, not understanding.

"The container … this, this thing …" *Fucking immigrants*, Harry thought as he slapped the red plastic jug.

Finally understanding, one of the men said, "Six, six," and pointed to the far side of the store.

"At least they can say numbers," he muttered as he headed for aisle six. It was as if he were a salmon swimming upstream as he dodged seemingly hundreds of shoppers, each pushing, carrying, or pulling something orange filled with supplies.

At the end of aisle six was a pallet stacked with the containers he sought, but they were going fast as a sea of customers grabbed what they could carry. With all the portable generators on the island, gasoline still had to be transported to them.

He picked up two of the highly coveted jugs and headed for the checkout area but stopped when he thought of another item he needed. He did so abruptly, resulting in the shopping cart behind him slamming into his backside. *Jesus, get me out of this fucking place.*

When he turned to see who the careless driver was, he faced his two foreign buddies from his former encounter. Their faces turned ashen as they backed away, bowing and saying, "Sorry ... sorry, sorry."

Hogan shook his head, swore to himself, and hurried to the paint aisles to pick up the respirator he would need the following day. He vowed it would be his last day shopping at Home Depot.

He paid cash for his items and headed back outside, where the wind velocity seemed to have doubled, and the daylight was receding.

Fifty

Mikee was usually gone by four, but the activity at the parking lot was frantic, and he still hoped to land a few hours of work. He'd spent most of the day shooting the shit with Vaso and Taito, hunkered down in the back seat of their Buick while the winds rocked the big cruiser.

He'd gotten to know the two Samoans and liked them for their kindness and unselfish dedication to safeguarding the day workers at the lot. They never took any jobs; they just hung around in their station wagon and looked after the temporary workers. Mikee figured they were independently wealthy and considered watching over those less fortunate their calling in life.

After saying his goodbyes to the duo, he stepped out into the maelstrom to return to his dingy apartment. It was only a ten-minute stroll, but with the wind howling, he planned on cutting that in half.

Looking up to be sure he wouldn't be run over by a pickup or a car, he tightened his John Deere ball cap, and that was when he saw the man Francis was looking for.

Hogan was the name he recalled, and Francis was sure this was the guy who had poisoned all those people. With his cheap second-hand cell phone, he called Francis's number.

"Yeah ... who's this?"

"Francis, it's Mikee ..."

"Hey, Mikee. Some shit this storm, eh?"

"Um, yeah, but Francis ... I'm looking at the guy you're trying to find."

"You're sure? Where are you?"

"I'm at the Home Depot lot. He's carrying two gas containers and a bag with something in it."

"What's he driving?"

"I don't know; he's walking away from the parking area. He could be on foot."

"I'm only a few minutes away. Can you follow without him seeing you?"

"I can try."

"I'll hurry; do the best you can."

Afraid of what might happen if he was spotted, he turned back to Vaso and Taito for help. As soon as the driver's side window was rolled down, Mikee shouted his predicament over the buffeting wind gusts.

While appearing passive and unaware, the brothers were very much attuned to their surroundings and felt it their duty to assist whenever called upon. They knew all about the psycho terrorizing the island they called home and were happy to help apprehend him.

"C'mon, Vaso, let's see where this guy's going."

The three men followed Hogan as closely as they dared, and once they were out of the enormous lot, they left a little more space between them and their quarry. The brothers had forsaken their treasured cowboy hats for Mariners ballcaps but had difficulty keeping them on in the forceful, gusty winds.

Hogan turned right onto Fourth Avenue without noticing the threesome of pursuers and then left when he got to Ely Street. The empty residential streets lined with maples whose leaves had departed months ago were now cloaked in rain, wind, and darkness.

Viewed from afar, it might have been a scene from a dark-humored comedy—two huge men and one small man holding their hats on with their hands, following a killer through a fierce storm on an island where the residents had no inkling of the drama.

Carrying the bulky containers with the respirator under his arm, Hogan was bent forward into the rain, his hat on backward to prevent the wind from tearing it off.

The narrow opening to the alley leading to the Growler Motel's back entrance was bordered by the same laurel hedge shielding its parking area from the main road. He arrived at the pickup, parked at the entrance to his room, and dumped the two gas containers into the bed. Still holding the plastic bag that contained the respirator, he wiped his face with his sleeve, finally clearing it of the raindrops that had pelted him since leaving the Depot.

He unlocked the passenger door, placed the breathing device inside next to the Mossberg, and closed and locked the door. As he turned to go to his room, he glimpsed something in the side mirror. Three figures had emerged from the hedge and stopped abruptly when they saw him.

***

Francis, driving as fast as he dared, arrived at the Home Depot just in time to see the backs of Mikee and the two brothers as they exited the ten-acre lot. After dodging pickups, vans, miscellaneous SUVs, and sedans, he finally found a spot, jumped out of his truck, and hurried to catch up, oblivious to the elements delivering punishing blows to his uncovered bald head. As he ran, the lot was plunged into darkness.

He was happy to see the brothers helping Mikee but was pissed that he'd now lost the trio. He called the last number he'd received and was thankful when Mikee answered.

"I'm here. I saw you and Taito and Vaso leaving, but I had to park and lost you. Tell me where you are."

Mikee described their route and told him they were now watching Hogan, who was putting his supplies into the old pickup he'd purchased.

"Stay out of sight; I'll be there in a few minutes. I'm calling the cops right now."

He tried Roger as he jogged but wasn't successful. He assumed the storm had knocked some of the cell towers down or their power was interrupted. He left a message and tried Kevin. Because he lived on the island's east coast, the cell towers from the mainland were often reachable.

"Kevin?"

"Yeah, I'm here ... Francis?"

"We found Hogan. Can you reach Roger?"

"I'll try, but there are trees and wires down all over the place. Our road is impassable, and the whole island is without power."

"Well, keep trying; it's a shitshow here too. I'll do my best to keep tabs on him."

He thought he heard Kevin telling him to be careful as their connection failed. He forged ahead through the stinging rain and wind, constantly wiping the water from his eyes.

Fifty-One

Hogan stood motionless for several seconds. He had been discovered, and he recognized the two big guys from his truck purchase. He wasn't sure who the little guy was and couldn't care less.

He opened the passenger door again, pretending he had forgotten something, and watched the trio move closer along the hedge. When they were no more than twenty feet away, he grabbed the Mossberg, whirled round while racking a shell into the chamber, and fired a double-aught buckshot charge directly into Vaso's face, blowing the giant Samoan backward.

The sudden violence froze the other two, giving Hogan a second to rack another shell, which he promptly fired into the chest of Taito, who dropped in a heap. The little guy turned to run but was methodically dispatched with a third shot to his back.

Under any other circumstances, the booming shotgun blasts would have drawn instant attention to the scene, but with the shrieking winds and exploding transformers, the sounds vaporized into the ether.

The hedge would hide the bodies for enough time to allow him to escape, but no way was he taking the pickup, since the entire island would be looking for it. It was unclear if these amateurs had alerted the authorities, but he wasn't taking any chances.

The only way they could have followed him was from the Home Depot. He remembered the two brothers wearing cowboy hats and sitting in an old Buick station wagon, and he hoped it was still parked there. He searched the pockets of one of them and came up empty. As he bent over to search Taito's corpse, a stocky, muscular bald creature with what appeared to be tears running down his face emerged from the laurel hedge.

Fifty-Two

As he hurried, staggering over fallen limbs and other debris, he hoped Mikee's directions were accurate. That was when he heard three evenly spaced blasts that he was sure weren't storm-related.

The only illumination was from occasional battery-powered emergency lighting, making any increase in speed impossible. As a result, he almost plowed into the hedge surrounding the Growler Motel.

He moved cautiously along the laurel until it turned right, and he was facing the rear of the shoddy building. Francis saw Harry Hogan, backlit by an emergency spotlight high on the corner of the structure, holding a shotgun while bending over a huge mound.

Coming to an abrupt stop, he saw Hogan look up then bring the gun to his shoulder. He turned, dove behind the hedge, scrambled to his feet, and began to run. He heard a shell being racked into the chamber and ran faster. A wrecking ball slammed into his shoulder, and the last thing he heard was the blast as he tumbled into the thick wall of foliage surrounding the Growler Motel.

Fifty-Three

I left three messages for Roger and even tried reaching Bill Owens and Matt Steele, but it was hopeless. We were lucky to get intermittent cell service from a tower in Everett directly across the Saratoga Passage, but that was spotty at best.

The news we could pull up on our phones when service was available was dire. At nine p.m. the peak gusts reached nearly eighty miles per hour—well above hurricane force—and lasted over three hours. Whidbey Island experiences its share of wind-related events, but this was unique.

Jenne, Emma, and I huddled together on the sofa in front of the fireplace amidst candles and battery-powered lanterns. We spent the night listening to the wind howl and the trees crash, eventually dozing off after midnight when the raging winds began to subside.

The prevailing storms in the winter, when the most severe events occur, are from the south and southwest, and many of those have gusts in the fifty-mile-per-hour range. This event's winds were from the north and northwest, meaning they were blowing against the growing direction of the enormous firs, alders, and cedars making up most of the forests on the island.

As a result, the number of trees ripped from the earth was unparalleled in the island's history. All roads were impassable, all power and communication lines were down, and all emergency services were stretched to breaking point.

Waking at dawn, we ventured outside to survey the scene. We were stunned by the catastrophic damage we could see from our driveway. At least twenty trees were strewn across the road with power and cable lines woven throughout them like so much Silly String. The sound of gasoline generators humming in the background was a reminder that although this storm was unequaled, occasional power outages weren't uncommon.

Our closest neighbors had decided to visit their grandkids in Seattle when the weather forecast turned ominous, and from the looks of the damage they'd sustained, they had chosen wisely. A 200-year-old fir had cleaved half the deck they had recently installed from their house and lay like some gigantic sledgehammer among the rubble.

We returned inside, made breakfast—thank goodness for propane—and found an old transistor radio in the junk drawer. As expected, the reports of the carnage on the island were front and center on the Seattle news stations.

The entirety of Island County—Whidbey and Camano—lacked power and cell service. Several hundred thousand residences were impacted by the power outage, including the islands and many on the mainland, but other than Island County, most had cell service. Emergency crews were being ferried to Whidbey Island to clear the roads to allow police and emergency services to get to those in need. The expectation was a week, possibly longer, without power, and they hoped to get the main arterial—WA-525—opened by day's end.

The only bright spot was the forecasted sunny skies and temperatures in the mid-50s for the day, with the promise of several more following. The nights would be in the low 40s and high 30s, but thankfully, our propane fireplaces would keep us warm. At the same time, most of the island's water systems had backup generators for emergencies.

"Still nothing from Roger?"

"Nope. Even if he got my messages, he's got to be swamped right now. At least he won't have to worry about the down power lines arcing. The feed over Deception Pass will take at least a week to restore."

"What happens if someone needs the EMTs?" Jenne was spot-on with her concern.

"That's why getting the main road clear is their highest priority. Once that's done, they can triage from there. I'm afraid we won't know what happened in Oak Harbor for a while."

"I'm worried about Francis."

"Me too, but he's a resourceful guy, and if anyone can handle a tough situation, it's Francis. Let's finish up and see how the other neighbors are faring and if they need help."

Fifty-Four

Roger Wilkie was exhausted. He had experienced nasty storms since moving to Whidbey Island, but nothing close to this one. With only his police radio system available for communications and its limited range due to the hilly terrain on the island, his ability to keep in touch with his deputies and team members was challenging at best.

The support crews from off-island reached him shortly after midnight, letting him know their plans. Clearing 525 was foremost, but powering up the remaining cell towers was a close second. The eighteen-wheeled flatbed trucks, loaded with portable generators, rolled off the Squamish ferry at 6:20 a.m. Several fuel stations on the island were using backup generator power, so gasoline wouldn't be a problem.

It was ten o'clock when he saw the first bars on his cell phone, and three minutes later, he saw the voicemail alert.

"Kevin ... Kev, can you hear me?"

"Yeah ... the thing scared me when it went off. They must be working on the towers."

"Tell me about Francis ... Your message said he found Hogan?"

"Yes. The last time I talked to him, he was following some guys he met, and they were following Hogan."

"Shit ... We need to get up there, but right now it's impossible. Have you tried his phone?"

"Yes—no luck. How about his brother, Jake? Maybe try him."

"Good idea, Kev, but I've gotta go. I'm still at home and need to do more chainsaw work before getting to the road. Wally's on Camano; they aren't quite as bad as we are, so maybe I can get him over to Oak Harbor."

"Wait ... Roger ... what about Bill Owens? They couldn't have had much damage in Bellevue. Maybe he could get up here and help."

"Maybe ... I'll give him a call. Call me if you hear from Francis. Bye."

It was noon before 525 was cleared enough to allow emergency responders access to the entire island. It was painstaking work supplying auxiliary power to the remaining cell towers. Still, eventually, most of the residents could reach loved ones and make necessary calls for emergencies.

In a rare display of selfless community service, Verizon, T-Mobile, and AT&T put aside their competitive predispositions to offer free service to all living on the island until the entire infrastructure could be restored.

Exhausted, Roger took a few minutes to review the messages on his phone. Because the service was intermittent, some came in immediately; others took longer. One of them was from Francis.

"Roger ... I'm chasing after Hogan ... Get me some help ..."

There was a message from Jake Early asking Roger if he knew anything about his brother, several from Matt Steele, and a few from the task force members. And there was a strange one from Chief Eddie Trevitt of the Oak Harbor Police Department, who requested an immediate callback. The call came shortly after nine a.m.

"Chief Trevitt, it's Roger Wilkie returning your call." Roger had a bad feeling about this.

"Hey, Roger, I know you've probably got your hands full with this storm, and I also know you're running the show on this Hogan thing."

"What's up?" He had little time for chit-chat with everything on his plate.

"What's up is I've got three dead bodies and another seriously injured. A Home Depot employee was heading to work this morning—they managed to get open, by the way—and she ran across them near the rear of the Growler Motel."

"Okay ..."

"One of them had his face blown off; the other two had holes in them the size of basketballs ..."

"Chief, please tell me why I'm talking to you ..."

The policeman continued, ignoring the interruption, "The guy still breathing took a load of double-aught in the shoulder and lost a lot of blood. We had a Navy chopper get him to Whidbey Health in Coupeville. Just before he passed out, he mentioned Hogan."

"Chief ..."

"The injured guy's ID says he's a Francis Early and lives in Freeland. Do you know him? Any relation to Jake Early, our county commissioner?"

"Jesus ... fuck ... sorry, Chief. Yeah, he was helping on the Hogan thing. I'm guessing this is his doing."

"We don't take too kindly to multiple homicides here in Oak Harbor, and when word gets out, folks are gonna be upset. It'll make more sense for you and your team to deal with this than me, but I need to be in the loop. Remember, this is my town."

"We'll get on it right away, Chief, and thanks for your professionalism."

"Yeah ... I'm sure. Bye now."

Cell service was slowly improving, but internet service wouldn't return to normal for some time, and most roads were still unpassable. Roger needed help from somewhere other than Whidbey Island. He picked up his phone and called the Bellevue Police Department. He'd try Owens first, then let Jake know what was happening.

Fifty-Five

With the only illumination coming from the emergency lighting on the corner of the Growler, Harry Hogan wasn't sure whether he'd killed the bald guy. He heard him collapse into the hedge, though, so he didn't care either way.

He was confident the storm's ferocity had obscured the shotgun blasts, but still, he needed to get away from the dead bodies before anyone saw what had happened. He hoped the keys he'd fished out from the dead Samoan's pocket would provide the answer.

He grabbed the containers and respirator from his truck and hurried through the buffeting gusts back to the Depot. With only emergency lighting now available, the store had emptied quickly, and the parking lot held only a smattering of vehicles. One of them, an ancient Buick Roadmaster wagon, was parked in the far west corner. He could still recall the two huge men sitting in it while he conducted his business with the old man.

He hit the unlock button on the key fob and was relieved to see the headlights flash from the wagon. After hurriedly dumping the containers in the back of the old relic where the third seat was folded down, he got behind the wheel. He was surprised at how clean the interior was, since it seemed the two brothers practically lived in the thing.

Turning the key, he was rewarded with the full-throated rumble of the 5.8-liter V8 engine, identical to those in the Corvettes of the same era. He dodged carts and debris from the storm and headed for the main highway on the island, WA-525.

The radio was already tuned to the news and promised hurricane-force winds within the hour, lasting through midnight. He needed to find a place to hunker down soon before the roads were littered with hundreds of tree carcasses.

Heading south on the arterial, he dodged limbs and fought to keep the eighteen-foot-long, two-ton-plus behemoth on the road. He passed the county seat of Coupeville, then headed west to Ebey's Landing. While exposed to the storm's fury, the 25-square-mile National Park offered something unique on the island—very few trees.

Great expanses of prairie and agricultural fields roll up to 200-foot cliffs with nary a tree in sight. This was where Harry Hogan chose to spend the night, waiting out the storm, whose peak gusts exceeded ninety miles per hour. These were recorded near the trailhead parking area, where Hogan was stretched out, considering his next moves.

The electrical power to his storage unit would surely be interrupted, but the incubators were insulated sufficiently to keep the bacteria alive. The cooler temperatures would slow down the growth of the microbes, but the temperature could drop as low as 40 degrees without any appreciable loss in viability. He wasn't worried.

The previous owners of his new ride had thoughtfully left pillows and blankets on the second-row seat, and when folded down, it made the wagon almost as comfortable as his room at the Growler.

Fifty-Six

With my battery-powered chainsaw, I was able to clear the debris from my driveway, but driving anywhere was still impossible. Jenne was helping me clear the limbs off to the side when we heard a rumbling diesel slowly approaching.

We made our way to the paved road in time to see one of the fallen alders being shoved into the ditch at the side of the road. Behind it was a John Deere 5E series tractor with a forklift attachment, and behind the wheel was Seth Robbins.

He shut down the engine, dismounted, and made his way over wires, branches, and trees, finally reaching us.

"Hey, you two, how do you like my new ride? Alice bought it for me to use around our property. I had the forklift attachment on it to move some stumps out back a couple of days ago, and then this storm hit. I cleared our drive and made my way up here. I've been shoving these trees as far away as possible. I should be able to make at least a single lane so folks can get out for supplies."

"Thanks for thinking of us. How did your place make out?"

"A little damage but not awful. We cleared the big trees away when we built the house, and we're glad we did."

"What's the road like on the way into Langley?"

"It's still a mess, but with all the farms around here, lots of heavy equipment is available, and everyone is pitching in. By day's end, you might be able to make it to 525, taking a few detours."

I thanked Seth and headed back with Jenne to continue the cleanup when my cell phone buzzed. The caller ID said it was Jake Early.

"Jake, how are you making out?" I knew Francis was in Oak Harbor, and being in a wheelchair without power would be difficult.

"I'm fine, Kev, but I just heard from Roger. Francis is in the hospital in Coupeville. It seems there were multiple murders, and Francis was the only survivor. They're pretty sure it was Hogan."

The last I'd heard from Francis, he was following Hogan, so I filled Jake in with what I knew.

"Roger said he was on his way there, and Bill Owens was coming up to lend a hand. I can drive the van, but I'd rather not chance it with the roads the way they are. I'm sure those two will have their hands full with the investigation, so could you make it out and maybe get to the hospital?"

The Early brothers were good friends, and we'd been through some rough stuff with them before, so I didn't give the answer a second thought. "Of course. The three of us will get there as soon as we can. We'll call you as soon as we see what's happening."

Emma, Jenne, and I climbed into my pickup and headed out through the rubble to hopefully make it to the main highway.

It was only a mile before we came to a stop. A giant alder had fallen across Saratoga Road, taking down numerous cable and electrical wires. We backed up and tried the small loop that went through the community of Bells Beach. It took some doing, but we managed to get by the impasse by driving off to the side of the road and under a fallen fir being held up by a utility pole. Emma was as nervous as we were until we were clear of the wreckage.

We took Lone Lake Road south without encountering any blockage until we reached Andreason. The short road leading to Bayview Road was completely covered with fallen trees, requiring us to backtrack to Goss Lake Road and then to East Harbor. The trip to Freeland—typically a fifteen-minute journey—was accomplished in ninety minutes, but we managed to get to the highway safely.

It was only another thirty minutes to Coupeville since it wasn't necessary to dodge any trees or utility poles. Along the way, we passed numerous crews working furiously to get the island back among the civilized. I mused that the folks on Whidbey were far more capable of dealing with disasters than those on the mainland, but that was probably because they saw more than most and were proud of their independence.

Arriving at the medical center, just off the main arterial, we cracked open the windows, left Emma in the truck, and hurried in to find our friend.

"Well, look who's here …"

As soon as we arrived in the waiting area, we saw my good buddy Bill Owens sitting beside Roger Wilkie.

"Somehow, it doesn't surprise me to see you two. Jenne, can't you keep him away from trouble?"

The fact that Bill was his annoying but lovable self told me that Francis would be okay.

"Knock it off, Bill; how is he?" I love it when my wife takes charge.

"He's going to be all right," Roger explained. "He's knocked out on painkillers right now, and he's weak from losing so much blood, but the doc assures us he'll make it through. They'll have to do some surgeries to repair his shoulder, and his recovery will take a few months, but they're encouraged by his toughness."

I was confident that Francis would be fine if willpower were the deciding factor. "Were you able to talk to him?"

"Only for a few minutes. He confirmed Hogan did the shooting and was sad about the other three victims. Said they were good guys, and if we didn't get Hogan soon, he'd kick our ass and handle it himself when he's out of the hospital."

"That sounds like Francis."

"Bill and I are going to the Oak Harbor police station to see the chief. Maybe you can hang out here and call Jake if you don't mind. I'm sure he's worried as hell."

"We'll do that. Would you let us know what you find out?"

"Why would we do that?" Bill was back to his old grumpy self.

Roger chuckled as they exited through the automatic doors and shouted over his shoulder, "I'll fill you in, Kev. Call Andie too, will you?"

I saw Bill punch him on the shoulder as they turned down the walkway. The two cops from different cultures and constituents seemed to have developed a kinship in the pursuit of a common enemy.

I broke the news to Jake about his brother's injuries and brought him up to date on the murders while Jenne filled Andie in on the goings-on. I promised to let him know when Francis was strong enough to take a call and told him we'd wait around until that happened. He told me he would do all he could to help in the investigation, and right now, he had a call to make.

Fifty-Seven

Even though the station wagon was parked in an area without trees, daylight exposed the storm's ferocity. The windshield was plastered with wet leaves from forests miles away and sand from the beach two hundred feet below. Even Harry Hogan was amazed at nature's power.

After folding the bedding, he climbed out of his mobile hotel room and took a few minutes to relieve himself while taking in his impressive surroundings. Although he'd lived on the island for years, he had never been to Ebey's Landing and never understood why folks raved about the place. Now, even in his confused and maladjusted psyche, there was a glint of appreciation for nature's majesty in this profound meeting of land and sea.

He scraped the storm detritus from the windshield and began planning his next moves. The radio news confirmed what he thought about Whidbey Island's entirety being powerless, with many roads blocked by fallen trees and power poles.

Even if he could make it to his storage unit to collect his cultured bacteria, getting to Langley and its reservoir might prove difficult. He figured the storm cleanup and resulting chaos would consume the local gendarmes, and he doubted they'd be looking for his new wheels. Sure, the four guys he'd shot would cause some consternation, but Oak Harbor was a Podunk town except for the Navy base, and the local cops would be in over their heads.

No, he'd wait one more day until the road crews had most of the trees cleared. Then, he'd proceed with his mission.

Hogan was hungry. With the massive power outage, only those places of business with generators were operating, mostly gas stations. He left his improvised campsite and headed east to the historic town of Coupeville.

With a population of nearly 2,000 souls, the Island County seat was a frequent stop for visitors to the island. Many of its quaint and historic structures along Front Street are the originals, built in the late eighteen and early nineteen hundreds.

It's the home of Whidbey Island's only major hospital and is considered the dividing line between the north and south ends of the island. Because of the storm, only the hospital and two fuel stations were operating on this day.

Hogan drove his floating behemoth past Whidbey General Hospital, where the O'Malleys waited patiently for Francis Early to regain consciousness just after Wilkie and Owens departed for Oak Harbor. The 45-KW generators providing power to the hospital could be heard as he drove by.

Pulling into the Chevron station a block from the medical center, he found enough energy bars and bottled water on the near-empty shelves of its convenience store to fulfill his needs. After satisfying his thirst and hunger, he returned to 525 and headed south. Still determining where he would spend the coming night, he preferred to get as close to his colony of microbes as possible. It would be the following day for certain.

Fifty-Eight

Chief Trevitt was a rotund man in his fifties and of small stature. Owens and Wilkie sat across from him, his ancient oak desk providing physical separation, their wooden chairs of dubious construction and lower-than-standard seat height reinforcing their diminished status.

"The governor tells me to extend any aid you need; it seems you two have some pull there. Does that seem about right?"

Wilkie looked at Owens, both men surprised by the local chief's offer even though it was tempered by his attitude.

"We'd like to know the details of that triple murder. We're part of the task force trying to get to this guy before he can do more damage. He's killed over a dozen other citizens besides these three. We understand that yours is a small community, and folks are scared, but unless we find this man soon, even worse things will happen."

Whether it was Roger's reasoned plea or a sudden empathy attack was unknown, but Chief Trevitt rose from behind his desk and beckoned the two policemen to follow him.

"Let's go to the conference room; all the stuff we have is in there. The two officers who responded are also here, and you can ask them whatever you'd like. They've been told to treat you as they treat me, which is how you'd like it, trust me."

They followed the portly chief down the corridor to a small room where two uniformed officers rose immediately from their seats. The chief introduced the men and then addressed Roger.

"You don't need me for this, but if you're not satisfied or want me to rattle some cages, call me. Use these two however you want." With that, the conflicted department head turned and waddled back to his office.

The two policemen who had been first on the scene shared all they had, including the crime scene photos and the legwork they had done in identifying the victims. While the event was tragic, those killed appeared to be innocent casualties whose only crime was possibly trying to help Francis.

They had interviewed the manager of the Growler Motel, who was of no help save for identifying the room that had been rented. The local crime scene tech had managed to get prints from Hogan's room, but since Francis had identified the murderer as Hogan, they would only be helpful in a courtroom.

They also identified the F-150 pickup in the motel parking lot as the one sold to Hogan a few days earlier, verified additionally by fingerprints.

"You men should be proud of your work; this has helped a lot." Bill Owens addressed the two officers.

"Any idea how he got away—what he drove?" Wilkie asked.

"Not yet, sir. We were going to work on that until the chief said to hold off," one of them answered.

"What about this Vaso and Taito Kiana? What did they drive?"

"Whatever it was, sir, we couldn't find a record of it. Those guys, as big as they were, didn't leave much of a footprint."

"Are you willing to do some more work on this? We can use the help."

The two men looked at each other and nodded enthusiastically, appearing to embrace the idea of reporting to anyone but their boss.

Roger told them to do their best to discover what Hogan was using to get around and that it was important. Then, he and Bill headed back to the hospital to check on Francis.

Fifty-Nine

"We spoke with Jake. He was relieved when he heard of his brother's condition, then told us he had to make a call," I told Roger and Bill as soon as they walked into Whidbey General. With the hospital on auxiliary power and elective surgeries cancelled, the waiting area was empty save for a few storm-related injuries.

"Whatever he said to the governor seemed to work. The Oak Harbor chief didn't seem too happy to share, but he did," Bill replied.

"Yeah, and the two cops on the case were helpful, and they're doing a little more legwork for us," Roger chipped in.

"Anything on where Hogan is?"

Roger grimaced before answering. "No. We were hoping that when Francis comes around, he might help with that."

I made a trip to the pickup to check on Emma, who was sleeping soundly on her bed behind the front seat, and when I returned, Jenne and the two detectives were gone.

"They're in with Mr. Early. You can go back if you like, but as I told them, you're on a short leash. The patient needs rest more than anything." The duty nurse indicated the way to go after addressing me.

I joined Roger on one side of the bed, with Bill and Jenne on the other. Francis appeared weak and pale but still sported a happy smile. "Nice to see everyone cares," he said.

"We do, Francis; you scared us," Jenne said.

"Any luck finding this asshole?" His condition hadn't lessened his resolve to nail Hogan.

Roger answered, "We're working on it. Do you have any idea how he got away?"

"It was dark, and I only saw him for a few seconds, but I think he was trying to get something from Taito's pocket—maybe his keys."

"Do you know what the brothers were driving?"

"It was a big old station wagon ... a Buick or Pontiac or something. It was tan but really faded."

"That's great, Francis, really great."

Roger turned to Bill. "Let's go. We need to get this out to everyone."

After they were gone, we called Jake and let him chat with Francis until he started dozing and the nurse kicked us out.

"This Hogan is evil, isn't he?" Jenne asked me as we climbed into my truck.

"Yeah, he is. I don't know how anyone gets that fucked up, but this guy doesn't care about anything but taking out people who don't see things the way he does. And he doesn't mind any collateral damage either."

We made our way back to 525 and turned south to go back to our powerless home. Hopefully, the road crews had made some progress in opening things up.

With few people on the road, the drive was uneventful. Many of the side roads had been cleared, allowing us to make the journey without any detours, and we made it home just before nightfall. We turned up the gas fire, turned on the battery-powered lantern, lit the candles, and settled in to listen to the tinny sound of the little transistor radio.

To be certain we had contact with the outside world, we'd made sure our phones were fully charged during our drive to Coupeville. We could cook, had running water, and, as long as we didn't open the refrigerator often, we had plenty of food to last for days. Emma didn't seem to notice any difference in her lifestyle.

***

"One of those Oak Harbor cops left a message for us." Roger addressed Bill Owens as they walked into the sheriff's office in Freeland. "They managed to talk to a few of the day laborers at the Home Depot who knew the Kiana brothers. They said the car was an old Buick station wagon, and the two practically lived in the thing."

"Can we get the word out on this?" Owens seemed doubtful, considering the lack of communication options due to the storm.

"We'll pass it on to all our people via radio and have them get it to the local police in the towns. We'll get it to the Clinton ferry terminal since they're under generator power and can easily spot him if he wants to leave the island that way. Everything is out on the north end, so if he's taking the bridge at Deception Pass, we're screwed. Maybe we'll get lucky."

"Can Matt help with this?"

"He texted me he'd try to be over sometime tomorrow, and he'll bring his crew. I'll get Wally here first and get everyone on the same page. What about you?"

"We've got our usual stuff in Bellevue, but if you'd like, I can stay for one more day."

"Thanks, Bill; I'd appreciate that. C'mon over to my place for the night. Andie's there, and we've got generator power; it'll be better than trying to find something here or in Langley."

After a simple dinner of burgers and salads, the three discovered much in common as they shared their life experiences. When the discussion turned to cop stuff, Andie, still tired from her ordeal, bid them goodnight and went to bed.

She was already sleeping when Roger lay down beside her two hours later. His mind wandered to his days in LA and the killers he'd brought to justice. As much as he tried, he never understood how a human could take another's life without remorse. Yet most of them fell into that category.

This Hogan, though, was a cat of a different breed. He was clever and calculating, and the mounting death toll he spawned indicated a committed, if deranged, individual. He was certain he'd catch the son of a bitch, and when he did, he doubted Hogan would be alive to make it to prison.

Sixty

Whidbey Island was famous for its dark night sky, where stargazing during the few clear winter nights was hard to match. With the total absence of power and a crystal-clear night, the celestial display was remarkable.

Unconcerned about nature's display, Harry Hogan headed south on 525 with only a vague idea of where he would spend the night. The good news was that the power outage and the absence of ambient light provided ample cover. The few deputies on duty would be consumed with other emergencies brought on by the storm and weren't likely to spot him.

Still, he would need to find somewhere to spend the night and then visit his storage unit to harvest his mutated E. coli bacteria. A thought struck him as he passed Greenbank and the lone still-operating phone booth on the roadside.

He turned off the highway to Smuggler's Cove Road, then took a left on the gravel drive leading to his compound. He figured correctly that the storm was occupying the island's civil servants, and monitoring his property would be useless after several days.

Now illuminated by his headlights, the heavy gate at the end of the drive was slightly ajar. For an instant his anger flared as he thought about deputies and FBI agents traipsing over his home, but he quickly parked the thought in the back corner.

He doused the headlights, proceeded to the massive swinging gate, and shoved it open just wide enough to allow the station wagon to squeeze by. If there were still cops around his compound, the gate would surely have been open.

Upon entering his home, he saw items strewn about, takeout coffee cups thrown on the floor, and remnants of candy bars and fast food wrappers. Again, it pissed him off, but he shoved the thought aside as well. His bedroom, too, was tossed, but at least the bed was still intact and a place where he could sleep for the night.

It was just after nine o'clock. He had fired up the propane iron stove to warm the house, eaten a few energy bars, and stretched out on the bed. As he was picturing his movements for the next twenty-four hours, he could see a problem.

The word would be out that he had taken the car owned by the big Samoans, so he would need to stay out of sight until tomorrow night. That meant he'd need to have his containers full and ready to go by then. He'd have to fill them before daylight tomorrow, requiring him to get his ass out of bed and do it now while there was no power and no lights.

He drove the three and a half miles to Whidbey Self Storage, slid the chain-link gate to the side, and proceeded to his unit. He was surprised to see a glow from the small office off to the side, but when he heard the generator's hum, he breathed a sigh of relief. At least there would be light inside his storage unit.

With his Mini Maglite in his mouth, he dialed the combination lock, removed it, and lifted the squeaky garage door, flipping on the switch for the single overhead bulb. He grasped the two five-gallon plastic containers and his respirator from the wagon, entered the unit, and lowered the door just in case.

The Lysogeny broth he used as a medium for culturing his version of E. coli had taken on an amber tint as the bacteria population had multiplied. The two-quart glass beakers inside the incubators containing the deadly microbes looked more like iced tea than the poison it was.

Making sure his breathing apparatus fit snugly, he carefully transferred the viscous liquid from the twenty beakers into the two red gas containers and screwed the caps on tightly.

He turned the light switch off before lifting the door again, then removed the respirator and placed the two tanks in the car. As he lowered the door and prepared to leave, he caught a rustling behind the Buick.

"Aren't you going to lock it?"

Startled, Hogan turned to see a twenty-something man in a hoodie looking quizzically at him. He was holding a flashlight similar to his own, and now Hogan recognized him as the owner.

"Goddamn, you scared me. What are you doing here?"

"I own the place. I was checking to see if there was any storm damage and saw you. Kinda late, isn't it?"

Although he would have preferred to shoot this asshole, he didn't want to jeopardize the mission when he was so close to achieving it. He took a deep breath and said, "I came to see if I could find a couple of lanterns I thought I'd put into storage. You know, with the storm and all ..."

"Did you?"

"Nah, must've been mistaken."

"Want me to help you look?"

This clown didn't give a shit when I leased the space, and now he's Mr. Helpful. "No, that's okay. I'll make do."

"You forgot to lock it."

"Shit ... yes, I did. Thanks."

He replaced the lock in the hasp, twirled the dial, and said goodbye as he climbed into the station wagon. As he drove through the gate, he looked in the rearview mirror and could have sworn the guy was still watching him.

Sixty-One

Our second dark night was only slightly better than the first. We had spent most of the day cleaning the storm debris from the yard and helping our elderly neighbors do the same.

Considering the undependable cell service and most of the police and sheriff's deputies with their hands full in response to the storm, it was no surprise we hadn't heard anything on the search for Hogan.

Jake had called and told us Francis was doing a little better, although he still needed additional shoulder surgeries. He said he had had to promise to let him know when Hogan was apprehended.

We managed a meal of cheese and crackers, a small salad, and a respectable pinot noir. Emma, of course, had her usual kibble with a couple of dollops of canned food scattered on top. Dogs are terrific; they never tire of the same food twice a day, every day.

Without Netflix, Prime, or football, Jenne and I had nothing else to do but talk to each other. I say this with a hint of sarcasm because working together side by side for a decade and a half meant we spent twenty-four hours a day with each other. We loved it, respected each other's opinions and talents, and never lacked for interesting conversation. This evening was no different. Still, it would have been nice to have the Seahawks on the tube. We hit the sack early, wondering what Sunday would bring.

December 1st arrived early in the O'Malley household. It was still dark at seven while we were having oatmeal for breakfast, and the sun wouldn't be up for at least another half hour. We were listening to the little radio, but most of the news was focused on other tragedies and crises in the world.

Puget Power said there were now 80,000 customers without power, including all of Island County, and it would still be a few days before any appreciable dent would be made in that number. The devastation on Whidbey required numerous crews that wouldn't be available until the mainland electricity had been restored.

Not fully grasping the intricacies of the cell phone infrastructure, I couldn't understand why some voicemails were received immediately, and others took hours or even days to arrive. I was reminded again of this phenomenon when I received notice of a voicemail that arrived at four a.m. but had been left at ten the night before.

"If you're the guy who left the picture of that asshole poisoning everyone on Whidbey, then call me. I just saw the son of a bitch. Oh, this is Tom at Whidbey Self Storage."

I played it again for Jenne.

"You've got to get this to Roger right away."

"Really? Ya think?" I knew she was caught up in the chase, and I still couldn't help being a bit of an asshole. "Sorry, hon, I'm doing it right now." I thought my recovery was acceptable, but the look on her face suggested otherwise. With any luck, my outburst would have a short half-life, and she'd forget about it.

I tried Roger and left a message, then did the same for Bill. The service was awful, and, based on my recent experience, I wasn't sure when they'd get the damn things.

"How about we take a drive out to Whidbey Self Storage?"

"Are you gonna be a shithead, or will you behave?"

See, I knew she'd forget about it right away.

***

Still skirting fallen trees and wires, we reached 525 and drove a mile north of Freeland to our destination. The gate was open, so we went through and up to the shabby little office and were surprised to see the door open.

We'd got within ten feet of the opening when I saw two legs sprawled on the linoleum floor and a puddle of congealed blood. The temperature was in the high 30s, but suddenly it felt much colder.

"Jesus, Kevin, he killed him."

"Yeah, he had to have done it right after he called me ... shit. I've gotta try Roger again."

I did and met with the same results. When I looked up, Jenne had stepped gingerly into the office, carefully avoiding the remains of the owner of the enterprise.

"Jenne, get out of there; it's a crime scene."

"Really, Kev? Ya think?" Now, I knew where my tendency for sarcasm came from.

"I know it is, but if Hogan was renting a space here, maybe we can find out which one."

A whiteboard hanging behind the gray metal desk listed the unit numbers and the dates they were rented and had a column to be checked if payment was owed. The entries were written in black felt marker, and the payment column was either red or green, depending upon payment, I guessed.

"When did the paper print the story about the task force visiting the farms and ranches looking for the lab location?"

I knew the weekly paper was distributed on Wednesdays and tried to remember exactly when the story was released. "The last couple of weeks have been a blur, but I think ... yeah ... it had to be around November 15th or close to it."

Jenne's eyes scoured the entries in the lease date column and stopped at two of them. "Here ... it looks like unit L-24 was leased on the 16th and this other one, M-15, on the 17th. Let's check them out." She stepped over poor what's-his-name carefully, and then we left the crime scene and walked over to L-24.

The gravel in front of the unit looked undisturbed, and the shiny Master Lock securing the door told us we weren't getting in the place unless we broke open the door. When we turned the corner to M-15, we noticed the roll-up garage door was open about a foot at the bottom, was unlocked, and had many tire marks and footprints.

We looked at each other with eyes wide open and nodded simultaneously. "Gotta be," I said.

"Careful, Kev. We don't know what's in there."

I waved okay at her and slowly lifted the door until the morning sun pierced the darkness of the interior.

"Holy shit!" She accurately voiced my thoughts.

A row of what I guessed were incubators lined each wall. Their doors were open, and dozens of glass beakers lay on the tables or the floor.

"We have to get Roger over here ... *now*." I rolled the door back down and gently guided Jenne back to the truck.

"Kev ... that's where the E. coli was growing."

"I know, but what bothers me most is that it's no longer there. The fucker's got gallons of that stuff with him now, and I'm afraid he's about to do something awful with it."

We arrived at the Freeland sheriff's office around eleven, just as Roger Wilkie and Bill Owens got into Roger's cruiser.

"Well, if it's not Holmes and Watson. Sorry, you two, we've got to meet with some deputies from Oak Harbor." I could always count on Bill for a little dig.

"Um ... we don't think so. Did you get my messages?"

"We've been a little busy, Kev, but no, I didn't. You, Roger?"

"Nope."

"There's been another murder, and we know where Hogan is—or at least where he's been," I blurted.

"Yeah, and it looks like he's got gobs of that poison with him."

"Whoa, whoa, slow down. What are you two talking about?"

I took a deep breath and told him about the call from Whidbey Self Storage that I had received.

"And you didn't think to tell us?"

"I left a message, goddamn it."

"Okay, easy, Kev, tell us what's happening." Roger always seemed the adult in the conversation.

We began relating our discovery at the storage place, trying not to miss anything, but three sentences in, Roger held up his hand. "Stop, give me a sec ..."

He reached inside the vehicle, grabbed his mic, and ordered two deputies to secure the scene. Next, he reached Matt Steele on his cell and asked him to drop everything and get to Whidbey. He said Andie was already here. He called her next and asked if she could meet him at the scene.

Then he turned back to us while Bill listened intently. "Go on ... no, wait, never mind. Follow us back to the storage place, and you can tell us there. I'll need to know exactly where you were and what you touched."

With a distinct lack of enthusiasm, we complied and followed the two cops back to the murder scene.

Sixty-Two

Driving away from Whidbey Self Storage, Harry Hogan was having second thoughts about his interaction with the young owner of the company.

Because he'd been so occupied with collecting his genetically modified E. coli, he hadn't noticed the guy come up behind him. *How long had he been there? Did he see me with the respirator? Did he recognize me?*

He asked the same questions repeatedly until he made up his mind. Then he pulled to the side of the road, made a U-turn, and hustled his ass back to the storage place. He parked just inside the gate, grabbed his Mossberg, and walked several hundred yards to the office. The desk lamp was still on and the generator humming, but the place was empty.

Exiting the office, he walked around to the rear of the building, where the noise from the Honda generator was much louder. An old Chevy pickup was parked a short distance away, suggesting the proprietor was still on the premises.

Rather than go back inside, Hogan decided to wait in the shadows, sure that the owner would return. He was rewarded when, after only a few minutes, the young man went inside and sat at the old desk. He looked up when Hogan walked into the room.

"It's you."

His smirk took on a malevolent glow as he nodded his acknowledgment. "How did you know?"

"Someone shoved your picture under the door with a phone number on it. I thought maybe you were the guy when I rented the space, but I wasn't sure until I saw you tonight."

"What's your name?"

"Tom."

"Well, Tom, that's too bad. Did you call anyone?"

He had, of course, but he had a bad feeling about what might happen if he admitted it. "No."

"Toss me your phone."

Tom's bluff was about to be discovered, so he had little to gain by denying it. "I mean, yes; yes, I did. I called the number on the picture."

"Who did you talk to?"

"Nobody. I just got a voicemail."

"What did it say?"

Tom was just a guy trying to live his life; he was no hero. "The recording said it was Kevin O'Malley."

"Did you leave a message?"

"Um, no ... No, I didn't." He wasn't sure why he lied, but he did.

"You know what I think, Tom?"

"What?"

"I think you're a goddamn liar. Stand up; we're going for a walk." As he said this, he pointed the shotgun at him,

Tom got up slowly, moved around the desk and in front of Hogan, then tried to bolt through the door when the Mossberg thundered.

Hogan shook his head at the futility of the escape attempt, then picked up the cell phone. The last number called only ten minutes ago had taken forty-five seconds. That was too long for someone who didn't leave a message.

He didn't bother to turn off the light or close the door; he walked to his station wagon and drove away, confident he would be the last visitor to Whidbey Self Storage tonight.

Sixty-Three

After arriving back at the scene of the latest murder, we stayed inside the truck until Bill Owens walked over to us. Several squad cars blocked the entrance, and yellow tape had been strewn everywhere. We rolled the windows down.

"Roger's got his hands full with the crime scene for a while. Why don't you tell me everything you saw and did here again?" He said this with none of his usual bluster or sarcasm as he placed a recording device on the dash. It reminded me how empathetic this Bellevue chief of detectives could be, and it was easy to see how he and Roger had become good friends.

We began with the message I had received from poor Tom, and by the time we had gotten to the discovery of the mess inside M-15, Andie had pulled up alongside us.

Bill acknowledged her arrival and held up his finger, asking for a moment.

"Anything else you remember? Jenne?'

"No, I think Kevin's said everything. If we think of anything, we'll let you know."

He turned off the device, then addressed us with a serious look, "Thanks for your work on this, both of you. I know it had to be a shock seeing this mess, but I also know our history, and I'm grateful for your contributions—even though you're a royal pain in the ass ... sometimes."

This last was said with a wide grin and a shake of his head. It was nice to have my buddy back on form.

Turning to Andie, he said, "They're going to need you inside the ropes; it looks like some nasty stuff in unit M-15."

As soon as Bill left to escort the microbiologist to Hogan's garage unit, we rolled up the windows. We were drained from the ordeal and weren't sure if we'd be needed again, so we parked outside the gravel entry where the sun shone through the tall firs and proceeded to nod off.

In what seemed like seconds, but my watch said it had been thirty minutes, a gentle tapping at my window startled me. Andie made a little wave with her fingers, and I powered the window down, waking Jenne.

"Sorry to wake you guys, but I thought you should know what you found in there." She indicated with her head the cluster of storage units inside the fence.

"Absolutely. How bad is it?"

"I got enough to sample, and it's evil. My field microscope is only 2000×, but that's enough to get a good idea of what we're dealing with."

"And?" Jenne looked frightened.

"Normally, E. coli cells will double every twenty minutes under ideal conditions. This stuff doubles every ten minutes, meaning one parent cell will become over a million in less than four hours. And he's been at this for a week. I won't know the lethality until I return to my lab at home, but based on his earlier attacks, I'd say this is among the deadliest bacteria on the planet. We're not just talking about diarrhea and cramps here. This stuff can potentially shut down every organ in the body in a very short time regardless of how healthy the subject is."

"Jesus ..."

"Maybe *he'll* be able to help, but my money's on Roger and Bill. I'm glad you two found this place, but please be careful. I've got to get to work on this."

"Andie?"

"Yes?"

"Is it possible to be infected by just breathing this stuff?"

"It depends, Jenne. If the concentration is high enough, and this is, the bacteria can easily aerosolize. When that happens and someone inhales it, it gets into the lungs and the circulatory system, and it's the same result. There wasn't sufficient density in there for you to worry about, though."

"How much was in there?"

"Based upon the number of empty beakers, I'd say he's got more than enough to contaminate over half a million gallons of water."

Jenne's face paled as she processed the damage the bacteria could inflict.

"Look, I need to get going on this. Why don't you two go home and try to get some rest? And guys ..."

"What?"

"Nice job." She turned and hurried back to her car.

***

Hogan packed his tools and left his compound before sunrise. Sooner or later, they'd come for him, and he needed a place to hang out until this evening. Whoever this Kevin O'Malley was, he knew he was back in the area, and it wouldn't be long before they raided his home again.

Passing through Langley, he saw several joggers, a few dog walkers, and a couple of food service trucks delivering to the local restaurants. He stayed well under the speed limit and proceeded south until he passed the entrance to the service road leading to the reservoir. He considered depositing his liquid poison immediately for a fleeting moment, but he couldn't take the chance now that the sun was almost up, and he needed to find a place to hide out until nightfall.

A billboard advertising the Island County Fair coming next July poked out from between two cedars on the right side of the road. Under it was the entrance to the county fairgrounds. He pulled off the road into the empty lot and shut the engine off. Several huge barns rose from the fairgrounds, with additional smaller buildings surrounding them. The structures had been in place since 1937; all were painted the same shade of red, and the impression was that of a ghost town from a bygone era.

The only entrance to the fairgrounds was guarded by a manual swing gate secured with a wrap-around chain and locked with a ten-dollar, four-digit combination lock. After inspecting it, Hogan returned to his vehicle, selected the Mossberg, and whacked the lock with the butt several times until it broke loose. After driving through, he swung the gate closed again and left the chain and broken lock where they had fallen. He drove to the rear of the largest barn, satisfied that no one could see him.

With the entire day to kill, he made himself comfortable in the old Buick along with his ten gallons of pure misery, ate his remaining energy bars, and envisioned what the next twenty-four hours would bring.

Sixty-Four

After the exhausting morning, we were glad to return home, and Emma acted as she always did—like we'd been gone for months. The sun was still shining, and the temperature had risen to a balmy 51 degrees, so we took the opportunity to take a stroll on the beach with our faithful companion.

"You think they'll catch this guy before he can use the bacteria?"

"I sure as hell hope so. According to what Andie said, that stuff could hurt a lot of people." I was afraid to say what I was thinking—that Hogan had been masterful at avoiding capture so far, and the infrastructure on the island was still in shambles.

"I've been thinking ..."

"Uh-oh, there you go doing that again." My reply earned me a punch in the arm.

"No, listen to me. Hogan is back here on the island's south end, right?"

"Judging by the dead body at the self-storage place, I'd say yes." My acerbity earned me another punch, so I decided to listen to my wife's words without being a wiseass.

"If he's here, then maybe what he's going to do with that stuff is here."

"Okay ... but maybe he's just here because his temporary lab was here."

"I thought about that, but he could have abandoned it and left the island after killing those men in Oak Harbor and injuring Francis."

"I suppose ..."

"He didn't because he's committed to doing something big, and it has to be somewhere nearby. That's why he killed the guy at the storage place."

"So you think he killed him for shits and giggles?"

"No, you idiot. He did it because the guy recognized him."

"Then how did he manage to call me?"

"I haven't figured that out yet."

"Let's say you're right. Andie said the amount of bacteria Hogan has now is enough for more than half a million gallons, right?"

"Okay ..."

"If he's still in the area, how many tanks that size are there on South Whidbey?"

"I don't know. Maybe he's going to do more than one."

"I don't think so, Jenne. Like you said, I think he's going for a big splash. It seems like all these smaller attacks were only for testing the efficacy of his altered E. coli bacteria. Andie seems to think what was in that unit is more virulent than any earlier versions."

"I agree. What do you want to do?"

"Let's get back home and do a little more research."

"How? The goddamn power is off, and so's the Wi-Fi."

Shit, I forgot about that.

"I've got it!"

"What?"

"We've got a little better cell service from here on the beach because we're using the towers from Everett, right?"

"Yeah, so ..."

"So I'm calling Shelly Owens right now. I'll talk her through what we're looking for, and she can search while I'm on the phone with her."

It's times like these that I'm still in awe of how resourceful my wife can be. I kissed her forehead and said, "How about taking a seat on that log over there while you and your buddy chat?"

After about twenty minutes on the phone with her best friend, Jenne said goodbye and walked the hundred yards to where I was throwing sticks into the Saratoga Passage for Emma to fetch.

"Well, how did we do?"

"*We* did just fine, thank you."

"Has Bill let her know what's going on?"

"Mostly ... she hadn't heard about this morning's events, so I told her."

"And what did *we* find out?"

"Freeland, Clinton, and Langley are the three largest cities, and they all have their own water systems. Langley's reservoir tank is the biggest—over six hundred thousand gallons."

"Bingo!"

"I think so too. It's the place most tourists visit; it's charming, and if their reservoir is poisoned, it'll kill hundreds of people and destroy the town. We've got to find a way to stop it."

"You try Roger, and I'll call Bill. There's a chance they're already on the same page, but it won't hurt to tell them what we've come up with."

***

By noon, the crime scene at Whidbey Self Storage was at the mopping-up stage. The medical examiner was gone, the techs had completed their work, and Wilkie and Owens were heading for Roger's cruiser when their phones began vibrating.

They looked at each other, then at their phones, and then back to each other again, both offering a wry smile and a slight headshake. They listened for a few minutes, said a few words, and then disconnected.

"Don't tell me ... Jenne?" Bill asked.

"Yup. Kevin on yours?

"Yup ... you think they're right?"

"It pains me to say this, but they seem right more often than not."

"Unfortunately, I agree with you. No matter how often I tell him to keep his nose out of police business, he sticks it there."

"Do you think he tries to, or is it one of those cosmic things?"

"Hah, maybe ... what do you want to do?"

"Let's put someone at the Langley reservoir tank. Matt should be here with some reinforcements by tonight, but for now, Wally can handle it."

The cell towers were slowly coming back online, but because each one required a generator for power, it was time-consuming. Owens and Wilkie headed back to the Freeland office to monitor the situation and figure out a way to find Harry Hogan before he could do any further damage.

Every deputy and small-town police officer on South Whidbey was aware of the presence of a mass murderer somewhere nearby. The difficulty with the search was balancing that need with the urgency of returning the island to normal after the storm's devastation.

Most secondary roads were now passable, thanks to the locals chipping in with DOT to cut up and remove the fallen trees. The downed cable and power lines, too, had been cleared. It was promised that Puget Power crews would arrive the following day to hang new lines to almost all of the island.

While Jenne's sketch of Harry Hogan was posted in every police vehicle, it was seldom noticed due to the mess created by the storm.

Roger's attention was divided by the two serious situations, while Bill Owens focused on finding Hogan.

"It's not like this end of the island is that big, Roger."

Wilkie had just looked up from a notice from Puget Power. "I agree. The problem is that there are lots of places to hide. If we had power, we could get the word out to the residents, and maybe we'd get a tip, but that's not going to happen.

"Our best bet is to catch him when he makes his move. We've got Wally at the Langley reservoir, and I've got another two deputies at Freeland and Clinton, just in case. This storm recovery doesn't help, but we'll have better coverage when Matt gets here tonight with his team."

"Is his compound still being watched?"

"No. After the FBI left, we needed every able body to help with the storm damage. Why? You don't think he'd go back there?"

"Probably not, but I think I'll go take a look. Why don't you catch up with what you're doing, and I'll be back after I see if anything's there."

"Thanks, Bill. Appreciate all your help."

Owens tipped his hat and left.

Arriving at the Hogan property, he first noticed the half-opened gate. He knew the FBI had scoured the place and spent several days waiting to see if anyone showed up. They tended to be somewhat messy, but leaving the gate open was out of character for the Feds.

After ensuring no other vehicles were in sight, he proceeded to the main house, pushed open the unlocked door, and went inside.

Whoever had staked the place out was a slob, something he'd talk to Steele about. He went to the bedroom and saw an unmade bed that looked like it had been recently slept in; on the nightstand were two Kind bar wrappers.

The outside temperature hovered around 50, yet the room was much warmer. He walked to the stove, held his hand over it, and felt its lingering warmth. *Son of a bitch, Hogan has been here.*

Owens called Wilkie immediately. "Roger, I think Hogan spent the night here. He's gotta be nearby."

"See if you can find anything else, and then come back here. We'll come up with something."

He checked the rest of the small house and, finding nothing, went to the barn. Before he was halfway there, he could hear the little goats bleating their heads off. They quieted for two seconds when he slid open the barn door, then began the deafening racket anew.

"Whoaa … whoa there, you guys … easy does it." His gentle tone seemed to have some effect. "What's the problem here? You hungry?"

They looked up at him with their horned heads and long goatees, seeming to understand his question.

He looked around and saw that their water trough was empty. He began filling it with a hose attached to a yard hydrant, but as soon as the water hit the metal bottom, the three pygmies nosed and butted him away. They gorged on the water he poured into the tank, now from the other side. *Cute little guys,* he thought, *but goddamn noisy.*

He found a way to leave the hose in the trough while filling it and looked around to see if they had any food. Their little door was open, so he figured they had some pasture to graze, and he thought that would hold them a little longer. He'd done all he could for the little dears; now, he needed to return to Freeland.

Sixty-Five

"Do you think they took us seriously?"

Jenne looked at me as if she were considering my question. "I don't know. Roger, probably ... Bill, maybe."

"What do you want to do?"

"Why don't we take Emma for a drive? It's almost three, and there's not much we can do around here without any power anyway."

"I'll get her in the truck while you lock up. Let's go see how things are in Langley."

We took Saratoga Road and headed for town, only stopping twice to wait for crews moving deadfall from one side of the road to the other. The already narrow road was still a single lane in a few spots that hadn't been cleared sufficiently, but it was still only a twenty-minute drive.

We went past the Star Store, still open under generator power, and proceeded south until we hit Langley Road, leading away from town.

Less than a mile from the village, we passed the entrance to the utility road for the town reservoir, and, sure enough, Wally Turpin was sitting in his cruiser doing something with his phone. We slowed enough for him to see us, beeped the horn once, waved, and continued.

"I guess they took us seriously enough," I said.

"Yeah, maybe so ... pull in here."

"Why? It's the Island County Fair entrance, and it's closed."

"I know, silly. It's so you can turn around, and we can go home. Now that they've got the reservoir protected, we can relax.'

I pulled off the road, drove up to the swing gate, and prepared to make a "K" turn when I heard my wife say, "Stop."

"What?"

"Look."

"What am I looking at?"

"The gate ... the lock ... it's not locked."

"So? Some maintenance person screwed up and forgot to lock it."

"Yeah ... maybe ... let's get out and take Emma for a stroll."

At the beginning of not feeling comfortable, I voiced my opinion. "Um ... maybe we should do this somewhere else."

"Why? It couldn't be that the fairground's property butts up against the hill that the reservoir's on, could it?"

"Jenne, I'll admit seeing the gate unsecured is slightly suspicious, but if anyone *is* in there, we're not the ones who should be checking."

Instead of answering me, Jenne was furiously working on her cell phone.

"Jenne?"

"Gimme a minute, I'm almost there ... the service sucks ..."

"They don't have all the towers working yet."

"I know ... I know ... wait for it ... wait ... there, I've got it."

"What have you got?"

"Dalton Road runs alongside the fairground property. We can take a right there and maybe see behind the big red barn."

"Jenne ..."

"C'mon, Kev, it won't take long, and there's no danger. We can take off if we see anything ... c'mon ..."

"Sheesh, okay, okay."

I completed my turn, took a right out the drive, and then took another immediate right onto Dalton.

"Go slow, Kev."

"Not a problem; there's so much crap in the road, I *have* to go slow."

We crept along at fifteen miles an hour, but the ancillary buildings blocked our view to the rear of the large event venue. That was until we reached a point where an ancient fir tree had been uprooted and crushed one of the single-story support buildings, creating a narrow opening exposing the area behind the huge barn. That was where we saw an ancient Buick station wagon and a smallish man exiting the vehicle.

Sixty-Six

ogan was becoming restless. Sitting in his ride and listening to crappy AM radio stations only distracted him for so long. His impatience beginning to get the better of him, he began to consider moving up his timetable. In another hour, the sun would be dropping anyway.

The access road to the town reservoir was just outside the fairground's gate to the north, so the chances of someone seeing him were minimal. He drove from behind the barn, swung the gate open, and turned left. The next left was the turn to the access road, but when he began to take it, he saw a Sheriff's Department cruiser parked at the chain-link gate.

Shit, how did they know about my plans? He continued north to a motel parking lot and turned around, then headed back to the fairgrounds to consider the situation.

Safely behind the barn again, Hogan went through his options and found that there weren't many. On the hill north of the fairgrounds was his target. He thought about climbing the steep embankment, which was doable, except that he'd be carrying almost sixty pounds of deadly bacteria, plus his tools. No, not an option.

As these thoughts marched through his brain, something caught his eye. Through a tiny sliver of space between the barn and an adjacent structure, he could see the front gate where a gray pickup drove up. He was too far away to see the occupant, but whoever it was sat there for a few minutes and seemed to be deciding something.

Hogan reached behind him and felt the reassuring barrel of the shotgun, but as he went for it, the vehicle turned around and left. It was late afternoon, and whatever he came up with had to happen soon.

His only option for accessing the ginormous tank was via the access road, but a cop was blocking it. He had to find a way to remove him from the scene.

Sixty-Seven

"Should we stop and see what he's doing?"

"I think we've done enough, Jenne. See if you can get Roger on the phone. It's time for them to take over."

I drove faster, still wary of the fallen limbs jutting into the road. Because it was a dead end, I made a U-ey and proceeded back the way we had come.

"Any luck?"

"Nope. I guess the cells are busy with only a few towers back in service."

"Keep at it. I'll head over to the Freeland office." As I spoke, we passed the fallen fir again, allowing us a peek at the car. This time, it was empty.

"Maybe we should tell the cop at the reservoir gate."

"We could, but I don't think he'd want to leave his post. Remember, we think that's the target."

"You think that's Hogan in there?" Jenne asked.

"I suppose it could be some maintenance guy or something else, but my money's on Hogan."

"If we think it's him, let's get to the cop next door. He's got a radio, and maybe he'll just go in there and arrest him and get this over with."

"*If* it's Hogan ... okay, I'm with you. Worst case, he can get Roger and Bill on his radio, and they can decide what to do."

We turned into the access road and drove up to the gate, where Wally Turpin was sitting in his cruiser, doing something on his phone. He looked up, startled.

"Jesus, you guys scared the shit out of me."

"Wally, we think Hogan is parked behind those fairground buildings."

"Huh? Why?"

"Because we saw this old station wagon parked there, and a guy was sitting there."

"A station wagon? What color?"

"It was a faded brown-yellowish thing, very old—maybe a Buick or Olds or something."

"It's him. Don't move." Wally held his hand out, ensuring we stayed while he keyed his radio, receiving nothing but static.

"Damn, these hills make it tough on the range of these things. Let me try the phone."

"We did."

"Well, both of you try again and again. So will I. We need reinforcements here now!"

Wally was in cop mode and was all business. He alternated between the radio and his phone, doing everything possible to reach another vehicle or headquarters without leaving his post.

Just as a voice broke through the static on the radio, a massive explosion rattled the air, and thirty-foot flames erupted from the fairgrounds next door.

"Goddamn ... Roger ... Roger, can you hear me?"

"Go ahead, Wally. What's going on?"

"Hogan's here. The O'Malleys found him at the fairgrounds, and I think he just blew up the barn."

"On our way. Do what you can. We'll get the fire guys there, too. Out."

"I want you two to go back up the street, pull into that motel parking area, and stay there until you hear from me. Got it?"

We both nodded. We knew Wally a little and always considered him an easy-going fellow with a live-and-let-live approach. Now that he was in a crisis, his professional yet urgent approach to the situation left little doubt that he was up to the task.

"Got it, Wally. Good luck."

Before we could follow orders, Wally fired up his cruiser and spun gravel as he peeled toward the fairgrounds. We did as instructed. Neither of us, including Emma, wanted anything to do with whatever happened next.

With sunset fast approaching, Hogan needed to find a way to get the cop stationed at the access road to move.

He entered the eighty-year-old red barn via a rear access door that was easily jimmied open. The musty smell of hay, farm animals, and diesel fuel assaulted his senses seconds before he flicked the bank of light switches. Almost a third of the space was filled with hay, while alongside one wall were orderly racks of pitchforks and other farm implements. On the opposite side, an enclosed cage held dozens of olive jerry cans; some said gasoline, but most were labeled diesel fuel.

Taking a pry bar from the tool cache, he snapped open the padlock in seconds and carried the gas containers over to the stacked bales of hay, where he emptied the contents and then tossed the cans aside. Next, he loosened the caps on the diesel cans and positioned them on top of the hay.

He unscrewed the last gasoline can, attached the spout, and poured a trail of the fuel from his makeshift bomb back through the rear door until he was outside.

After lighting the gas trail, he watched it go to the gas-soaked hay and burst into flame. With only a few minutes before the diesel was hot enough to explode, he left the fairgrounds and retreated to the motel parking lot to wait.

The explosion was more than he had hoped for, but he still gave it another ten minutes to ensure the deputy left his post.

As he left the motel lot, he passed a pickup that might have been the same one he had seen earlier, but he discarded the thought; his schedule required focus. He had one more job to do, and hopefully, the entrance gate to the reservoir was now left unmanned.

Wally Turpin screeched into the Island County Fairgrounds parking lot as the flames were leaping from the storied red barn that had adorned posters since the late 1930s.

The intense heat from the fire prevented him from getting anywhere near the barn, but his real concern was finding Hogan. He made a quick circuit around the entire perimeter before concluding that he'd missed the son of a bitch.

He made it back to the entrance in time to see the fire department beginning their well-choreographed moves and the arrival of two squad cars. Roger and Bill ran over to Wally the instant he turned off the ignition.

"Anything?"

"Nothing, Roger. I did a loop around the whole property and nada."

"The reservoir?"

"I left it to come here. O'Malley said they saw his car here."

"Okay, you stay here. Bill and I will go and check on the reservoir. When Matt arrives, have him search the area, including the whole town, if he has to."

"On it, boss."

Sixty-Eight

The flaming inferno of the old barn cast an eerie glow in the dark sky ahead of us as we drove to the motel. It was the reason we clearly saw Harry Hogan going by us in the opposite direction.

"You think he saw us, Kevin?"

"No way ... those flames were directly in front of him. I think even seeing the road would be a problem."

"You think he's headed back to the reservoir?"

"I'd bet on it. He must've set the barn on fire as a diversion."

"What do you want to do?"

I reached the lot, did a quick turnaround, then answered my wife. "We've got to let Bill and Roger know."

I floored it. With the conflagration in front of me, I was convinced Hogan couldn't have seen us.

We arrived at the fairgrounds and found at least a half-dozen emergency vehicles blocking the entrance. "Jenne, get out and see if you can find Roger. Tell him and Bill to get to the tank as fast as possible, and I'll meet them there."

"Are you gonna do something stupid?"

"Hell, no. I just want to be sure that's where Hogan is going. I won't even get out of the truck."

Just before she threw the door closed, I heard her say, "You'd better not."

I drove up to the reservoir entry road, where the gate was crushed. Hogan hadn't even bothered to get out of the two-and-a-half-ton Buick and instead used it as a battering ram to clear the entrance.

For some reason beyond my comprehension, our GSD, Emma, possessed a supernatural ability to sense danger or trouble whenever it presented. Her fur had been bristling, and she'd been fidgety since our first stop at the fairgrounds, and now, with her mom absent, she was downright uncontrollable.

While she panted, paced, and whined in the back seat area, I climbed the gravel road leading up the heavily wooded hillside to the thirty-foot-high concrete tank. I took the bend in the road to the thicket of alders that obscured the reservoir and almost plowed into the Buick Roadmaster. It was empty.

With a sliver of moon and the glow of the fire from the fairgrounds, the top quarter of the domed concrete tank was barely visible above the thick skeletal trees surrounding the structure. At almost ten meters high, it would be years before they managed to obscure the Langley water storage tank entirely.

I stepped out of the truck and opened the rear door, allowing an increasingly agitated ninety-pound German Shepherd to bolt from the vehicle. She galloped directly toward the reservoir, already picking up the scent of what she perceived as a threat.

By the time I caught up with her, she was barking furiously at a figure two-thirds of the way up the ladder leading to the vent stack and the inspection port on the tank roof.

Even in the dim light, I could see Hogan struggling under the weight of two large containers. With the narrow steel steps and difficult visibility, one slow step at a time was all he could manage. It appeared he had strapped the plastic holders around his shoulders with rope, allowing him to grasp the rails on both sides.

He looked down at us for several seconds and seemed to think we weren't a threat. Then, as he looked at the top of the ladder, he managed a deep breath and focused on taking another step. I guessed an old guy in his sixties and a dog who couldn't climb were easy to dismiss.

I left Emma and returned to the truck to wait for reinforcements. She'd make sure Hogan would think twice about coming back down, and if Jenne arrived with Roger, I could always pretend I had obeyed her and stayed out of harm's way.

Sixty-Nine

Convinced that his diversion was successful, Harry Hogan drove past the flaming fairgrounds and arrived at the now unattended gate to the Langley reservoir. With everything that had happened, he knew he had precious little time to accomplish his mission.

Instead of stopping to open the gate, he used the vehicle's weight to smash the chain-link barrier aside and continued up the steep, poorly maintained road to the top of the hill.

Along with a small collection of tools stuffed in his backpack, he lugged the two containers of bacteria-saturated culture medium to the base of the weathered concrete tank, now illuminated by the glow from the fire below.

He knew the stuff would be heavy, but he hadn't planned on the narrowness of the ladder, and he couldn't afford more than one trip to the top. He rushed back to the Buick and rifled through the odds and ends the Kiana brothers had stored in the luggage area behind the second row.

There wasn't much help there, save for a short length of one-inch battle rope. He grabbed it, jogged back to the ladder, and fastened a container onto each end. He looped it over his shoulders and backpack and began to climb.

Hogan wasn't a big man, but an active lifestyle and a respectable diet had managed to keep his body in reasonably good shape. Still, the climb carrying almost seventy pounds of weight proved excruciating. By the time he reached the twentieth rung, he was exhausted, the sweat pouring off him even in the chilly night air.

Pausing a moment to catch his breath, he heard the fierce barking of a dog that unexpectedly appeared at the bottom of the ladder. When he looked down, he saw a German Shepherd looking up, its mouth showing an uncomfortable number of teeth. As he turned to resume his climb, an older guy showed up, and the dog seemed to calm down, if only a little.

He didn't think he'd seen the guy before, and judging by his age, Hogan didn't consider him a threat. When the old-timer left, and the dog didn't, he figured it wouldn't be long before he had a lot more company, so he took a deep breath and resumed climbing. The remaining dozen rungs to the top of the tank were challenging, but the added adrenaline from this new threat propelled him to the top.

The first thing he did was to put the heavy plastic jugs down and remove the backpack. He was drenched with sweat and gulped the cool night air.

This tank's rooftop layout was unique and slightly different from the others he had conquered. The vent was twice as large as the others and was made from corrugated steel. There were two bolted covers, similar to the manholes in the streets. The small saw he'd packed wasn't going to do much damage to the steel vent stack, so he had to find another way to get the deadly microbes into the tanks.

After inspecting the closest cover, he instantly eliminated it as a potential opportunity. The bolts were rusted and looked like they hadn't been touched in years. The second cover, on the opposite side of the roof, was slightly smaller, but his tiny flashlight showed the bolts had been recently removed. They did have a little rust, but it looked like they'd been sprayed with WD-40 or some other lubricant to loosen them.

He retrieved his pack, returned to the smaller cover, and removed the small adjustable crescent wrench he had thought to bring. The first of the eight-inch-and-a-quarter bolts turned without much effort, but the undersized wrench constantly slid off the six-sided head, slowing the process.

It was another seven minutes before he had the sixth bolt removed, and the goddamn dog was still down there barking. He wasn't sure where the old guy was and didn't care. In another couple of minutes, the entire town of Langley would be drinking or brushing their teeth or maybe eating something they'd washed with water contaminated with a genetically modified bacteria as lethal as any known to science.

With the seventh bolt finally removed, and the eighth one loosened sufficiently, he rotated the cover, opening the hatch, and donned his respirator. The thought of millions of tiny organisms flowing through the Langley municipal water system made him catch his breath.

Seventy

When Jenne ran to their car, Bill Owens and Roger Wilkie were about to leave the fairgrounds. "We just passed Hogan on the road; we think he's headed to the reservoir."

Bill asked, "And where's Kevin?"

"He followed him there but promised to stay out of trouble."

"I'm sure he did ... c'mon, Roger. Let's get over there before my good buddy steps in it again."

"What about me?"

"Matt Steele will be arriving in just a little bit. Bring him to the reservoir when he does."

"Bill?"

"Yeah?"

"Make sure Kevin doesn't do anything dumb."

"I plan on it."

The two cops arrived at the site, blew through the damaged gate, and tore up the access road, where their headlights revealed the old station wagon and O'Malley's pickup. They were both relieved when Kevin hopped out of the truck and hustled over to them.

"Talk to me, Kev." They snatched their tactical flashlights from the rear and were out of the cruiser before he got to them, and Roger spoke first.

"He's up on top of the tank."

"Are you sure?"

"Do you hear that dog?"

"Yeah ... Emma?"

"Yup. She's at the bottom of the access ladder, and Hogan's not going anywhere."

"Good job, Kev. Stay here and tell Matt the situation when he arrives. Have him contact someone from the city and figure out how to shut down the system. If Hogan is successful, I don't want to end up with a town full of dead people."

With their bright LED lights leading the way, they arrived at the ladder, where Emma was still excited and barking. She quieted as soon as she picked up their familiar scent.

"Good girl, Emma, good girl." Roger patted her on the head and gave her a scratch before she trotted off to her master, confident that things were under control.

"You think he's armed?"

"I don't know, Bill, but if he manages to get that stuff into the tank, it won't make much difference."

Owens, the younger of the two, didn't wait to discuss tactics. He grabbed the side rails and began climbing the ladder with Wilkie close behind.

In less than a minute, the two policemen arrived at the top of the tank. Quietly peering over the top rung, Owens could faintly make out a figure hunched over something sixty feet away. He carefully climbed onto the rooftop and motioned Wilkie to do the same.

"Get ready," he whispered.

Pulling his service weapon, then turning his 900-lumen flashlight beam on Hogan, he shouted, "Freeze, Hogan—it's over!"

With his light, Wilkie scampered ten feet to the right, his weapon also drawn and aimed at their prey. The beams revealed a man with a respirator mask covering his face pouring amber liquid into the tank. He casually looked up but seemed to chuckle and continued what he was doing.

"Put it down, Hogan, or we'll shoot."

Hogan ripped off his respirator and flung it at them. "Fuck you. Do whatever you want; it's too late. See these two jugs here ... they're empty." He stood and kicked them as he spoke, their hollow sound confirming the truth.

Now Wilkie stood and approached him, his light in one hand, gun in the other. "Down on the ground—do it now!"

When he'd been in LA, Roger had encountered a number of sadistic, deranged criminals, but none with the look of smug satisfaction he now faced.

"I don't think I will. Within hours, you'll have over a thousand dying people on your hands. Maybe you should start worrying about them."

As he spoke to Wilkie, Owens began circling in the opposite direction, attempting to outflank Hogan.

"Hold on, pal, I can see you over there." He addressed Owens. "What are you gonna do, shoot me?"

The cops ignored their prey and continued to advance on him from opposite directions. If he didn't comply, they would make him.

When they were less than twenty feet away on each side of Hogan, he abruptly dashed to the edge of the tank and jumped. They heard the leafless alder branches snapping as he tumbled thirty feet to the earth.

Seventy-One

By the time Bill and Roger had descended the ladder and looked for Hogan, he was gone.

"I would have thought that jump would have killed him," Roger said.

"Yeah, me too. Maybe the branches slowed him down, and the hill helped mitigate the fall. We'll get the word out and make sure he doesn't get off the island. Right now, we've got bigger problems."

They jogged back to where the vehicles were to find Matt Steele, Jenne, and a couple more agents standing by. A large older gentleman was also there, dressed in sweats and a purple hoodie.

"Matt, glad you're here."

"Hogan?"

Owens let out a disappointed sigh and answered, "Son of a bitch jumped off the tank, and when we got down, he was gone. Problem is he managed to dump the bacteria into the tank. We need to do something before this stuff gets into the system."

"Bill, Roger, this is Chuck Edwards; we picked him up as soon as Jenne told me what was happening. He's the chief engineer for the city and knows the system better than anyone. I've already told him what might happen, and now that it has, maybe he can help."

The engineer, probably in his seventies and sporting a four-day growth of white whiskers, seemed nervous to be the center of attention. He appeared to have missed very few meals in his life.

Matt started the conversation. "Chuck, tell them what you told me about shutting down the system."

"The city wanted to upgrade things a few years ago, so we installed new twelve-inch motorized gate valves in the main discharge line."

"So let's close them." Bill was getting impatient.

"We can't. No power."

"You're kidding. No generator backup?" Roger asked.

"Well, we're sorta in the process of wiring things for that very situation, but there are some parts we're waiting for."

"Jesus ... there's gotta be some way to shut it down manually."

"Theoretically, you can remove the motor package and manually turn them off, but we were going through that exercise last week, and one of the guys snapped off the stem. Now it's stuck open until we get the company that makes 'em out here. We've never had to shut it down, so we weren't too worried about it."

While this discussion continued, I stood on the sidelines with my wife and dog, letting the authorities do what they did. They were the pros, after all. I kept thinking about all the folks living in Langley, unaware of the poison that would be discharged from their faucets shortly.

I raised my hand to get Roger's attention, but he was too busy to notice. Then I yelled at him, "*Roger*, over here ..."

Perturbed at the interruption, he nevertheless walked over to us. "What? We're kinda busy."

"Get Andie over here."

"Huh? Why?"

"She's a microbiologist, Roger; she knows this shit. Maybe she can find a way to neutralize the bacteria before it can do too much damage. Can you get her on the cell?"

"Damn ... of course. Great thought, Kevin. Let me try."

He faced away and worked feverishly at his phone until he finally put it up to his ear. Then he disconnected and turned back.

"I got her. I told her what's happened, and she said she had to do some math first, then she'd call when she was on her way."

"Anything else?"

"Yeah—she said there's not much time before the bacteria gets mixed with the tank water sufficiently to become toxic downstream, and we need to alert the people on city water."

"How?"

"I'll get Matt and his crew on it, maybe ... wait, it's Andie ..."

After what seemed an eternity but was really less than a minute with lots of grunts and head bobbing from Roger, he disconnected.

Roger yelled, "*Everyone ... your attention ... now.*"

The night air was silent save for the crackles of the still-roaring fire below.

"Andie's on her way. She says we can neutralize the toxin with bleach, but we need eighty gallons. She says that's a significantly higher concentration than is currently added, but it's still below the amount that will cause harm to anyone. The water will smell like a swimming pool and taste shitty, but she says we need to increase the saturation to kill these super microbes.

"Matt, we need people at every grocery store on the south end. If they're not open, break in and get every jug of Clorox you can find.

"Bill, try to find a way to alert as many town residents as possible, then have them contact everyone they can. We need to try to buy some time. While you're at it, see if they have Clorox at home; we'll need all we can get.

"Chuck, see if you can get some of your people up here and find a way to rig up a pulley system so we can get the bleach up top fast when it gets here."

Everyone looked at each other for a split second after the assignments were handed out. Then the urgency set in, and a flurry of vehicles sped down the hill, everyone anxious to avoid the demise of the little town by the sea.

Seventy-Two

He hadn't planned to jump off the enormous concrete tank but saw no other option. The hundreds of spindly alder branches scraped, gouged, and buffeted him as he tumbled through the willowy trees, but when he finally hit the ground, he was still in one piece.

With the fairgrounds fire on one side and the access road on the other, Hogan saw no alternative but to head west into a thickly forested area used for hiking and nature walks.

The adrenaline now leaking from his body, he began to feel the bruises, scrapes, and contusions resulting from his ordeal. He supposed that was why his energy was dissipating so rapidly.

Because there was very little ambient light in the dense woods, he stumbled and fell over a tree that the storm had uprooted. With some difficulty, he picked himself up and sat down to catch his breath.

He felt flushed and jittery but attributed that to his ordeal. At least he could complete his mission, and now the people of Langley would soon be feeling the wrath of Harry Hogan. He suspected the authorities were too occupied with the imminent disaster to focus on him for the moment, and he would have a small window to escape.

He stood to continue on his way but suddenly felt a little dizzy. Sitting back down, he noticed that the slight cramp in his lower abdomen, attributed to his fall, had developed into a huge mass of pain that seemed to be moving through his intestines.

Breaking into a sweat even though the temperature was in the mid-40s, he began to shiver uncontrollably. He slid off the fallen tree and clenched his knees to his chest to ease the pain without success. The leaves and branches on the forest floor were the only witnesses to his agony.

Just after he felt his bowels explode and just before he passed out from the pain, he recalled throwing his respirator at the cops on top of the reservoir. His last conscious thought was that maybe he had done it too soon.

Seventy-Three

A ndie arrived at the town reservoir twenty minutes before the first gallons of Clorox began showing up. She brought respirator masks for anyone working near the open port to the tank and immediately scaled the ladder to distribute them and supervise the operation.

She knew the standard water treatment using chlorine was about .5 parts per million, but her lab work showed that wouldn't be nearly enough to do the job. They would need to increase that concentration to close to the highest tolerable level of 4 ppm to be sure to destroy the genetically modified bacteria.

We had settled Emma in the truck to make sure she was out of the way and did our best to help those carrying the gallon and quart bottles of bleach to the base of the tank. Chuck Edwards had rigged up a small wooden platform that could be hauled to the top via a pulley system, making it faster to get the plastic jugs to the opening.

Over the next hour, Clorox bottles arrived continuously. Bill Owens's crew even delivered ones and twos from the townspeople. They had alerted 90 percent of the residents about the danger and were doing their best to reach the remaining few.

Andie, Roger, and two of Chuck's crew handled the operation on top of the tank while Wally Turpin supervised the receiving and distribution of the bleach at the bottom. Jenne and I pitched in where we could.

There was little conversation among those hoping to avert disaster, only determination. Finally, we heard Andie yell from above, "*That's it!* We're done."

Everyone working on the ground froze. There had been such a resolve among them that stopping seemed irrational. We stood there until Andie and Roger were on the ground and addressed us.

"We've got enough bleach in the tank to kill the bacteria and make the water safe for consumption. We will still use caution and ensure no one drinks the water until we can test it both in the tank and downstream at the residences." A cheer rose among the group as Andie finished her comments.

Then Roger spoke. "I'd like to thank everyone here, especially Bill and Matt and his crew, Wally and you, Kevin and Jenne, and particularly Andie for making this happen. Let's all get some rest. We'll start looking for Hogan tomorrow, but I think the danger has passed."

The tests on the water the following day all proved negative, effectively signaling the eradication of the genetically modified Shiga toxin developed from the E. coli bacteria taken from the feces of the pygmy goats.

Andie notified the CDC and the DOH and let Jake Early deliver the news to the governor. Once again, the national news crews descended on little Whidbey Island to inform the public of the dangers of raising pygmy goats and the need to register every animal known to be in the US.

Many Langley residents were interviewed and told the world how lucky they were to have escaped a terribly agonizing death. Having been through the onslaught once before, Roger and Andie avoided the reporters, allowing the Island County sheriff and the director of Homeland Security to share the credit. Since we were only bit players in the saga, we managed to stay under the radar.

The local police, Matt Steele, and the FBI searched every nook and cranny on the island, looking for Hogan without success. They finally concluded that he must have found a way to the mainland and vanished.

Within a week, the news media had exhausted every possible facet of the events. The scuttlebutt was that Harry Hogan was now in Canada brewing up another batch of misery, and soon, they moved on to a more sensational story about a former president being indicted.

Shortly before Christmas, after three weeks of constant rain, a survey crew identifying boundaries for protected forest land stumbled upon the badly decayed and mostly eaten body of Harry Hogan. The raccoons, porcupines, and coyotes had damaged the disease-ridden corpse enough to make it unrecognizable.

Only after finding a fingerprint from one of the few remaining fingers was the sheriff's office able to confirm it was the deranged killer. Upon further examination, the cause of death was determined to be massive and complete organ failure due to infection by a genetically modified bacterium similar to E. coli 0157.

Seventy-Four

Roger and Andie invited everyone connected with the bacterial attacks on the reservoirs to a Christmas Eve party at their home on Lone Lake.

We were there, as was Emma, the Earlys—Francis was finally out of the hospital—Seth and Alice, Bill and Shelly, Wally Turpin and his wife, Matt Steele, Jim Lovvorn, and Chuck Edwards.

It was early evening, and the drizzle we had driven through on the way had now changed to snow, a rarity on Whidbey Island.

The guests had broken into smaller groups and were discussing anything but the events that had brought everyone together when Roger tapped his glass with a spoon.

"I'm glad you all could come despite the weather, and I know most of you have families to be with at this time of year. We wanted to tell you how much we appreciate you and couldn't have gotten through this without everyone doing their part.

"We also wanted to let you know that Andie and I are married. Chuck here is an ordained pastor who performed the ceremony just before everyone arrived."

It was quiet for a second, then Jenne began clapping, and everyone joined in. The guests took turns hugging Andie and Roger and congratulating the couple. When they eventually moved to other conversations, we were able to chat with the newly married couple.

"We're so happy for you two," Jenne said.

Andie replied, "If it weren't for the O'Malleys, we wouldn't be here. Thank you for your friendship and help."

"I wish we had known. We would have brought you something." I guessed what I'd said was inappropriate, judging by the look from my wife.

"Why do you think we did it this way? Besides, we ended up getting the same thing for each other.

"What?" Another look from Jenne.

"C'mon, you're not interested?"

"Sorry about my husband ..."

"Nah, follow us. We're dying to show you, and we couldn't be happier." Andie turned, and the three of us followed.

We went out the back door, where the snow was accumulating on a narrow path. During the short walk to a small barn, it crunched under our feet, and a dim light crept under the battered door.

The faint noise from our footsteps must have been a giveaway because we heard the three of them even before she slid it open. *Meh-eh-eh, meh-eh-eh.*

Cast of Characters

Jenne and Kevin O'Malley, retired interior designers
Deputy Roger Wilkie, Deputy Sheriff
Dr. Andie Saunders, microbiologist, University of Washington
Harry Hogan, bad guy
Bill Owens, Bellevue PD detective
Shelly Owens, Bill's wife
Matt Steel, FBI SAC
Jake Early, Island County Commissioner
Francis Earl, Jake's brother
Wally Turpin, Deputy Sheriff
Jim Lovvorn, FBI agent
Mikee, day laborer
Vaso and Taito Kian, guardian angels
George Weber, Uber driver
Eddie Trevitt, Oak Harbor police chief
Alice and Seth Robbins, neighbors
Liam Mallory, CDC director
Dale Olmsted, Homeland Security director
Maria Geddes, State DOH representative
Chuck Edwards, Langley utilities director
Emma O'Malley, GSD

Acknowledgements

Tanks is a work of fiction, and any similarities to people living or dead are purely coincidental. From time to time I use real names, because it's too damn tough to make them all up, but rest assured, only the names are real, not the people.

It is true that there are many private water systems on Whidbey Island, and to my knowledge, they are all monitored religiously by professional water companies. As far as I know, any bacterium known to man is neutralized by adding minute amounts of chlorine to the water supply.

The town of Langley is just as I described it—a quaint, charming community on the shores of the Salish Sea. It seems no visitor to Whidbey Island can resist a visit, and almost all of them dream about living in such an idyllic place.

Pygmy goats have been around for years but lately have become popular as pets due mostly to their adorableness. They are cute as hell and, compared to most farm animals, relatively easy to care for. That being true, I spend most of my time dissuading my wife from getting one.

Once again, my deepest thanks to my wife, who endures being the guinea pig in reading through my first draft.

Thanks, Baby!